The
Cross
Maker's
Champion

The Cross Maker's Champion

JACK A. TAYLOR

THE CROSS MAKER'S CHAMPION: BOOK 3
Copyright © 2020 by Jack A. Taylor

Print ISBN: 978-1-4866-1860-6
eBook ISBN: 978-1-4866-1861-3

Word Alive Press
119 De Baets Street Winnipeg, MB R2J 3R9
www.wordalivepress.ca

WORD ALIVE
—P R E S S—

Cataloguing in Publication information can be obtained from Library and Archives Canada.

This book is dedicated to the family members who love to the end, starting with Gayle, Steve, Dorothy, Kathy, Leon, Bryan, Gerry, Nancy, Charles, Sheila, Al, Barb, Edgar, Colleen, and Len.

Acknowledgements

Champions call us to reach deeper and excel further by showing us the way. I acknowledge the early champions who pushed me toward professional excellence in my faith, work and, studies: pastors like Doug Harris and Campbell Henderson; professors like Don Hills, Harold Dressler, and D.A. Carson; and all my colleagues at Rift Valley Academy in Kenya.

The current champions in my family and at Faith Fellowship spur me on to not give up on the dreams God has planted. Again, I acknowledge Evan Braun for his polishing of another story that fought to live outside the hidden caverns of my mind.

The true champion is the one who fought the greatest fight at the cross and won it for all of us. It is to him I entrust the hopes of all who ponder the deeper story behind this series.

Chronological Note

The events of this novel take place ten years after *The Cross Maker* and *The Cross Maker's Guardian*.

Chapter One

He was the last man standing - a black avenger. Twenty-two warriors lay lifeless on the bloodied sand. One man knelt before him gasping for breath - a crimson froth bubbling through his lips.

The setting sun glinted off the blade poised for the mercy stroke. Still Nabonidus waited as he held his foe up by his hair. The glassy eyes of the defeated gladiator dimmed.

A broken javelin shaft, blade half-buried in his own thigh, drew his attention. Dropping his sword, he screamed with rage, yanked out the weapon and thrust it into the jugular of the dying Saxon.

A roar like a thousand crashing ocean waves washed over him. Without waiting for the spoils of victory, he stumbled from the arena.

Shadows from the dark clouds above trickled over terraced hills, gathered momentum near the shops and alleys of Ephesus, flowed like a river at flood stage among the residences, and settled a short distance out of town in an inky pool by the courtyard of the Temple of Artemis. The darkness carried an icy touch, almost as if an evil presence inhabited the very clouds.

Two prominent features towered in the seaport to tie the residents to Rome. One was the twenty-five-thousand-seat arena and the other was the temple, considered one of the seven wonders of the world.

A gladiator's shouts had faded. Blood had been shed. With the battle over, the crowds dispersed, fumbling their way through mundane tasks. Rome had offered its meal of violence and the Ephesians had gulped it down.

A young merchant shuddered involuntarily as he pulled his cloak tighter. Sacred priestesses gathered up their colorful, form-hugging garments, shrank behind the massive white columns, and slipped into the porticos and side rooms set aside for them, their ankle bells fading with each step. Abandoned invalids, sprawled on the six stairways, moaned. The copper smell of blood, mixed with frankincense, drifted heavily on the breeze. The scene was lit by two torches near the temple entrance, struggling against the strengthening wind. A raven rested on a post, watching over it all.

Dozens of desperate souls crawled across the courtyard, moaning and beseeching the aid of Artemis, the goddess of healing. They had been brought to the temple, and sometimes abandoned, by family members and friends. Open sores, twisted limbs, coughs, and fevers drew supplicants to brave the costs that would be demanded for relief.

Snakes, agents of the goddess, coiled and slithered throughout the invalids.

Meanwhile, a lone barefoot warrior limped into the arena of flickering torchlight and stood among the resultant nest of venomous serpents. A cobra with eyes like dim coals suddenly struck like lightning, but the man's Roman sword was quicker, splitting the forked-tongued attacker in two.

The warrior stood silent and still, his sweaty black skin glistening in the torchlight. The cold and darkness barely punctured his grim visage. A memory of his home in Persia sprang to mind, clutched at his soul, and stole his breath before he shut it down with his will.

One torch gave up its light as smoke and incense swirled around the warrior, and the sound of an infant crying penetrated the realm of terror.

What is this dark magic which suffocates and exposes me? he wondered. *Is this evil or innocence I face?*

"Nabonidus!" called the voice of a woman. It dripped like fresh honey onto the carefully polished marble floor.

The warrior Nabonidus, sword in hand, shifted weight to his good leg, clenching and unclenching his fists. His rippling muscles hardened and he puffed out his broad, scarred chest. Clad only in a loincloth, he made no attempt to answer the woman.

"My Persian prince, champion of the people, warrior of Artemis, slave of Rome, what brings you to my throne?" the woman asked. "What brings you to the Temple of Artemis, daughter of Zeus, sister of Apollo, mother goddess of earth, the Artemission for all Ephesians, one of the seven wonders of the world."

The woman stepped out into the open and Nabonidus saw that she was a seasoned maiden, attired in a short white tunic. The wavering torchlight gained strength at her presence, illuminating her golden ear and nose rings. Glittering bangles ran from wrist to elbow. A crescent necklace graced her neck, matching the ones around her ankles. Her raven-black hair was coiffed into a circled tower on the back of her head.

At last, the woman extended a bow and aimed it at the warrior.

Whispered incantations, mixed with the plucking tones of a ten-stringed lyre, floated like phantoms around the nearby columns. A multi-breasted statue at the center of the courtyard resonated with energy. Its sightless eyes pierced the darkness. Its tongueless mouth seemed to speak instructions.

The cry of the infant sounded again, and Nabonidus's gut twisted. A deep sense of loss enveloped him.

Will this darkness steal my very will?

The maiden enchantress stepped closer. "Twenty-five thousand tongues screamed the name of Nabonidus only hours ago when you slew the champion from Britannia. The world was at your command. Yet here you stand."

"I come in peace."

"Yet my guardians lie dead by my door."

"Their fear made them fight." In truth, Nabonidus thought, they had been no more than children pretending to be men.

The arrow from the maiden's bow dipped and a flash of torches lit up a circle around the courtyard, each held by a young girl accompanied by a huntress. Smoke hung over the temple like fastened clouds, sending wisps to crawl into the back of his throat. Nabonidus coughed at the irritation.

In the middle of the temple courtyard, the two halves of the slain cobra ceased to wriggle. A swarm of other serpents darted for the crevices notched under the nearby stairs.

Six young men, their leather breastplates marking them as temple guards, stepped into the courtyard and carried off the sick and dying who had been ignored up until now. The moans of these desperate souls vanished into the darkness.

The ring of torches wavered in the breeze before gaining strength, overcoming the darkness again. In one choreographed motion, the torchbearers moved as a unit to surround the gladiator. Healers walked in their wake.

The maidens in their short white-skirted tunics, their bows set with razor-edged arrows, slowly descended toward the floor where Nabonidus stood his ground. Towering cedar doors folded away from the arched entryway and the jasper and marble columns around it. The glory of the one hundred twenty-seven marble columns stretched sixty feet high, supporting a structure four hundred fifty feet long and two hundred twenty-five feet wide. The gleam of torches against the marble transformed night into day in the courtyard. Erotic images and paintings stretched on every surface as far as the eye could see. Immense sections of the cedar roof lay open to the starry sky.

The maidens halted fifteen feet from Nabonidus, and only the lead maiden continued until she was within an arm's length of him. She glanced at the gaping wound in his thigh, still oozing blood down onto his ankle and feeding the red smear along the floor behind him.

She lowered her bow and arrow to the floor and knelt, exposing her neck. "The gladius," she said.

Nabonidus relaxed the grip on his short Roman sword and held it out to another maiden who stepped forward and retrieved it. He dropped five denarii on the ground. The coins clattered and spun in place. A young girl in a plain tunic and veil sprinted forward, crouched, scooped up the coins, and returned to stand by the archer for whom she held a torch.

The kneeling woman removed the lower portion of her skirted tunic to reveal an even shorter skirt. She motioned into the darkness and another young girl, carrying a clay pot, scampered forward and poured cool water onto the removed skirt. Nabonidus realized the kneeling woman was going to tend to his wound.

She wiped his ankle clean and slowly moved up toward the wound on his thigh. Nabonidus stood as still as a statue.

"The pain from this wound is shallow compared to the wound in your heart," the healer chanted quietly. "Death is your constant companion and shall continue to be until you find the love you seek. The love you seek is more than what you now see…"

One of the maidens carried forward a vial of myrrh, and the healer applied a few drops. She then rubbed hyssop on the wound.

Nabonidus shuddered at the smell of death.

When the cloths were saturated with blood, another maiden stepped forward to offer her skirted tunic, and then a third. Other maidens removed theirs to wipe up the trail of blood marking the warrior's footsteps across the courtyard. Several young girls now shuttled in jugs of water and ferried out soiled tunics.

"What traps the heart of the warrior?" the healer asked. Nabonidus stood silent. "Are you truly trapped by the decisions and labels of others, or is it only your mind which tells you so?"

The raven that had observed the scene from a nearby post fluttered to rest on the edge of a multi-breasted gold-and-silver statue of Artemis.

Elsewhere, two priestesses dressed in glistening saffron, indigo, and crimson emerged from an alcove and descended the stairs carrying an alabaster box and woven bag. The healer accepted these gifts and glanced into Nabonidus's eyes.

"A poultice of warm cabbage to stench the blood flow," she whispered. "When the physicians of the ludus cannot save you, the goddess is ready to work."

She applied the purple mix and wrapped it with yet another tunic offered by another maiden.

Entranced, the two priestesses ogled the impressive gladiatorial specimen before them. Their seductive positioning demonstrated their interest in him.

They see you as a marble masterpiece, Nabonidus thought. *Nothing more.*

"Pleasure will have its season," he said.

The lead priestess bowed and backed away. "Artemis awaits your pleasure."

The maidens who had removed the lower half of their tunics moved back into the shadows, their torchbearers joining them in retreat.

In the darkness, a single cobra poked out its head to peer into the courtyard. The infant's cry once again pierced the darkness.

Either evil wears the mask of innocence in this place or innocence is trapped by evil, he thought. *Artemis will have to find another champion.*

General Titius Marcus Julianus, trained thespian assassin, paced back and forth through the Syrian governor's gardens while his wife Abigail ambled through the rows of flowers, statues, and hedges. The role he had once pretended at had been confirmed once he'd regained his estate through law. His father's legacy had swayed the courts to make him a general.

The breeze sent his red cape billowing behind him. The sun glistened off the golden breastplate which marked his rank. Under his left arm, he tucked his ostrich-feathered helmet. His gladius, a short military sword, hung off his right hip.

A Roman officer sat quietly in a chair nearby.

"Julian," Titius said to the officer. "I will miss you. You have served Rome well. When others hesitated to stand with me, you were there."

The officer smiled and handed over his gladius. "This is my last act of loyalty. My fights are finished. Your new man Marcellus will serve you well."

"I can hardly believe you're leaving the life of open warfare to join the ranks of the thespian assassins. That life is not all you imagine it to be."

"I know you speak from experience, but I figure if they let someone like you into the brotherhood, it will be routine for me."

Julian rose and the two men embraced.

"May you truly find the purpose you have always longed for," Titius said.

Titius took a deep breath and swivelled to survey the group around him. A Roman prefect, two legionnaires, and a phalanx of imperial guards stood under the marble-pillared arches of the open courtyard. A Germanic maiden poured fresh mugs of wine while an Egyptian eunuch arranged a tray of fruit, cheese, flatbread, and fresh vegetables.

"Marcellus, what is this mandate from the emperor?" Titius asked, glancing toward the prefect. "What wisdom is there for Caligula to order the erection of an image of himself in the Temple of Jerusalem only because he was rebuffed in Alexandria?" He paused to take up a mug of wine and a handful of grapes. "His appointment of a new governor in Damascus, Publius Petronius to Damascus, showed insight and leadership, but this edict undoes all he hoped to accomplish here."

Marcellus, the newly appointed prefect over Judea, nodded. "The Greeks in Jamnia erected an altar in honor of the emperor and the Jews there tore it down while instigating a riot. This insult cannot be tolerated. The emperor needs to affirm his control everywhere."

Titius sat on a marble bench and motioned for the prefect to join him. Setting his helmet down beside him, he pondered the situation. "Herod Agrippa has just added Galilee and Perea to his domain, and the Jews won't take another attack on their faith and homeland." He finished off his grapes and stood to pace again. "Two legions have been ordered to enforce Caligula's edict, and that includes my legion. How can I tell Abigail I'll be working to force her countrymen to commit sacrilege in their most important place of worship?"

Marcellus stood to walk alongside the pacing Titius. "General, the Jews have significant economic influence in this part of the Empire. Perhaps you can persuade the governor about the wisdom of delaying the implementation of the emperor's mandate."

Titius turned and watched his wife, Abigail, bending over a red rose. The gold necklaces dangling from her neck matched the bracelets around her wrist and ankles. The thin leather straps of her sandals wrapped themselves around her shapely legs like vines around a trellis.

"Ever since she was a girl in my gardens in Rome, she has loved red roses," Titius remarked. "It was a red rose which helped me find her again in Jerusalem. I can't lose her now. Governor Petronius has studied Jewish philosophy. Surely he'll understand."

Marcellus took up another mug of wine and chewed on a date. "He has already commanded the statue be made in Sidon, but he's in no hurry. He's written a letter to the emperor encouraging a delay. He's also putting together a negotiating team to meet with the Jewish leaders in Tiberias. Perhaps you can be appointed to that team."

"Yes, I know Tiberias well." Titius watched a pair of doves nestle in a small alcove near the carvings of pomegranates at the top of one of the marble columns. "Thousands of Jews already demonstrated against our legions in Ptolemais, and they're already neglecting their harvest, threatening to undermine our ability to raise taxes and meet the demands of Rome. There is the threat of famine."

A messenger stepped through the curtained entrance to the garden and bowed before Titius, who drew his sword and tapped the young man on his shoulder.

"Rise and declare the news," Titius commanded.

The man, still on his knee, delivered a scroll marked with the emperor's seal. "This is for the governor, but I have intercepted it as you requested."

"Well done, Hermes," Titius commended as he broke the red wax seal and unrolled the manuscript. He nodded, read, and then dismissed the servant with a wave.

"What is the news?" Marcellus asked. "What does Caligula—excuse me, Emperor Gaius Julius Caesar Germanicus—declare for those of us who cannot resist him?"

"Come with me," instructed Titius as he moved deeper into the gardens, away from the ears of legionnaire and palace guard alike.

Marcellus followed the general toward the gurgling fountain of Apollo. There, he waited patiently as Titius shook his head, withdrew his dagger, and held it at the prefect's throat.

"This news must never be told beyond this garden," Titius declared.

"On the life of my two sons, not a word will escape my lips."

Titius handed him the document. "The emperor demands the governor take his own life if he fails to secure the image in the Temple in Jerusalem. I fear the accusations of insanity against this emperor may be truer than we believed."

Earlier that same morning, beneath the golden glow of satin curtains and a tiled fresco of dancing wildflowers, Caleb ben Samson cuddled his wife Suzanna and whispered his love over the woman of his dreams.

"The Almighty has given me the greatest gifts any man could have," he murmured. "True love, deep faith, and great hope. We will tell everyone here in Cyprus about the Messiah and the peace he will bring to us all. No more will I build crosses for the Romans."

Suzanna nuzzled her nose into her husband's thick beard and sighed. "You truly are a man among men. We must think strategically in sharing the good news of our Messiah. This island has four districts and we can spend a year in each one. We start here in Salamis, then Pafos, Amathous, and finally Lapethos. When we finish the island, we will head to Germania."

Caleb chuckled. "My sweet Suzanna, always wanting to conquer the world." He ran his fingers through her long hair, massaging as he did. "Twenty years ago, this island was devastated by an earthquake and now you intend to rock it again. I'm relieved to be away from all those Romans and their endless obsession with crucifying anyone who objects to their demands."

Suzanna pushed away from her husband and sat up on the mat that had been serving as their bed. She pulled a blanket over her shoulders to warm herself against the cool morning air.

"Have you seen the temples everywhere, the magicians, the superstitions these people practice?" she asked. "They seek protection in an empty power. We must share the truth God has opened our eyes to."

Caleb propped himself up on an elbow and rubbed his wife's back. "Of course, we must. God has brought us to this place, but first he brought us to each other. There will be time to transform the world."

Two hours later, as they wandered the marketplace observing the vast displays of wine, grain, oil, copper, glass, timber, and minerals, they chanced upon a man with distinctive Hebrew garb and features. A fine belt girded his expensive robe, marking him as a man of wealth. He strutted like a proud rooster and bartered aggressively with a linen merchant for a tunic.

Triumphant at last, the thickly bearded man turned and held up his purchase toward the sun. "Praise the Almighty for his gracious gift," he crowed. "The Sons of Levi have found their champion and we are blessed."

Caleb stepped forward and greeted him. "Shalom, my friend. May the Almighty continue to bless you and your family."

The Levite lowered his purchased tunic and smiled in welcome. "Shalom, my friends. My praise is to the Almighty for his blessing. Clearly, by your speech, you are Galilean."

Husband and wife nodded in unison.

"There are some truths not worthy of hiding," Caleb said. "I grew up in Nazareth as a carpenter."

Barnabas gasped. "Nazareth. The home of Yeshua, our Redeemer." He surveyed the heavens. "Praise the Almighty. What is the news of his followers?"

"You presume much, my friend." Caleb swatted at a small swarm of gnats hovering near his head. "We're actually new in following the Way and fled with everyone else when persecution broke out after Stephen's martyrdom."

Barabbas nodded. "Yes, Saul of Tarsus dared to poke the heart of God, and Caiaphas and the Sanhedrin reaped their vengeance. Now God has claimed Saul for himself, although many doubt the reality of his conversion."

As they walked, Caleb jumped to avoid a donkey who had stopped to relieve itself right on the pathway. The owner beat the heavily loaded beast and tugged it off the path and under a canopy.

"We were warned of Saul," Caleb said. "The most dangerous zealot is a proud one who feels bested. He would do anything to prove himself."

"He was all of that, without question," Barnabas agreed. "But things have changed. He narrowly escaped assassination in Damascus and tried to meet the apostles in Jerusalem." Scooping up three oranges from a vendor, the Cypriot flipped a coin to the woman without missing a step. "Everyone was afraid that his intention was to trick them… and trap them." He gently threw up two oranges, the first for Caleb and then for Suzanna to catch. "I intervened for him, letting them know he had met Yeshua in a vision."

Suzanna watched a flock of pigeons fluttering down to consume a small scattering of seeds that had fallen as a merchant unloaded his sacks.

"Is Saul still in Jerusalem?" she asked.

"No, he wouldn't stop debating the Hellenists in their synagogue," Barnabas said. "There were constant riots. His life was at risk and the church was divided with all the chaos. We finally sent him back to his home in Tarsus to sort out his life."

Caleb pushed past a cart filled with baskets of fruit. "Do you think you can confine a man like Saul? You've not heard the last of that renegade."

An hour after Nabonidus walked past the two prone guards he had chopped down at the entrance to the stairs of the Artemission, he emerged holding his sword. The red stain blotching the satin tunic around his thigh had stopped growing in size, the wound having been staunched by the poultice. The healers had done their job and he was grateful.

He glanced at the brothel where priestesses welcomed the final seasoned worshippers for the night, then noted the merchants closing up their shops and packing up their wares. Bats flitted in swooping circles around the plaza, darting after gnats and flies.

The hilltops of Ephesus blended with the midnight sky and a pantheon of stars emerged in the moonless canopy overhead. Groves of willows waved gracefully in the breeze near the temple walls. Fire smoke irritated his eyes and stuck in the back of his throat.

He cleared his throat and marched away, ignoring the throb in his thigh. But the haunting cry of the infant still echoed in his soul.

A cool, steady rain drizzled down on him. Droplets rolled off his bald skull and into the small tuft of black curls taking refuge on his chin.

Within a few hundred steps, he pivoted back toward the hundreds of covered torches surrounding the temple. A raven took to the skies and flew away over the city.

From amongst a contingent of bodyguards, his handler Selsus stepped forward and positioned himself in front of Nabonidus. As handler, Selsus arranged gladiator matches, organized training regimen, and worked on publicity to promote the warriors he represented. He was like a second skin, hovering over his warriors, controlling their every move.

The bodyguards took up position on either side of their leader.

"By all the gods of Rome, restrain your pleasure for this one night," Selsus said. "Allow yourself to heal."

Selsus was a German giant, blond, blue-eyed, bronzed, and two inches taller than Nabonidus. The Persian gladiator glared down at the man's white hand, planted firmly against his black chest.

"Pleasure is the last thing on my mind, especially if you continue to stand in my way."

"Listen to me!" Selsus warned. "When the Roman authorities sent you to us off that galley, they told us you were crazy, rowing like you had to power the whole ship by yourself. And now we send you to fight and you're out of control."

Nabonidus poked his finger into the German's chest. "I don't care who you send into that arena. I'm in control until I see a death stare in the eyes of the warrior who kneels before me with my dagger at his throat."

"You're crazy, and today is done."

"Today is never done," Nabonidus muttered. "Get out of my way."

"One night! Visit the Artemission in daylight and make your sacrifices where all can see. Perhaps one of those virgin daughters from the Way."

Nabonidus pushed through the others. "You're lucky you have no daughters of your own."

Selsus raised his club. "Before Zeus, I swear to you, the walls of Babylon, the hanging gardens, the pyramids of Egypt, and the tombs of the Caesars are poor imitations of glory compared to this home of the gods. Return when your strength can satisfy a hundred priestesses."

Nabonidus stepped away from him. "Priestesses will never satisfy my needs."

Chapter Two

Nabonidus was glad to have escaped the suffocating guardianship of Selsus and his sidekicks, who were no better than bullying nursemaids determined to prove they still had dignity despite being slaves themselves. He feigned an urgent need to relieve himself and slipped out an alternate doorway of the ludus he'd discovered on a previous excursion.

The ludus, or gladiator training school, was no place to spend all your free time. It was just a prison and a school disguised as a playground for killers. The cool breeze across his cheeks refreshed him after the stale and stuffy quarters under the arena.

Outside, raindrops clung to the oak leaves before plummeting to the damp earth below.

The gods must be crying over this wretched place, he thought.

Sometimes he had to run, to outrace the night terrors chasing him and threatening to tear his soul apart. A fire burned in his belly, a longing so deep nothing could reach it. Faces and visions from long ago haunted him, mocking him, never letting him say goodbye. Dragons prowling the corridors of terror-filled dreams.

Sprinting across the street known as the Sacred Way, Nabonidus merged with the crowd entering the agora through the Mazaeus and Mithridates gates. He knew the search was already on for him, but he wandered the seaside markets and breathed deeply of the fresh salty air. The stench of low tide was past with its rotting seaweed, sewer outlet puddles, and collection of discarded fish waste. Fishermen sorted their catch on the docks, sailors scoured the booths for quick enjoyment, and a showman entertained passersby with a small pack of barking dogs.

Pelicans skittered above the diamond sparkles of cresting waves and disappeared behind the towering sails of an Egyptian trading vessel. Were the birds omens? If only he had wings to fly to the far horizons.

A small convoy of Roman galleys bobbed alongside an extended wharf as centurions barked orders at the disembarking troops. Sunlight flashed off their swords and shields.

Never again will they take me to that hole of darkness, he vowed.

Strong memories of the five years he'd spent shackled to the oars of such a galley sent an involuntary shiver up Nabonidus's spine. Those had been endless days and nights. The Romans had taken him as a hostage to ensure his master Caleb stayed true in his trade as a cross maker.

His neck and shoulder muscles tensed like a drum skin as he recalled the cursed stroke-setter pounding out a rhythm that competed with the whip to motivate hopeless captives into giving of themselves twice what they physically could spare. A deep breath slowed his panic as he released his clenched fists.

Focus on your freedom. Nabonidus turned away from the rising thunder of hobnailed boots reverberating on cobblestones. *Spare your wrath for when you need it.*

Merchants called for his attention, hawking everything from fish to dates to slave girls. These were thieves, shaving the weights, cutting the corners… anything for a profit. He had stolen an extra-large red tunic from behind a senator's home to cover the tattoos which marked him as a gladiator. The navy blue cotton shawl on his shoulder was flecked with delicate golden stitching. The rich wardrobe drew the attention of vendors eager for a sale.

"Just breathe!" he admonished himself.

Phoenician women, with-bowl shaped woven reed baskets on their heads, strolled between the undulating canopies. They hawked spices, jewelry, and carvings. A pair of guardians in grey tunics followed them with two-edged daggers in hand, ready should a thief or beggar get too close. Nabonidus knew they'd last two minutes in a real arena.

He stopped at the stall of a young woman wearing a striped head covering.

"Jewish," he mumbled to himself. His previous owner had been Jewish.

Nabonidus sampled the peaches, grapes, and figs the young woman offered but declined to make a purchase. He allowed the sweet taste and rich flavor to fill his senses. He ignored the merchant's irate screams for payment as he shouldered his way through the crowd.

On his way back to the latrines, Nabonidus stopped to survey the exotic villas expanding like a field of mushrooms along the crest of Mount Koressus. Only one gladiator he knew had escaped the arena by accumulating enough victories to claim a place on that hill of esteem. One day, he would be there. Perhaps then the fire in his belly would die along with the rage consuming his soul.

Clouds rolled in to block the sun and a trickle of ice crept like a glacier over the gladiator. Two ravens called from a nearby olive tree.

Another omen.

He hid the red tunic in a corner of the latrine rafters. It would serve his purposes at another time. For now, he had to eat. Only the ludus, with its robust fare, would satisfy the cravings in his belly. For now, he would breathe and wait.

"Is anything else happening?" Caleb picked through an assortment of clams, mussels, and crabs dumped into a shallow wooden vat filled with seawater. "It amazes me people eat these things despite the laws we've lived under."

Two gulls hopped along a railing, calling to him for attention. He ignored their efforts and turned back toward his Cypriot friend.

"This looks like a good place for you to preach," Caleb said.

Barnabas frowned as he surveyed the flowing mass of people milling around the shopping area. "Caution, my friend. John's brother, James, was killed by Herod in Jerusalem. Peter escaped only by miraculous angelic intervention. This place is prosperous, but we must be careful about our proclamations. The Empire isn't a friendly place for followers of the Way."

Suzanna rubbed her index finger across the jumble of golden bracelets on Barnabas's wrist. "How do you do so well if the Romans are against you?"

"I have a place outside Salamis. Come and stay with me while you decide your next steps. We can learn about Yeshua together."

She reached out her hand to allow a butterfly to crawl off a sunflower onto her finger. "And what work do you do at your place?"

Barnabas pointed toward a booth filled with glass-blown jars and glasses. "I own the first glass-blowing shop on Cyprus. This is a new art for a new world. The jars are good for lotions, wines, juices, sweets, and anything you want to carry and display."

From nearby, an Egyptian saleswoman called out to Suzanna. "Come, exchange your plain attire for something to raise your man's desire. Why be a person who others scorn? Dress for Cyprus, not where you were born."

Suzanna stopped in her tracks and eyed the attractive blue himation, cloak, and brilliant white chiton undergarment. She rubbed the fine silk and linen vestments between her fingers.

"Your poetry is as fine as your clothes," Suzanna remarked. "My husband's desire rests mainly with prose."

The women laughed at the wordplay, then continued to barter as the men surveyed the passing crowd.

Caleb spied a gilded litter being carried by four Ethiopians. "Who rides in the royal carriage?"

Barnabas chuckled. "Sergius Paulus, the proconsul. He prides himself on representing Rome, but he's merely the puppet of a Jewish sorcerer named Bar-Jesus. He's intelligent enough but is too easily swayed by that which impresses him."

"I haven't seen any Roman legions here to support him," Caleb noted. "What authority does he have?"

"He'll act as judge in cases where the local council or magistrate can't rule. He sets up the high priest for the Imperial cult and he'll consecrate statues of the emperor. He ensures aqueducts, roads, theatres, and other things get built... the usual."

Suzanna pointed out several large buildings higher up the hill in the central part of Salamis. "What are those structures?"

Barnabas followed her gaze. "Those are administrative buildings. We might not have much of an official Roman presence, but those immensities are constant reminders of who's in charge here. The quaestor and his ten board members handle all the tax collection for the island. The shipbuilders have their offices there, too."

Caleb glanced back toward the market and pointed at a large pile of copper ingots. "This copper ore, is it local or imported?"

Barnabas shrugged. "The copper is mined here on Cyprus, but from the towns of Soli and Amathous. We just export them." He led them toward the booth. "The local coppersmiths also create images of Aphrodite at the temple. The myths say she was born from the sea foam of this island. There are huge festivals for her here."

"Pretty religious place, is it?"

"Also political. They have temples and statues to Augustus and Tiberius. They think every emperor will prove to be a benefactor. So far, nothing for Caligula."

"Are there no goddesses beside Aphrodite then?" Suzanna asked.

Barnabas indicated the statues outside a nearby temple. "Those are the daughter and wife of Augustus, now declared here to be Julia the Goddess Augusta and Livia the Goddess known as the New Aphrodite. There are statues everywhere on this island. Every third man seems to be a priest of some cult."

Marcellus set his feet and placed his right fist against his breastplate. "General, I am ready with my report."

Titius waved away the Egyptian slave, who had lain out the copper bowls with water for washing, and planted himself face to face with the Roman prefect. "Tell me, Marcellus, what exactly does a prefect like you do for someone like Governor Petronius? How much can you be trusted by those who might see things differently than the emperor?"

Marcellus relaxed, even though the general hadn't given him permission to do so. "I maintain law and order in Damascus, and in all of Syria. I ensure there is good government here and that the emissaries of Rome are safe while they're here."

"And how do you do that?"

"I command the Praetorian Guard, oversee the civil administration, and execute judicial powers when Governor Petronius is away. I organize taxes on the citizens to appease Rome."

Titius shuffled through a handful of scrolls and opened one, examining it with a frown. "And you want me to join this taskforce to lobby Petronius against the emperor's wish to place his statue in the Jerusalem temple?"

"Yes. You're more persuasive than most men I know. You have his trust and he'll hear you."

Titius released the scroll and watched it roll up on itself. "You seem willing to risk my neck by encouraging rebellion against Caligula, but you refuse to stand up and speak for yourself."

"It's my duty to keep the peace through wit. It's your duty to enforce it by strength. Sometimes words can be stronger than swords—if they're used well."

"Swords aren't usually stronger than necks, and mine will be the one exposed."

Marcellus stuffed a date into his mouth. "Herod Agrippa has gone to Rome to appeal on our behalf. He's the only voice the emperor will listen to." He swallowed the fruit and popped in another piece. "This place is a cauldron of death and superstition, but it serves us well as a buffer with the Parthians."

Titius paced with his hands clasped behind him. "For four years Caligula has hunted us with misery. He's not like his father or like his mother, or even like his grandfather Augustus. We all know he killed Emperor Tiberius to seize the throne, yet we can do nothing to stop him."

"Guard your tongue and bide your time, my friend," Marcellus cautioned. "From the time Caligula was a child, he has walked in soldiers' boots beside his father in Germania. The previous emperor spent his last years together with him. Caligula knows how fragile his life is while he's in Rome."

Titius moved closer to Marcellus. "He's ambitious, paranoid, pleasure-seeking, cruel, and perverse—and the Empire cannot last long under his reign."

Movement behind a nearby curtain caught Titius's attention and he turned to look in that direction with suspicion.

"Someone's been listening," Titius said. "Find him, quick, before we're reported. If we're lost, nothing will stop this statue from being placed in the temple. And if that happens, the Jordan will turn into a river of blood. No Jew will allow their holy place to be defiled like this."

Nothing about the young woman resting at the fountain set her apart from the other beautiful women who threw themselves at Nabonidus. The soft light caressing her olive skin and charcoal hair only enhanced the fine features of her face. Her lips moved slowly, as if chanting a song to a baby, and the gladiator's soul longed to hear the words.

His childhood memories of travelling in camel caravans with his mother, father, and younger sister haunted him. His mother had been singing to him when the bandits had attacked. His sister had cried out as the attackers murdered his father and wrenched him from the arms of his mother.

From that moment on, slavery had been his life.

The young woman at the fountain raised her eyes, as if aware of his gaze, and hesitated before glancing away. She pulled at the edges of her shawl and tucked a strand of hair behind her ear. Her shoulders hunched and she leaned forward to intently examine something in her basket.

A shaft of light fell through tree limbs and produced a halo effect around her. Even others near the fountain stopped to stare at the phenomenon. It awakened a yearning so strong in Nabonidus that he wanted to shake off everything he knew and run with her to wherever she might go.

He took a step in her direction.

Thwack.

He buckled to the ground as a result of the simultaneous blows to his knees and the back of his head. Were they bandits? The attackers fought valiantly to immobilize him, but he rolled away and sprang to his feet.

Among them was Selsus, with four armed warriors. They encircled him, carrying clubs and swords, spears and shields. Selsus held the whip.

"So the mighty Persian has the weakness of every man—a woman," Selsus said, laughing. He made a crude gesture with his sword. "This is a curse, perhaps one we should fix to keep you focused on the arena. Perhaps Apollo or Diana will satisfy you in their temples. Don't waste your life or mine on what you can't have."

When Nabonidus looked around the square, he couldn't find the woman. Had she been a phantom? The shaft of light had gone as well, and slaves and free people alike lowered their eyes and went about their business. There was nothing to see.

Except for a crow which stared him down with its beady eyes.

Selsus prodded him with the butt end of a spear. "Your choice—the galley, the arena, or the lions. Now, drop your tunic!"

His humiliation complete, Nabonidus stiffened his back, set his shoulders, raised his chin, and marched toward the ludus where his training would continue in the gladiatorial arts. His soul bubbled like a volcano ready to blow.

Chapter Three

The first time Nabonidus attempted to escape, he discovered just how trapped he was. He tucked his sandals under his cloak while he crept barefoot in the darkest crevices of the walls along the white-marbled Curetes Street. Torches probed the darker corners of the thoroughfare and pedestrian traffic was minimal and sporadic.

He lingered in a grove of olive trees by the Temple of Hadrian, watching the marching patterns of the temple guards and Roman centurions. They marched without purpose.

The gaps near the gates were almost negligible, and anyone approaching had to yell out for attention and wait until they'd been completely searched by the armed sentries.

As the Persian warrior returned to the ludus, he discovered a row of barrels resting against the Memmius monument. The memorial had been built by Augustus to honor the grandson and son of the dictator Sulla, who had conquered Mithridates after the Pontic leader had slaughtered eighty thousand Romans. By piling the barrels, he figured out that he could scale the wall. He'd just need to find a rope to help him down the other side.

Next time when the moon is sleeping, he thought.

On his way back to his quarters, Nabonidus rounded a corner near the columned library of Celsus. There, he spotted a woman sitting in a balcony alcove feeding pigeons. Was it another phantom? It was an odd time for anyone to be active here.

He stepped back into the densest darkness, but when she raised her hand and waved it became clear that she had seen him.

The alcove was ten feet off the ground, on the second story of a stone-block mansion. The woman wore a sleeveless white stola, suggesting that she was a young noblewoman.

Suddenly, he envisioned himself back in the Artemission with the archers who had helped heal him. Had this woman been there?

Yes, he realized. *This is the healer who worked on me.*

The woman rose, waved away the birds, and dropped a bag into some bushes nearby. He stooped to retrieve the bag and return it, except when he looked up again she had already disappeared inside.

The thunder of hobnailed boots pounded nearby and it became clear that a Roman cohort was entering through the Magnesian Gate—and moving in his direction. This spurred him to step quickly back toward the ludus.

Safely in his room, he opened the bag and discovered frankincense inside. The powder was designed to rub on a wound to prevent infection. He mixed the powder with a cream and created a salve. As he applied the salve, he glanced out the window and noticed two men in the shadows of an olive tree. One of them was pointing in his direction with a dagger, and four others were already moving toward his cell.

By the time Selsus stepped into the doorway, Nabonidus had positioned himself to rest comfortably on his mat in the corner.

The towering German stood over him. "I can smell the frankincense. I don't know how you got it, or how you got past the guards, but I'll make you an example for anyone else who dares mock my rules."

From dawn to dusk for seven days straight, Selsus punished Nabonidus in every way imaginable. He carried heavy beams up and down hills, fought new recruits unarmed hour after hour, ran pointless through the streets, tasted the lash, treaded water, dug holes and filled them in again… Through it all, Nabonidus felt his hatred for Selsus grow stronger.

One day, German, you shall meet your gods!

Caleb and Suzanna had been staying in Barnabas's spacious mansion for two weeks before they felt safe to accompany their host back to the market. Through his stories he had given them a virtual tour of the city, detailing the four gymnasiums, the fifteen-thousand-seat stadium, and the Temple of Zeus. They wanted to witness these things for themselves.

On the way, they were led by the bearded Cypriot to a cemetery with little more than a dozen natural caves interspersed with numerous hand-crafted mausoleums. Many appeared to have epitaphs.

Caleb halted near the entrance to the cemetery as Barnabas walked on ahead.

"Barnabas," he said, "the Scriptures call us to avoid the houses of the dead."

Barnabas pivoted and glanced around at the statues, icons, flowers, and other displays set up for the dead. He pointed toward a cave in the center of the cemetery. "Even Abraham secured his wife and family members in a cave like this. Don't worry. I haven't dedicated this place to any Roman deity. As you can see, the only sign on this tomb is the sign of the fish—to acknowledge that I am a follower of the Way."

Suzanna reached out and took Caleb's hand in her own. "Come, my husband, have courage."

Caleb hesitated until Barnabas walked back to join them.

"This is the only memory I have of my wife, my son, and my daughter," their host said somberly. "They passed away in a plague while I was with the apostles in Jerusalem. I have no illusions about where they are, but sometimes I come to pray and thank God for the years I knew them. Feel free to wait here until I return. Or feel free to pass through and find the market on the other side of the forest."

"We'll go to the market," Suzanna said, tugging at Caleb's hand.

"When you're in the forest, watch out for wild dogs and bandits," Barnabas warned.

Caleb indicated a circle of raised boxes set off near the entrance to a smaller cavern. "Why are coffins decorated so lavishly? Why don't these people bury their dead in the ground as we do?"

Barnabas walked over to the memorials Caleb had pointed out. "This is a generous noble family who were once great in our city. When the earthquake struck, their roof collapsed and all were killed. The people didn't want their memory forgotten and so they set up this place to honor their good deeds."

Suzanna released Caleb and walked over to read the epitaphs. "Caleb, they were Jews. This man was a rabbi. There's a box here where people have left jewelry, pottery, glass vials with perfumes, and small gold wreaths."

Caleb stepped closer. "Look, they even have a clay lamp to burn when things get dark."

Barnabas ran his fingers over the unlit memento. "It helps keep the memory of their life alive."

"Doesn't anyone steal these gifts?" Caleb asked Barnabas.

"Only if they want to be cursed by the gods. One day, family members will come and claim what is rightfully theirs."

Suzanna noted the darkening clouds overhead. "Come, let's get to the market and return quickly before we're drenched."

Barnabas chuckled. "Take your time. The larger market is colonnaded and has enough canopies to keep you dry."

"We'll be back as soon as possible," Caleb said.

Barnabas turned toward his family memorial. "I'll meet you back home when I'm finished here. Move quickly through the forest and you won't attract the dogs. Hurry now."

The city of Tiberius rose like a crown of glory alongside the glistening waters of Lake Kinnereth. The Galilee region was a bustling center of international trade and a key outpost in the Roman's stand against the incursions of the Parthians. First, the city of Sepphoris had been restored to serve as the central jewel for Herod, and now Tiberius had risen as a token of gratitude for the emperor's favor.

A brilliant double rainbow sparkled in front of the darkened sky over one end of the lake.

"The promise of the Creator," a tribune said. "These Jews will be confident in their own strength. This is art for all to see."

Today, however, Titius didn't focus on the beauty around him. He wasn't distracted by the dozens of fishing vessels along the shoreline. He wasn't enthralled by the hundreds of gulls, kingfishers, and other birdlife whirling above the waters. His legion stood still, blocked by countless Jewish peasants whose bared necks dared the Romans to kill them all.

Marcellus slowly made his way up the hill toward the lookout. "They dare us to kill them all," he reported. "They have lain on their faces for almost forty days, refusing to eat and refusing to move."

"Governor Petronius is on his way from Damascus after being thwarted in Ptolemais," Titius replied. "He had ten thousand soldiers with him and couldn't get his way. This position on the negotiation team is putting my own neck at risk. He doesn't even know about the letter from the emperor requesting his suicide."

Marcellus removed his bronze helmet and tucked it under his arm. Sweat poured freely down his face in the hot summer sun. "If only Emperor Caligula would rescind his order to put the statue in the Jerusalem temple. Perhaps we need to make an example by crucifying some of the leaders."

Titius took a few steps to get a better view of the road. "I think we're too late for that. The governor's entourage is coming. The Jewish farmers have already refused to plant their crops. If they're willing to starve their own families and bare their own necks to our swords, then the emperor's image won't make it through to Jerusalem."

Marcellus took up his position at the side of the road to await the governor.

"I blame Pilate for trying to put those Roman standards in the temple grounds," Marcellus said. "When the priests and others resisted his efforts, he backed down and forever made us look weak. Caligula was right to recall him to Rome."

Titius stood next to the prefect and took off his own helmet with the ostrich feather. "Did I ever tell you I met the Messiah, Yeshua, right down there on that beach? He changed my life. I've seen the power of these people when they believe their God and are convinced he's worth dying for."

When the carriage stopped in front of Titius and Marcellus, Publius Petronius, governor of Syria alighted. He observed the tens of thousands of brown-tunicked Jews kneeling in the dust and wiped the sweat off of his brow with his forearm.

"This is worse than Caesarea," said Petronius. "What are you doing to meet with their leaders? The emperor will not be pleased."

Titius observed the proper salute and motioned for the entourage to follow him toward the crowd. A mile down the road, though, they found themselves unable to move forward. Neither horse nor archer nor swordsman, convinced the peasants to so much as flinch.

"Send us your leaders," Titius commanded. "We are here on order of the emperor. Who speaks for you all?"

Three elderly Jews near the front rose and stepped forward, but they soon dropped again to their knees, baring their necks. Titius was sure he had seen some of these faces during his time of desperation searching for Abigail along the lakeside.

"State your names," Titius commanded.

"Isaac of Capernaum," the first said clearly.

"Joshua of Nazareth," the second declared.

"Benjamin of Bethesda," the third proclaimed defiantly.

Titius sighed and asked his questions, already knowing the answers. "Why will you die? Will you leave your wives and children without someone to care for them? Who will till your fields? Who will make the pilgrimages and lead your worship if you are all dead?"

Isaac of Capernaum raised his head. "The Almighty will care for his own. When our sanctuary was defiled before, Judas Maccabeus rose to deliver us. If you kill us all, the Almighty himself will raise up a deliverer to demonstrate his power even as he did against the Egyptians long ago."

Petronius attempted to walk through the crowd, to reach the palace, but the men knelt shoulder to shoulder and stood in his way, refusing to move. He beckoned for Titius to give him a sword.

Titius remained in place. "Governor, none of us will leave here alive if we try to prove our force today. We have nothing to negotiate with."

The governor retreated, spied a yellow flower at the side of the road, and deliberately crushed it under his heel. "Do you dare take the side of the rebels?"

Petronius scanned the crowd, looked over his own force, then turned and headed back to the carriage.

"Marcellus, join me," Petronius commanded.

Titius was left standing with his legion as the governor's entourage headed back to Damascus. In the distance, they heard the mighty roar of tens of thousands of Jews celebrating their risky rebellion against the emperor.

The shrill call of dueling trumpets pierced through the pounding shouts and foot-stomping of twenty-five thousand bloodthirsty spectators hungry for death. Blood-sucking vampires bored with their meaningless lives.

Nabonidus emerged from the tunnel of the arena armed with a club and spear to find himself face to face with a Gaul outfitted as a murmillo. Tucked into the back of his own loincloth and belt was a coiled whip.

The murmillo was fierce with a large bronze helmet and ornate grilled visor over his face. His sword flashed back and forth in his right hand while his left hand held a large rectangular shield. His lower limbs were protected by a thick leather belt with metallic décor, an armguard, and thickly padded feet.

"Two denarii on the murmillo," a voice shouted nearby.

Other bets were completed as the warriors walked their way to the emperor's box, made their pledge, and advanced to the center of the sandy fighting pitch.

Nabonidus examined the murmillo's helmet, featuring a sculpted fish at the front. What was his story and what was he thinking in the face of death? This gladiator didn't come from his own ludus, and he had no idea of his opponent's fighting skills.

He analyzed the strengths and weaknesses of the man's shield, the gaiter on his right leg, his padded feet, and the two-and-half-foot gladius in his hand.

Nabonidus set himself for the inevitable attack, but another gate opened and a massive Ethiopian warrior ducked into the arena. No doubt, this was a surprise designed to entertain the bloodsuckers in the stands with too much money to spend. This black-skinned giant was dressed as a retarius with a trident and net, but he had no helmet. Only a metal shoulder shield protected his neck, and twenty victory-strings dangled from his wrist. He swung the heavy net as if it were a fairy's wand.

Another unknown combatant.

The crowd erupted into roars, and one section near the boxes set aside for the nobility waved white towels.

Next, a trio of lions padded into the arena. Slaves, strategically placed, pelted the lions with stones until the cats were enraged enough to trot into the middle of the arena. Beasts and men alike recognized their plight almost simultaneously as the roars of the crowd rose again. The three gladiators, having formed an unofficial pact, worked together to dispatch the animals.

Once the lions were left writhing in the sand, the warriors turned on each other.

"Ten denarii on the retarius," shouted someone from the crowd. Wagers were made as rich and poor, noble and commoner, Roman, Greek, or foreigner all focused on the death match.

The contest was over within ten minutes, much to the crowd's displeasure. The murmillo, assuming a form of truce with the retarius, attacked Nabonidus with his shield raised and gladius swinging. The retarius then betrayed him, throwing out his net and snagging the feet of the murmillo, forcing him to tumble to the ground. A trident in the back fatally wounded the falling gladiator before he could regain his balance.

With his net still wrapped in the feet of the murmillo, the retarius was an easy target for Nabonidus, who dropped his club, grabbed his whip, and unleashed it around his opponent's right ankle. Nabonidus then dispensed of him with his spear and began clubbing the body.

A doctor rushed out with his assistants begging the Persian to stop. The law forbade the dissection of anyone who had already died; cutting up the dying was the only way for medical practitioners to learn the art of how the human body worked. The assistants examined the murmillo and retarius before bundling them up on a board.

An opium brew, a few stitches, and a good massage left Nabonidus fading into a sleep of exhaustion. A sleep filled with the faces of home.

As he drifted off, he remembered that a win in battle was usually rewarded with a day of unattended freedom. A wound like his could mean a week or more free from training.

Chapter Four

Nabonidus was given two weeks off to recover from his latest battle, and he chose to spend some of that time returning to the fountain where he'd met that woman. He'd become convinced the meeting hadn't been a coincidence. Every day for a week, Nabonidus loitered in the place where he'd seen the charcoal-haired beauty, and on one such visit he noticed a small, crude drawing of a fish that had been etched into the stone along the fountain's edge. It puzzled him. He'd seen such small drawings of fish around the city, and at first he'd thought they perhaps pointed towards nearby fishmongers. But indeed, they seemed to have no such connection.

Anyway, no one questioned his presence here, although men brought their young boys up to him from time to time and asked that he touch their heads in a blessing.

Being a hero and a champion brought up confusing feelings in him. While he was a terror to his opponents in the arena, he was beset by his own inner terrors… terrors which worked hard to consume him. And the battle in his head was worse than the one in the arena. If he didn't harness the rage releasing him to destroy others, it would soon destroy him. The peace he sought was so elusive.

Having been abducted as a child, he hadn't learned the faith of his father or mother. The faith of his former owner, Caleb, had been strange in that he'd had no visible deity to worship. That religion hadn't had a place for outsiders like Nabonidus. And the Romans seemed fixated on images from all over the world, as though they were attempting to placate any and all deities to cover their own transgressions.

The fountain provided its own solace. Birds were numerous here, with sparrows, sunbirds, jays, and wrens being the most populous. Pigeons and doves settled in the trees overhead and watched the busy humans below. It was a great comfort for the soul after the pandemonium of the arena.

An old sailor, missing many of his teeth, rested next to Nabonidus on the second day.

"Did you know the legend?" the man mumbled.

Nabonidus answered so as not to be rude. "Which legend?"

The old man seemed startled. He examined Nabonidus as if noticing him for the first time. "You're not my son."

Nabonidus glanced away but the sailor tugged on his arm.

"Did you know the legend about the boar and the fish?" the man asked.

"No. I fight in the arena."

The old man picked up a pole he'd been holding and placed it on his lap. "Our city was founded by Androclus a millennium ago after the Delphi oracles showed him the way."

"The way to where?"

"Well, first Androclus fried a fish over the fire and the fish flopped out of the pan into a bush. A spark ignited the bush and a wild boar charged out."

"I don't know what you're talking about."

"Our city," the man said. "Androclus was told he needed to pay attention to the boar and the fish. When the bush burned, he built a new settlement and called it Ephesus."

Nabonidus rose and walked away. There wasn't enough time in the day to listening to such stories. The previous day, he'd been told the city had been founded by an army of Amazon women setting up a place for their goddess.

By the third day of sitting and pacing, Nabonidus grew curious about the variety of offerings displayed by a fishmonger who had set up shop nearby. As the gladiator stood near the table, he gained an appreciation for the choices. The merchant gave away samples, and the aroma drew people in. He even instructed his customers in the best way to prepare the fish.

"Madame, you'll love the bluefish. A brush of olive oil will give it the perfect touch before you grill it. My friend, I see you like the bonito. That fish is so big and will be perfect for a large family or a banquet with friends. Grill it after brushing it with olive oil. Sir, the red mullet! You have fine taste. Add garlic, herbs, tomato, and spices and you'll have a delicacy your diners will talk about for years. Step up, my lady, and stand in awe at this sea bass. Roast it with a side of this wahoo as an appetizer. Just pickle these little guys in a brine of lemon juice, some salt, and store it in olive oil until you're ready. You, sir, you look like a discerning chef. Smell this up close. Fresh. This turbot, cut into thick strips, coated with flour and fried, will leave your whole household wanting more. Friends, come now before it's gone. Fresh sardines wrapped in vine leaves and grilled to perfection. Get a taste and take it home to share. Get it now, while you can… mackerel, pandora, anchovies… get it all right here."

On the fifth day, Nabonidus was given another opportunity to learn something new. An old Persian trader stepped off a cart loaded with spices and sat beside him.

"Son, why are you sitting here?" said the trader. "Have you lost an understanding of who you are?"

Nabonidus shrugged his shoulders. "I'm a champion of the arena. I live to die."

The man squinted and gently hit the side of his own head with the palm of his hand. "Who fills your mind with this pulp? What did your mother and father teach you about being Persian?"

Nabonidus raised his chin and looked him in the eye. "My mother and father were killed by bandits when I was five and I've been a slave ever since. I know nothing about being Persian."

The old man clasped Nabonidus's forearm and nodded in empathy. "My name is Anoshiruvan—it means 'the immortal soul who knows.' First let me feed you Persia's best food and then we'll talk about who we are in our blood."

He rose and disappeared into the chaos of the market.

Three hours later, Nabonidus heard the distinctive click of a cane and saw the man return accompanied by two Persian girls around nine or ten years of age.

"My daughter, Adrina, which means 'flaming lights,' and my daughter Atossa, which means 'free flowing.' They have tried their best to prepare what their mother has taught them."

The girls set down two steaming dishes in front of Nabonidus and a crowd quickly gathered.

The old man pointed at the first dish. "This is Fesenjan—we use it in weddings. There is pomegranate, duck, walnuts, onions, saffron, cinnamon, sugar, and perhaps some other things which are a family secret."

Adrina spooned out a generous helping into a clay bowl and handed Nabonidus a wooden spoon.

Once Nabonidus had eaten several spoonfuls, Atossa removed the lid of the second dish.

"This is Bademjan," the man continued. "The golden-red tomatoes have turmeric, lemon juice, grapes, eggplant, onions, lamb, and some seasoning which is part of our family recipe. You eat this with rice."

Atossa stepped back and let him examine the contents. Nabonidus ate until he was satisfied. He hadn't tasted food like that in forever.

The girls removed the dishes and Anoshiruvan settled himself down for further instruction. "First, you must know that Persians don't practice spirituality as the Romans do. We have no monuments or temples. God is above all."

Nabonidus nodded. "We're like the Jews who worship the unseen Creator."

Anoshiruvan grunted his agreement. "Yes. We cultivate his earth. We were the ones who brought pistachio nuts and sesame seeds to this land. We manufactured linen from flax. We brought many new fruits and vegetables to the Empire. We brought alfalfa for the animals to forage. We introduced irrigation!"

The gladiator nodded again. "So we work the creation we have been given?"

Anoshiruvan pursed his lips wide. "We also create as the Creator does. We set up a system where riders can carry messages from place to place. We also trained pigeons to carry messages between homes."

"So we spread our influence wide."

"You are a Persian and must be very proud," Anoshiruvan insisted. "You are the best of peoples and should never bow to any man. What was your family name?"

"Maimonides."

"And where was your family home?"

"Susa."

"And when were you taken?"

"Twenty-three years ago."

Anoshiruvan ran his knuckle back and forth across his wrinkled brow before nodding in confirmation. "It must be true," he said. "Around the time you say you were taken, a young prince disappeared with his family. Many people still believe this prince will return to restore justice to our lands."

"I know nothing about that," Nabonidus said. "All I know is that my parents were killed by bandits and I've been a slave ever since."

"One day you must return to Persia and prove your identity. In the meantime, I can prepare the way for you."

The lesson was over. The old man and his daughters hobbled away without even saying farewell. A piece of Nabonidus's home vanished with him.

On the eighth day, after loitering at the nearby medical school and library, Nabonidus saw the beautiful woman again. She carried the same basket, sat in the same place at the fountain, and looked like heaven come down to earth. When she saw him approaching, she made no effort to look away or run.

The scent of roses filled the air as he strode purposefully toward her. When he came close, she reached into her basket and pulled out a peach hidden among the flowers. Nabonidus accepted the gift and did his best not to crush it in his shaking hands.

"Who are you?" he asked.

The olive-skinned woman smiled. "A messenger."

"From whom?"

"A friend."

"What is the message?"

"Love is stronger than hate."

Nabonidus's furrowed brows betrayed his deep thought at the message. *What kind of message is this for a gladiator? Who would send such a message? Is it meant to torment me?*

The woman removed a clay cup from her basket, dipped it into the fountain, and raised it up to the warrior. "Quench your thirst. Salve your parched throat. This cup is offered in the name of your friend."

Nabonidus drank the cool liquid in a single guzzle. He then returned the cup and the woman placed it back in her basket.

"Have you ever worked as a healer in the temple?" he asked. He hadn't focused on her face during that first encounter, when she'd healed him, but he was sure this was the same woman.

"My former life is a path of shadows gone forever," she replied.

"Aren't you the one who healed me? Didn't you put cabbage on my wound? And later, did you not throw down the bag of frankincense to help my infection?"

"I have done what was needed, but now I am a free woman, no longer bound by the chains which trapped my soul."

"Why don't you speak plainly, woman?"

"I can only say what is true."

He hesitated. "What is your name?"

"Daphne," she said. "I'm a student of the apostle John and a friend of Mary, the mother of Yeshua of Nazareth."

A shiver went up his spine. Yeshua? Was that the same Yeshua known by Caleb the cross maker?

Daphne rose. "I must go. My duty was only to deliver the message. Your duty is to receive it."

He watched her blend into the crowd of the agora without glancing back at him. No shaft of sunshine highlighted her path this time; she was simply a messenger retreating after doing her duty.

Yet the conviction within him grew. This Daphne, this follower of the apostle, was the very healer he had met in the Temple of Artemis. There could be no doubt.

Titius and Abigail stood on a hill overlooking Damascus. It had been a week since he'd been warned by Marcellus that the governor was determined to destroy him.

A flock of vultures circled high overhead. Caravans crawled out of the desert like an army of ants toward the oasis near the city. Oxcarts plodded over the steep hills hauling cargo from the ports of the Great Sea.

Abigail held her indigo veil tightly over her nose and mouth as the wind tugged at her rich red robes. Mountain ranges rose up to their west with Mount Hermon towering above the rest. Great fertile hills spread out to the south and desert dunes to the east.

Titius pointed toward the city. "That larger temple is dedicated to Jupiter. The Romans built it recently out of Grecian marble and local limestone. The river through the mountains over there is the Euphrates, which flows right over to the land where God began all of life with Adam."

"Don't forget about Eve," Abigail said.

A dry arid wind scratched at their clothing and disturbed puffs of dust at their feet.

"It's hard to believe," Titius said, "but this place and Jericho are two of the oldest continually inhabited cities in the world. This place on the Barada River sits at the crossroads between the land of the Ethiopians and the Persians and all points beyond. If we go south, we'll face lions, elephants, and leopards. If we move east, we'll face bears, tigers, and other perils."

"Must we go?" Abigail asked. "I feel we've run enough. First Caeserea, then Antioch, Corinth, Athens, Alexandria, and now Damascus. It's been almost ten years and I want to share the good news of Yeshua's victory over death."

"If I'm going to continue my role as a Roman general, I have no choice but to live as one. We lack for nothing. We have freedom to move, and we meet followers of Yeshua everywhere we go."

"Living as a general's wife isn't as easy when I've spent most of my life as a slave. I fear every day someone will discover who I am and turn me over to the lions in the arena. More than anything, I would like a child and a home to call my own."

Titius reached out and took her hand in his. "You are the wife of General Titius Marcus Julianus. There's no better woman in this country. Just because Saul created so much havoc here doesn't mean the Nabataean King Aretas will be back to extinguish us. He's dying back in Petra. Emperor Caligula only gave him this city to calm him down after Herod Antipas divorced the king's daughter…"

"What about Ananias?" Abigail asked. She had lived independently for many years and didn't quit. "How can we leave him alone to build up the church in Damascus? His wife and children work hard to welcome people while he preaches. I'm tired of moving around."

Titius suddenly pushed Abigail behind himself protectively.

"Wait! There's a half-dozen camels racing out of Damascus in this direction," he warned her. "Something's happening. The spies may have found us out."

"What will we do?" she asked, sounding afraid.

"Hide down in that gulley." Titius indicated the hiding spot. "And if anything happens to me, find Ananias here or John in Ephesus."

Titius watched as Abigail bundled up her red robes and scuffled her way down an embankment to hide behind a rocky outcropping in the gulley outside Damascus.

Up ahead, the six camel riders were urging their mounts on while a small caravan of traders pulled off to the side of the road to get out of the way. Splashes of sunlight glimmered off the riders' swords. Titius drew out his own and made a plan of defense. He took up position in a copse of olive, walnut, and chestnut trees banded together near a wadi a few hundred feet from the road.

Despite rolling up his scarlet cape and sheltering on the lower limbs of an oak tree, Titius knew he'd been seen. His pursuers didn't hesitate to charge into the copse of trees. They soon surrounded his hideaway.

"General, we bring news," the leader yelled.

Titius stepped down from the tree and walked without fear into the midst of the mounted soldiers.

"You must come with us," a soldier said as he pulled his camel into a kneeling position. "Your time has come and we've been ordered to bring you back to Governor Petronius."

The camel ride into Damascus took the rest of the afternoon. The caravans, carts, and pilgrims crowding into the city reluctantly made way for the caravan as they pushed toward the main gate.

A niggling sensation of danger captured Titius's awareness. Dark clouds had crept across the plain—but they weren't clouds out of the sky; they were swarms of bees! Pilgrims and traders appeared oblivious of the advance, but the insects' hum grew louder among the braying of donkeys and creaking of loaded carts. The bees descended into the crowd. Soon the people were screaming, panicking, howling as they dispersed in all directions.

A donkey cart in front of the camels pivoted and clipped the legs of the camel carrying Titius. The animal bellowed in pain and collapsed under him, tossed him into the path of a galloping troop of legionnaires.

His reflexes kicked in so quickly that he had no time to consciously process what was happening. One moment he was in the path of deadly hooves and the next he had rolled to the side, leapt onto the neck of a new mount, and kicked the rider off onto the roadway.

Yanking on the reins, Titius lurched his horse out of the mob and galloped away from the city. He chanced a look over his shoulder as he rode and saw that the soldiers had all dismounted to care for the injured camel; they hadn't even noticed his disappearance yet.

Titius detoured toward a small village, shedding his Roman gear on the way. On the outskirts, he dismounted, stripped down to his common tunic, and searched through the pack still attached to the saddle. He removed a few provisions that had belonged to the horse's previous owner, including a simple cape. He then exchanged his leather sandals for a pair of worn ones lying outside the door of a cottage. At another cottage, he helped himself to a woman's tunic and left the horse behind.

Five minutes later, from his perch atop a cedar tree, he saw two camel riders and four legionnaires tracking his escape route. One was holding up the crimson cape he had abandoned. It wouldn't be long before he had nowhere to hide.

Halfway through the forest path toward the market place in Salamis, the first drops of rain landed on Suzanna.

"We need to find a good tree or run for the market," she warned.

Caleb noted the angry clouds rumbling overhead. Lightning flashed, and moments later the thunder shook the surrounding trees. A deluge soon fell like a waterfall overtop them.

At that moment, a pack of wild dogs howled into the space between husband and wife and advanced toward Suzanna. Caleb snatched up a handful of small rocks and hurled them at the lead dog, gaining a yelp for his efforts. All but one of the pack turned in his direction and gave chase as he ran for the nearest branches.

Suzanna raced off into the undergrowth as another dog picked up her pursuit. As she glanced over her shoulder, she saw the animal's bared fangs opening wide to bite her.

To her relief, the dog suddenly disappeared under the tusks of a raging boar. The dog yelped, growled, and bit at its attacker, but it was no match for the attacker's tusks as they gored into its side.

The lightning and thunder shook the forest in bursts of flash and fury as the clouds poured out the full weight of their burden. Suzanna became soaked as she watched the boar retreat into the forest. The injured dog lay whimpering in the brush and finally stopped moving altogether.

She looked around and realized that in the chaos she'd gotten lost. Determined not to be caught by the rest of the pack, she pushed through the brush until she found a deer path. Once on it, she ran. She fell three times, getting caught up in the branches before she broke through onto a hill above the cemetery they'd visited earlier. She breathed in relief at the sight of the marble monuments, carved idols, wilted flowers, and limestone reliefs.

As she reached a small knoll, the earth shuddered and ripped apart as if it were nothing but a piece of unleavened bread. A wide, dark fissure opened up under her and a scream escaped her lips as she fell into the depths.

The cold sweat on Nabonidus's forehead accompanied the shivers consuming him as he curled up under a bear skin blanket, sprawled on a straw mat. The gash in his thigh, a wound gained from a momentary lapse of attention against a newcomer in practice, burned like the rest of his body. The lanista, the one who had purchased Nabonidus and took responsibility for his overall care, had summoned the local physician and now the two hovered over him, discussing his condition. The dark room deep in the heart of the ludus was devoid of natural light.

"The wound is infected," the physician mumbled. He poked and prodded Nabonidus until the gladiator groaned in pain.

"Can you help him?" asked the lanista. "He's my best warrior and is scheduled to fight in two days."

"He's too weak to fight." The physician examined Nabonidus's teeth, eyes, and throat. "You might as well send a goat."

"I'll pay you well to cure him."

The physician carried a wooden box and burlap sack from the other side of the room. "Fortunately, the Greeks have taught us much. Healing depends on balancing the four fluids—the black and yellow bile, the phlegm and the blood. Perhaps bloodletting and time in the baths will help. First, we must induce him to vomit. I have the perfect ingredients."

"Are there not incantations or sacrifices we can make?" the lanista queried.

The doctor waved him away and tied Nabonidus's ankles and wrists together. "If you wanted superstition, you should have taken him to the Temple of Aesculapius. That Son of Apollo and Coronas is said to have learned his art from a centaur… if one can believe in such myths. No, we must use what we know. Hold him down while I pour this solution down his throat."

Chapter Five

It took Nabonidus a month to recover to full strength from his infection, and during the final two weeks of his convalescence, he had been making regular visits to the temple healers.

The Temple of Artemis appeared only half as evil in the light of day. The sacred prostitutes still plied their trade at the entrance and the merchants continued to craft and sell their images of the goddess. The jade and golden columns glinted in the sun. Priestesses lured worshippers into the cavernous halls, and the erotic paintings and images were still as explicit and lurid.

The blood stains of the temple guardians he had slain months before had been polished away and the marble gleamed as white as ever. New sentries stood calmly in place, watching the sick and dying being dragged into the courtyard. The healers recited their incantations and applied their remedies while collecting their coin from the desperate.

Today, Nabonidus hadn't come seeking healing; he'd come seeking answers. After speaking with Daphne by the fountain, he had decided to speak with the governess at the temple. She was the one responsible for overseeing the priestesses, apprentices, and other women connected with temple worship.

Selsus, the flaxen-haired giant, strode confidently down the stairs toward him.

"This woman you seek, Daphne, is no longer in the city," Selsus announced. "The governess says this woman was released from her spirits by the followers of the Way, whatever that means. I paid her well, but she then told me to seek someone she referred to as the apostle John."

"In this whole empire, only Rome is larger than Ephesus," Nabonidus remarked. "A quarter of a million souls live and die on this soil. How in the name of Jupiter do we find a man named only John?"

Selsus just shook his head. "If this woman has fallen prey to some cult, it means she is weak-minded and not worth your effort. Spend your pleasure on someone who longs for you. If you continue to be distracted, the arena will claim your heart before she ever does." Selsus gave him a hard shove. "I just wish they would let me fight you. I'd cut you to pieces and feed you to the lions without hesitation."

Nabonidus shuffled to a nearby stone bench and slumped down on it. "She healed me, and I wanted to thank her and her maidens."

"Perhaps it was only your delirium," Selsus said. "You know how women play with the mind of a man. Perhaps they were nothing but hags enchanting you to steal your coin."

"You wouldn't know a hag from a princess," Nabonidus muttered. "One whore is as good as another for you."

Selsus slapped the Persian across the face but Nabonidus refused to respond.

"I thought so," Selsus said, mockingly. "You have the fury of a lamb, and the power of a child."

"If you weren't as pitiful a prisoner as I am, I'd snap your neck. Be careful where you sleep. I might not be able to wait until you grow skilled enough to face me in the arena."

"You're nothing but a pitiful slave, worthy of the dung heap."

Nabonidus smirked. "I recently met a Persian named Anoshiruvan who thinks I might have been born a prince in Persia."

Selsus lowered his head in mock adoration. "If you're a prince, I'm an emperor."

"If you were the emperor, every senator and slave would be in rebellion. Who would bow to your demands?"

Selsus crossed his wrists over his chest and took a deep breath. "Even now, I've been gathering children from the streets to take to a nearby farm and raise as my own. Every one of them honors me. One day, they'll be ready."

"Ready for what?"

Selsus reached for his sword and held it out at arm's length. "They will be ready to fight, to love, to rule... whatever I desire for them."

Two centurions riding in a chariot suddenly clattered up the cobblestone streets and onto the marble courtyard of the temple. The one holding the reins wore a golden helmet with a large ostrich feather arched on top. He drew his sword.

"Gladiator, get up," the centurion commanded. "You are summoned to the governor's residence immediately."

The second centurion stepped down from the chariot and drew out a whip. He snapped it at Selsus, daring the giant to interfere in the snatching of his charge.

Nabonidus slowly walked toward the back of the chariot and allowed himself to be hoisted up and fastened in place by the wrists. He ignored the furious glare of Selsus as the chariot raced away.

Caleb crawled higher into the cedar tree as the wild dogs growled savagely on the ground below. He could see the roof of the Temple of Zeus, but the noise around him made it impossible for his yelling to be heard that far away. When the howl of a wild dog sounded from the forest through the roaring thunder, two of the pack peeled off and raced after it.

As he watched the dogs run into the forest, he thought of Suzanna. He had a feeling they were pursuing her, but the sentries below kept him from helping.

"God, help her," he prayed. "Suzanna! Suzanna!"

The only response to his calls was a thunderclap and flash of lightning.

Caleb broke off small branches and hurled them down at the remaining dogs below, but this only served to agitate them. They snapped their jaws hungrily at him.

After a few minutes, he climbed higher to see if he could see someone he could call for help. From a higher perch, he saw a small waterfall where a stream poured into a pool hidden by the forest undergrowth. An old man was hunched at the top of the falls, holding a small fishing net.

But the fisherman was too far away to hear above the storm and surging waters.

When Caleb was ten feet from the top of the tree, he also noticed two boys running together away from the forest. They didn't hear him either, his yells lost to the pounding rain.

Without warning, the branch he'd perched on broke. Losing his grip, he hurtled down through the branches, grasping desperately for a hold. He lost all sense of up and down and soon hit stomach-first on a thick branch near the bottom of the tree, knocking the wind out of him.

A faint blur of snapping jaws inches from his face energized him to tighten his thighs and reach up for a handhold. He had nowhere to go as he gasped for air.

Eventually the dog stopped leaping and lay on its belly, tongue hanging out.

Caleb maneuvered his arm up to grab a smaller branch as an anchor. He pulled himself until he could straddle the branch. He dragged himself inch by inch until he could wrap his arms around the trunk.

Hours passed before he gained the confidence to stand again and peer down at the wild dogs.

Meanwhile, a deafening crack resonated through the forest as a tree was split in two and crashed to the ground. Half of it fell directly onto the pack of dogs. One dog took a direct hit across its back and lay squirming under the shattered trunk. Two others, pinned by branches, yelped and struggled until they were free. They then licked themselves and limped around trying to help their fallen pack member.

––––––––––––

Suzanna sat neck deep in mud as more water and earth caved into the crevice that had been created by the earthquake. Semiconscious, she worked to raise her arms out of the pit. The rain was cool and images of her childhood, dancing in the rain near Hebron, distracted her until her chin dipped into the mud.

A dog's bark somewhere overhead filled her with enough terror to jerk fully wake. She extracted her hands and grabbed a protruding tree root. Pulling with all the energy she had left, she adjusted her legs so she could kneel. From there, she planted her right foot and pushed up to free herself from the slimy grave. The mud came up to her thighs and rising and a pair of dogs were hovering over her, baying at their trapped prey.

The rain continued to beat down on dogs and woman alike, and Suzanna felt freezing cold right to the core. Numbness prevailed in her limbs as she attempted to step onto a branch now buried in the mud to free herself. The dogs only leaned in close.

"Yeshua," she prayed. "Help me!"

––––––––––––

Titus, disguised as an old grandmother, watched as a line of legionnaires trotted their horses past him. He hobbled around as the riders searched for the runaway general, knocking on doors and calling out for villagers to be alert for the escaping Roman.

Titius pulled up the headscarf over his nose and continued into an apple orchard where a group of children ran giggling past, mocking him as they ran toward the well where the soldiers had called everyone to gather. The youngest child, around six years of age, picked up a stick and attempted to throw it at Titius. He glared, and in response the child retreated, tripping over a goat and falling on his back. Everyone who noticed laughed and continued on their way.

Titius kept his head lowered and shuffled deeper into the trees. Once safely away, he snatched up a new pair of clothes from outside a cottage and walked away from town, this time dressed as a field hand.

He moved in and out of convoys, travelling in plain sight while remaining invisible—an art he had perfected.

When Titius was certain no sentries or legionnaires had persisted in their search for him, he dropped to the side of the road and waited by a tree as the afternoon slipped by. Safe again, he jogged back toward where he'd left Abigail.

But no matter how long he searched, he found no sign of her.

The slave at the governor's mansion wasted no time ensuring Nabonidus was washed down and then outfitted in white leather. His loincloth, belt, wrist strap, and sandals, all leather, had been cut from the same hide. The twenty-three streamers attached to his wrist strap spoke of his triumphs in the arena, although the symbol of glory was truly a trophy of shame.

As shadows crossed the floor of the great hall where he waited, he looked up at the walls covered with the heads of lions, bears, leopards, zebras, and even an elephant. An Ethiopian slave was at the far end of the room, lighting a candelabra. Another slave left a platter of dates, figs, cheese, and apricots.

The apricots toyed with his memories. Caleb the cross maker had chased down Barabbas by tracking apricot sellers in Caesarea. It was the fruit of treachery…

Nabonidus smelled roasted meat as a steward arrived to escort him to the governor's hall. His stomach growled in protest.

Entertainers and kitchen staff lingered around the corridors, curious to examine the colossal specimen of humanity being put on display. The longing gleam in their eyes matched those he had seen among the priestesses at the Artemission.

Lust isn't limited by wealth or class, he reminded himself. *It's but the desire to have what isn't yours…*

The steward halted before a set of scarlet curtains. "Five Roman senators have joined the governor inside. All the elite of Ephesus are here. Perform well and you will be rewarded."

"Perform? What does the governor expect?"

"There's no time to explain."

The steward parted the curtains to reveal a massive lounge filled with the glitter and glamor of the city's nobility. Flickering torches danced in rhythm with drums, zithers, flutes, and lyres.

"Do what you know and do it well," the steward said as he departed.

Abigail hurried along the streets of Damascus, intent on her destination. Titius had told her that if anything happened to him, she should find Ananias, and that's exactly what she intended to do.

But when she got to the road where the man and his family lived, she stopped in her tracks. A group of Roman soldiers were loading Ananias's children onto a cart while his wife stood off to the side, weeping hysterically.

Not knowing what else to do, Abigail turned and fled.

As she passed a clothesline, she borrowed a few items of clothing and ducked into a copse of willow trees to put them on, exchanging her bright red garments for the plain brown tunic of a common Syrian. The cloak, wrapped around her waist, added bulk and gave her an entirely different body shape. The shawl completed the disguise.

She pocketed the few coins Titius had given her and used them to purchase figs, dates, and olives from the market. She then set her sights on travelling to Ephesus and reaching the apostle John. That had been her husband's other suggestion, in the event that something had also happened to Ananias.

Abigail left Damascus through the west gate, hitching a ride with a small caravan of traders heading north to Tarsus. From there, she'd cross west to Ephesus.

By the time the torrential rains ceased and the thundering skies quieted, mud had risen to Suzanna's armpits. Evening was fast approaching and the cold had penetrated to her bones, but she held onto the tree branch with every ounce of her diminishing strength. At least the wild dogs appeared to have left.

"Yeshua, giver of life, save me in this place," she prayed. "Free me to share your truth with those who need it here."

Suddenly, she heard a man's voice. "Is that the voice of the dead? What spirit might you be?"

"Help!" Suzanna shouted through the dark of the cemetery. "I am not a spirit. I'm down in this hole."

"Have you come from the pit of Hades itself? I call on Apollo and Zeus to free me from this terror."

Suzanna stretched herself, getting up onto her tiptoes. "If you abandon me now, I pray all the curses of the gods fall on your head. I am buried under this tree in a hole caused by the earthquake. Save me!"

A bearded face appeared above her in the dimming light. The man held a torch. "By the mercies of Diana, what evils have you committed to be buried in such a manner?"

"I have committed no evils," she said. "I was walking to the market and the ground opened up beneath me. Please pull me out."

The man worked his way around the hole and tested the firmness of the branch she was clutching by stepping onto one of its limbs.

"I dare not test the Fates," he mused. "Surely you have done something to bring about your own judgment. Confess your evils, make your sacrifices, and all will be well."

"How can I make sacrifices buried up to my neck? Release me from this pit and I shall confess my sins to the only true God of life."

"And who might that be?"

"Release me and I'll tell you."

"I came to this place to end my life this night." He reached behind him and produced a rope. "This rope was meant to hang me from this very tree. I came to take my place among the dead. No god has ever heard my cries for help before now... why should I help someone who's clearly under a curse from whatever god she follows?"

"Who do you think destroyed your tree of death and made it into a ladder of life for me? Use your rope and pull me to freedom. My God has reached out to offer you life."

Suzanna reached for the rope, hoping her would-be rescuer would do his part.

When Nabonidus stepped into the room containing the Ephesian nobility, he found two centurions in the middle of a skirmish while the rich men of the city watched from the sides of the room. The skirmish was more theatre than actual battle. At least, that's what Nabonidus assumed by the awkward thrusts.

As time passed and the bout continued, however, the noblemen shouted for blood and the thrusts of the soldiers became deadlier.

Suddenly, a gladius grazed Nabonidus's own arm and he reacted from instinct. Within moments, he had decapitated both of the squabbling centurions. The noblemen roared their approval, cheering and clapping the gladiator's performance.

Shortly after, Nabonidus was dismissed into the night as if nothing had happened. He changed into his street clothes and walked out the door.

Painted prissies drinking themselves stupid, he thought as he left, imagining the night's entertainment finished.

As he approached the gate, another centurion waited for him, looking angry.

"Before this night is through, your head will be in the same place where you left the heads of my men," the centurion had said.

Nabonidus had continued into the night, but he soon heard footsteps behind him and realized the angry centurion was giving chase. This set him to running through the streets of the city.

The alleys off the main residential area of Ephesus were like a maze in the darkness and Nabonidus soon got himself lost. Rats scurried around his feet amongst the garbage.

As he ran, a vivid image of his older brother Yanti stabbed into his memory. Rats had bitten his feet in their home in Persia, attempting to eat the remnants of grapes he had been stomping on in the family vat. The small bit of flesh lost to the teeth of a rodent had seemed small and insignificant for a twelve-year-old, but the fever had taken Yanti slowly over days and weeks. He had complained of pain, but the redness and swelling had seemed to respond well to salt baths. The weeping pus oozing out of the wounds had gone unnoticed for days as his mother and sister had focused on placing cool cloths on his head and dripping water onto his parched tongue.

The vomiting had been sudden and vicious. Yanti had clutched his temples as his head threatened to explode. The rash had raged across his body like a fire out of control, his throat continuing to swell. It had been a mercy when the priest arrived to put him out of his misery.

Nabonidus shook off the memories.

That's what happens when you love someone, he thought. *You lose them and get left with nothing but pain.*

Drunken shouts and howls emerged from inns and homes as the people fell prey to their addictions and terrors. A small campfire burned at the end of the current alley and a dozen shadowy figures huddled together attempting to warm up in its glow.

The voice of the centurion screaming at someone in the darkness behind him stirred Nabonidus to quick action. He scaled a small fence and hoisted himself up onto a balcony. Shuffling along the precarious edge until he reached a broader ledge and pulled himself up through a window opening.

As Nabonidus peeked over the sill, the centurion and a dozen legionnaires marched past the home and confronted the group huddled around the campfire. Those who ran fast enough escaped the beatings.

Give me a minute in the arena with that Roman rat and we'll see how well he can take a real beating, Nabonidus thought. *May Mars feed him to the scorpions until he screams for mercy.*

As he backed away from the window, he bumped into someone—someone who let out a squeak of pain. Hearing the commotion, the centurion on the street turned and looked at the window where he had just entered. Stepping across the prostrate bodies around the campfire, the centurion hurried toward the home where Nabonidus had taken refuge, his men following behind.

Nabonidus ran.

Titius decided to look for his wife in the most obvious place he could think of—Ananias's home in the city. But when he arrived, he found the home empty. Huddled in the darkness, he watched as Roman legionnaires went about the business of questioning the neighbors about the whereabouts of Ananias. From the terrified pleas of the peasants, it seemed that Ananais's wife and children had been taken to the governor's dungeon—but the man of the house had not yet been found.

Titius determined that Ananias was clearly being hidden by other followers of the Way, that he was safe for now.

Titius snaked his way through the alleys until he reached the governor's mansion—a fortress for the worst of prisoners. He berated himself for having discarded his clothing as a Roman general. With that role, he could have penetrated the security detail.

Caleb outwaited the wild dogs long enough that the moonless night soon covered his descent from the cedar tree. He shook leaves out of his tunic when he reached the ground.

Climbing trees had been such a great part of his childhood. Having the freedom as a boy to roam the forests near Nazareth had confirmed his love of wood. The neighbor lad who had grown up to become Yeshua the Messiah had simply been another carpenter learning his father's trade. Together they'd planed and whittled and shaped the oak, cypress, olive, and juniper pieces left over from their fathers' projects.

Those days seemed long ago indeed.

Taking a big breath, he caught the pleasant scents of evergreen box trees and red sandalwood. Feeling safe, he heard nothing but the croak of frogs and the chirps of crickets.

He assumed Suzanna must have found her way back to Barnabas by another route, so he intuitively sensed his way through the darker patches of forest. His progress was slow, but he soon came to a boulder which he remembered; it had been near the entrance to a path.

Before he could gain much confidence, though, he heard a leopard's snarl.

His hope draining, Nabonidus rounded the corner a mere three hundred yards ahead of the trailing legionnaires.

Looks like you've done it this time, he told himself.

As he ran through an alley, the sound of a lute, a cithara, and a lyre drew his attention. A door was opening and a woman emerged to dump a pail of water. Daphne! He raced toward her, and Daphne held open the door, motioning him inside. It seemed almost too good to be true!

He raced inside and up some stairs, hearing the door bolt shut behind him. A moment later, he heard the pounding feet and thunderous shouts of passing soldiers. He had gotten away.

Looking around, he realized he'd been let into an inn. Was Daphne an innkeeper?

Nabonidus was still bent over, catching his breath, when someone knocked loudly on the door downstairs.

"Open up!" demanded the voice of the enraged centurion.

He froze, wondering where to go next, when Daphne answered the unspoken question for him. She pointed toward a blanket hanging on a wall, then pulled it aside to reveal a hidden doorway. Was it an escape—or a trap?

Having no choice, he turned the handle of the door and stepped through as Daphne lowered the blanket again behind him.

He found himself standing at the top of a stairway going down. As he crept cautiously down into the darkness, the pounding on the door to the inn grew more insistent.

The sound grew more distant once he reached the bottom. He was standing beneath the inn's floorboards. Just above him, the door to the inn finally slammed open and the centurion pushed his way inside.

"Give him up, you wretched hag," the centurion demanded. "Where are you hiding him?"

Nabonidus ran his fingers along the moist walls and found a passageway leading away into the darkness. From his sense of direction, it seemed to pass beneath the street itself, turning into a tunnel shored up with strong timbers.

Without torchlight, the space felt like a crypt.

Suddenly, as clear as day, the image of a purple-faced ghoul rose up in front of him—it was the face of his first slave master, Maimonides. Nabonidus remembered cowering in a wagon as the man poured buckets of fish over him.

Nabonidus shook away the memory, but still he crouched on the ground and waited for the horror to pass. When it finally did, he crept forward, toes and hands outstretched. He brushed away thick cobwebs which wrapped themselves around his body like a mummy's shroud. Apart from spiders, only one other lifeform made its presence known in this tunnel—rats, the spawn of Hades.

He gagged on the stench of rat feces long accumulated in the dank earth, covering his nose and mouth with the crook of his elbow.

Despite the sturdy timbers overhead, dirt sprinkled down on him as he pushed on. It seemed as though the heavy march of Roman soldiers might cave in the very roof of his refuge.

He hunched in the darkness and replayed the evening's events. On the tables at the governor's mansion, the nobles had snacked on the orange fruit Nabonidus himself had loved as a child. It had momentarily brought back memories of his mother's table—of dishes of pistachios, almonds, walnuts, pomegranates, mint, grapes, saffron, and heaps of special rice.

Never had he been free to eat his fill of the food of kings, though.

That's going to change, he thought to himself. *No Roman pig will stop me from getting what I want. I've earned my freedom in the arena and no one will take it away from me again.*

He slowly rose and faced the darkness ahead.

Chapter Six

The faintest speck of light filtered into the tunnel as Nabonidus kicked at another rat running over his sandaled foot. He crept the last few hundred feet until his hand touched a slightly opened door. He tried to peer into the room, and suddenly the door swung open to reveal a grey beard and a hooded face buried in shadows.

Nabonidus took a step back and almost twisted his ankle on a brick lying at an angle. The old man reached out and grabbed him by the wrist to steady him.

"Whoa, my Persian friend," the man said with a chuckle. "There are easier ways to find the Lord than hiding in the darkness."

Being designated as a friend gave Nabonidus the confidence to step into the room where four clay lamps lit the faces of a dozen men and women huddled around a loaf of bread and a cup of wine. They wore anxiety and fear on their faces.

The old man shut the door to the dank passageway and covered it with a blanket. He then cinched the belt around his tan robe and pulled at the prayer shawl laying across his shoulder.

"We heard the noise and thought perhaps Daphne was coming to warn us of trouble," he said. "The Romans were searching every home in this area. Would that someone be you? Are you a believer?"

Nabonidus brushed off more of the cobwebs from his face and arms as he surveyed each person. Three women wore the finer garb of house slaves. Two of the women had Roman togas with purple stripes, marking them as nobility. A few of the men were tradesmen, possibly carpenters. One was a fisherman. No one was familiar except a girl he had seen once at the marketplace.

"I mean no harm," Nabonidus said. "I am a gladiator."

"We know who you are Nabonidus," the old man replied. "I'm John, the one you've been searching for. The Lord Jesus has brought us together at last."

The curtain on the other side of the room parted and Daphne stepped through to take her place at the table.

"Sorry to delay you," she said. "The Lord's work is always full of surprises. I see you've met Nabonidus. The Romans must think he's a phantom."

Nabonidus accepted the chair offered by John and sat back to watch the proceedings. John shared a story about Yeshua meeting with him and his friends to share a last meal before his death. Yeshua had spoken about bread being like a body and about the wine being like blood. Apparently it was all part of a new agreement which God had set up to save his people.

Nabonidus was intrigued. "What is this new agreement you speak of? What was the old agreement?"

John nodded thoughtfully, raised his eyebrows at those waiting with pieces of bread in their hand, and turned to his questioner. "The old agreement set by God was that if we successfully obeyed every law set down by him, we would be given a life which lasts. If we fell short of his demands, we would die. In place of our own deaths, though, we could sacrifice a perfect animal in our place, as a temporary covering each year."

"I've seen this with an older master of mine," Nabonidus said. "What's the new agreement?"

"The new agreement says that Yeshua—that is, Jesus Christ—obeyed the law for us, took our place in death as a perfect sacrifice, and gained for us eternal life."

Nabonidus frowned. "I don't know what this means, but my former master grew up with this Jesus in Nazareth and said he was a very good man."

John moved closer and put a hand on the gladiator's shoulder. "I too knew Jesus, although we called him by his Hebrew name, Yeshua. I walked with him for three years and stood at his feet when he died on that cross. He's far more than a good man."

"You're a follower of the Nazarene?" Nabonidus shook off John's hand from his shoulder and rose to his feet, towering over the apostle. "Do you know what they're doing to the followers of the Nazarene? Right here, in Ephesus? When they're not soaking the sand with the blood of gladiators, they're soaking it with the blood of Christians!"

"We know," John said.

Nabonidus walked over to Daphne and stared into her eyes. "Your children are being sacrificed to Artemis, your women given in pleasure to barbarians, your men torn apart by beasts… you know this and yet you stay?"

Daphne reached for his hand and held it gently. "We fear death some days as much as any other person, yet we long to embrace a life that will never end. It's only a matter of time for all of us."

The gladiator whirled and strode to the curtain he had watched her come through. "You are all deceived. When I enter the arena, I fight for my own life and for my freedom. None of your people are given a weapon when they enter the area. There's nowhere to run."

"We don't need to run," she said.

The compassion in her eyes broke into a deep part of the vault in which he'd barricaded his heart.

"The worst of curses is to die by the cross—or the beasts." He paced back and forth, shaking the jowls on his great bald head. "What kind of God would feed his people to death in such a dark way? Surely you want life as much as anyone. If you're so courageous, why are you hiding here in the heart of the earth?"

"We hide to shelter people like you," she said. Tears trickled down her cheeks. "And to celebrate the One who already died for us."

"You better hope no one finds you," Nabonidus said. "I don't want to see you burning on a cross, or being torn apart by wild dogs."

With that, he turned and fled out into the night.

Caleb froze in place at the leopard's snarl. He waited for the inevitable attack, but nothing happened. Perhaps it had merely snagged a deer and was warning him not to interfere with its dinner. Or perhaps it had gotten caught in a trap and was unable to advance on him. Perhaps it feared him as much as he feared it…

Past experience assured him that running wasn't the right response. He did his best to make himself large and to face the unseen black demon of the night. He knew the animal would stalk him, circling and waiting for a lapse in judgment.

Caleb reached out and felt the bark of an oak tree. He searched for a branch, but there were none within easy reach. He moved slowly to put his back against the trunk and explored the ground around him to see if a branch might be available for a defensive weapon.

His ears picked up sounds which frayed his nerves. An owl hooting. Crickets and frogs. The snap of a twig.

"Lord Almighty, Yeshua, God of my Fathers, save me!" he prayed. "Deliver me from evil."

At that moment, a boar crashed through the underbrush and raced by him. The snarl of the leopard erupted again from behind him and it was clear from the squeals and thrashing the cat had found another target for its hunt.

Caleb didn't hesitate. He found another tree and climbed it to wait out the night.

Suzanna rested her feet in a pan of warm water next to a bristling fire as her rescuer worked with his sister to prepare a warm meal.

"It took the strength of Hercules to pull her out of that pit, I tell you," the young man was saying as he lowered pieces of meat onto a skewer. "Zeus himself would have been hard-pressed to have wrested her from the pull of the demons bent on destroying her in the grave."

"Hush, Diogenes, you've told me enough of what a hero you are," said the man's sister. "I want to hear more from Suzanna about this god of hers who called you from death to life. Imagine what would become of me if you had hanged yourself on that tree!"

"Hemera, what hope do you have with me here? Nothing has changed."

Suzanna raised her head and turned to the siblings. "I don't want to contradict the heart of the hero who rescued me," she said, "but everything has changed. Yeshua has called you. You've been given life. You have reason to live and love again."

Diogenes walked toward her and laid the skewer of meat across the grate above the fire.

"I trust you're warmed enough now to tell us more," he said. "My sister took a fright when I carried in your muddied form. From the gash on your head, we thought you might be dead. Not since our parents perished at sea in the last storm have we had anyone in this home."

Suzanna adjusted the rag wrapped around her head. "What sadness you must feel."

"Sadness is a distant memory," Diogenes replied. "Now I'm consumed with guilt, because they died while going to the mainland to purchase a pan flute I insisted on. My soul is numb and my mind burdened with a weight I'm sure will never be gone."

"My God can forgive you and heal you," Suzanna assured him.

"Perhaps, if that was all. But there's more." Diogenes paced across the floor and bent to turn the meat. "Without our parents, we had nothing. I stole from the markets so we could survive. I've always known it was simply a matter of time before the authorities caught me and hung me. I went to that cemetery to die. I *chose* to die by my own hand rather than through public disgrace."

Suzanna wiggled her toes. Searing pain sizzled her unthawed nerves. "I appreciate your desire to save your honor, but God is great and he can do more than we imagine. You can trust him."

"I want to trust him," Diogenes said as he and Hemera sat down with cups of tea.

"Perhaps I should rest some," Suzanna said. "My head continues to pound despite the potion you gave me. I can't even remember why I would have gone out in that storm at such a time."

Hemera handed Suzanna a mug of steaming liquid. "Try some more of this. My mother, Zeus rest her soul, used to give me this in my distress. It's a dreadful thing that you can't remember where you live…"

Diogenes turned the spit of meat and breathed in contentedly. "A good meal is all she needs. I'm sure whoever's missing her will be looking for her shortly."

"Tell us this story of Yeshua," Hemera urged. "Just what you remember."

Suzanna had hardly started her story when they heard a pounding at the door.

Hemera was terrified. "Run! Hide!" she whispered to her brother. "I'll stall them."

Titius crawled on his belly like a snake, worming his way toward the one tree whose branches breached the perimeter of the governor's mansion. During his time as general he had warned Marcellus about this opening, but nothing had been done. Now six sentries stood at all times within twenty feet of the tree, except when they went through their elaborate routine of changing the guard—a routine Titius knew well.

At three o'clock in the morning, he made his move up into the tree, along the branches, and down onto the manicured lawn lit by torches. Crawling in and out of alcoves he inched his way toward the hidden entry for kitchen staff.

At four o'clock, an Egyptian slave would empty the chamber pots into the gardens. Right on time, the clean-shaven servant pushed open the door and propped it wide with a rock. Still sleepy, and tasked with an unpleasant responsibility, the Egyptian held out the clay pot as far from his nose as possible.

By the time the servant had reached the garden, Titius had gotten inside and disguised himself as a house servant.

Few were awake at this time of day and none assumed any trouble on the premises. The two cooks didn't even glance up as he walked by the kitchen, picked up some bread, and headed for the hallways that led to the dungeon. The guards continued their rounds as he infiltrated the locked area, stopping only long enough to open the gate so he could feed the prisoners their daily portion.

Governor Porteous had instituted a policy to constantly change out the personnel in the governor's mansion to ensure no one had opportunity to conspire against him. This policy now worked in Titius's favor; the guards didn't even lock the door behind him as he raised his torch to glance at the sleeping faces of the prisoners.

He found Ananias's wife, son, and two daughters in the third cell. He lobbed the bread toward them and it landed right on the son's neck. He awoke with a start and flinched at the torchlight.

"Wake your mother," Titius whispered. "I've come to take you out of here."

The son shook his mother until she acknowledged his efforts. He whispered to her and she crawled out from under her blanket, coming over to the grate where Titius stood.

"You must pretend your children are sick," he instructed. "Tell them to groan loudly. I'll call the guard and let him know I can assist. If you're convincing, we'll get you out of here."

Within five minutes, the drama was underway and Titius had persuaded one of the guards to accompany him to check out the suffering children. When the guard had turned the key in the lock to open it, Titius knocked him unconscious, dragged him into the cell, and exchanged clothing with him. He gagged the unconscious sentry, locked the cell, and led the woman and children out through the passageways.

With the keys in hand, he walked boldly through the garden gate and locked it as they exited. But a moment later, yells from within the governor's mansion alerted them that their escape had been discovered.

"Follow me," he whispered urgently. "Unless we move fast, we'll be feeding the lions at the games later today."

Nabonidus's futile attempt to sneak back into the ludus after leaving Daphne's inn was almost comical. Selsus spotted him loitering in the marketplace without any personal guard and immediately sent a squadron of legionnaires to capture him.

The punishment he received was just as brutal as expected. The lashes across his scarred back hardly fazed him. Five years on the oars under a Roman dragon's whip had made this seem like child's play. He had learned long ago to focus on other lands and other faces to endure the deep flesh wounds. He considered it training for the arena. He also considered it the price for maintaining control of his own life.

In his imagination, he pictured the white-robed priests chanting in the temple around the leaping fire as he'd hidden in the dark shadows as a child. The chants had called him to purity through the flames. He'd sensed angelic and demonic spirits hovering, gaining power from the chants. He'd focused on the fire and imagined it burning his back, purifying him, strengthening him…

Nabonidus had bolted from that temple screaming in terror. Two days later, bandits had killed his entire family and stolen his life. He'd known better than to invade the sacred territory of the gods. And yet something within him had called to the divine for help.

A bellowing yell pulled his attention back to Ephesus. It was Selsus, making his presence known long before arriving at the cell block. He mocked the manhood of the guards and challenged them to a fight in the arena during an elimination match. All of them.

When Selsus walked into view, Nabonidus noted that he was inebriated. The German man smashed his club against the bars of iron and ranted and raved at the prisoner.

"Did Artemis steal your mind again, you fool?" Selsus sneered. "I hope whatever woman you spent time with was worth it. You just signed your death warrant and there's nothing I can do to stop it."

Nabonidus hung his head and tried to ignore the string of vulgarity which followed.

Chapter Seven

Nabonidus lay flat out on the stone bench in the cell as a slave carefully applied salve to the deep wounds on his back and sides. A small barred window permitted a sliver of light. Selsus towered over him muttering incantations and curses.

"What bothers you now?" Nabonidus inquired.

Selsus smashed his fist into a wall and stared at the blood that flowed from his knuckles. "The emperor rides through my homeland of Germania, like his father, mocking my gods. And now he rallies the Empire to conquer my enemies in Britannia without me."

"Be glad you aren't near that man," Nabonidus cautioned. "Everyone near him seems to die of poisoning or torture."

Selsus leaned back against the wall of the ludus. "Guard your tongue, gladiator. You only live so you can die entertaining him and his kind. You're an ant to be crushed underfoot. Another word and you'll be like those he tries to eradicate."

"How did you end up in the gladiator games?" Nabonidus asked. "You and your people speak as if you're invincible. Yet here you are."

Selsus spat in the dirt. "You Persians understand nothing. Why should I humiliate myself before you?"

"So you confess that the Romans humiliated you and your people?"

"One day I'll show you whose people are humiliated," Selsus retorted. "Give me a razor-sharp framea and I'll thrust it through any Roman or Persian shield. If the Romans hadn't attacked us when we were all weak with fever, we would have destroyed them."

Nabonidus shifted to watch the German carving notches in his club.

"At the Battle of the Teutoburg Forest, we ambushed and destroyed three entire legions of Romans—twenty thousand trained warriors. We slaughtered those invaders. They've never since been able to conquer us east of the river."

"Too bad you couldn't defeat Germanicus."

Selsus tossed his notched club up into the air in a spiraling motion and caught it coming down again. He peered overtop of it at Nabonidus.

"Germanicus had thirty-five thousand men against our tribes. My grandfather fell to him. I was still a boy."

Nabonidus rested his head on his forearms and allowed the slave to massage the salve into the rest of his body. "I hear if Emperor Tiberius hadn't reassigned Germanicus, he may have wiped you all out."

"And now his son is the emperor, dreaming of expanding this empire even more."

"What happened to your gods?" Nabonidus asked. "Were they not strong enough to deliver you? Didn't your seers warn you about what was to come?"

The German paused thoughtfully, stroking his club. "From the time I was born, I only knew the worship of Tiwaz. Our seers ruled all our lives." He stood and paced toward the doorway. "They determined our marriages, declared the bounty of our harvests, and predicted our victories in battle." Selsus set his foot up on the bench and leaned on his forearm. "Yet they were wrong. I had to find the head of my father, the arm of my uncle, and the body of my brother among hundreds of my people. The Romans were merciless. One in ten were crucified, the rest sold as slaves. My gods let me down in the same way your gods let you down when they allowed you to be captured and sold as a slave."

"So what did you do?"

Selsus glared down on Nabonidus. "I decided that if the Roman gods were more powerful than my gods, I would serve them and learn all I could to become the greatest warrior in the Empire. I sold my soul to Artemis."

"What if there are gods still more powerful?"

"There are no gods more powerful than Artemis. I've seen the champions of every nation fighting in this arena, yet none of them prevails over death. Artemis claims them all—"

"What do you know of the followers of Yeshua?"

Selsus stopped in his tracks and sat back down on the bench. "You mean the followers of the Way?" He swatted at the air as if batting flies. "Vermin, sorcerers, cannibals, pagans. They're cursed above all others."

"Why do you think Caesar pours out his wrath on such a gentle people?"

57

"Gentle?" Selsus crouched before Nabonidus. "These people abhor all gods. They refuse to bow the knee to the emperor. They claim that a crucified criminal is somehow their living god. They're no more than food for the lions—worthless, deceived, to be pitied above all men."

"They seem free of fear when they face death."

"What do you know of them?" The German sprang to his feet and swung his club against the cell wall. The thud drew the curse of the sentries outside. "Don't tell me that woman you chase is a follower of the Way! If so, I'll personally crucify you and feed you to the lions."

Abigail curled up under the leather tarp of an oxcart as it rocked back and forth in the fall rain. The air was cool as the convoy travelled out of the mountains and down toward the sea. They'd spent three nights camping by fires along the roadside, all of which had been lonely even though the family she'd sheltered with had done their best to include her in their dancing and celebrations.

While working at the governor's mansion, it had been her job to attend to the slave market—and while she lay under the tarp, the memories came flooding back. On one of those trips, she had selected four young men and a woman to serve the governor. She'd known they were Jews—emaciated, unkempt, uncultured—but she hadn't been able to resist plucking them from the auction block. Few others had wanted them and their price was right.

Even washed and in new clothes, though, they had sagged, looking like they had no hope at all. Inventing jobs for them had been challenging. She'd been sent to purchase bricklayers for the governor's new bathhouses, and these ones would have been fortunate to hold a broom. She'd hoped they would fit in without her to cover for them.

Two of those male slaves had proved to be keen with numbers and had served to increase the governor's profits. The woman had served well enough through garment-making. The final two men had served briefly as bricklayers before abandoning their positions and running away.

She remembered her own journey as a slave in Rome, working for Titius's father. Her older sister had taken on the hardest tasks while she herself wandered the rose gardens and dreamed of freedom, only to fall in love with the senator's son. But the senator had forced himself upon her and the man's wife had sent her back to her people in Galilee.

There, a distant relative had adopted her to work as a fishmonger selling pickled herring. She had fought off the advances of many men over the years until being reunited with Titius and coming to find true peace in the Messiah.

Now she feared that all she had loved was lost.

The leader of the expedition continuously exchanged news with those who passed them on the road. One particular horseman, carrying a message from Governor Petronius, informed them that there had been an escape from the dungeon and a woman and her children had somehow disappeared into the city.

Abigail knew instinctively Titius had somehow been involved in freeing Ananias's family. She knew by the time she reached the apostle John in Ephesus, Titius would likely already be there waiting for her.

Dozing off, she dreamed again of her walks in the gardens in Rome where she'd first met her husband. She relived her days as a slave girl in Rome, as a fish monger in Magdala, and as a new follower of Yeshua. The years elapsed quickly and her bones rattled as the cart jostled.

As she drifted off to sleep, she was startled by a sharp yell from someone along the road: "Turn your wagons, quickly! Bandits ahead!"

The oxen were slow to respond on the narrow road and within minutes the convoy leader ripped the tarp off the cart.

"Bandits ahead," he said to her. "Run for that crevice in the hills and stay there until the fight is done. If we lose, you're on your own. If you know a god, pray!"

Suzanna stayed quiet as Diogenes slipped out a back window and Hemera asked the door-thumpers to give her a minute while she dressed. The thumping didn't stop, and when she finally did open it three men pushed her aside and burst into the home.

"Where is the thief?" the men's leader shouted. "Turn him over or we'll burn this house down."

Hemera backed up against a wall. "If you're searching for my brother, he's not here. And I can't tell you when he'll be back."

The home only had two rooms, so it didn't take long for the men to confirm that their quarry was gone.

"I guess that only leaves us one option," said the leader. "We'll burn it all down."

"And what do you hope to accomplish by burning it down?" Suzanna asked.

The men appeared to notice her for the first time. The leader stepped up, grabbed hold of Suzanna's chin, and turned back to Hemera. "A Jew? You have a Jewess in your home soaking up your heat and hospitality? A Jewess who doesn't know when to keep her mouth shut?"

The man turned to his two comrades, who now held Hemera between them.

"Perhaps there's another way to get our money back," he said. "The slave market in Alexandria will reap us a rich reward for a couple of beauties like these."

Caleb stood on the steps at Barnabas's home and scanned the horizon again. He'd been up and down every road and path between this house and the city. There was no sign of Suzanna and no one had seen or heard from her.

Barnabas had gone to meet with the church in Antioch and left Caleb to locate his wife. Several of the local merchants had been alerted to keep their eyes open for Suzanna.

Since sunrise, though, Caleb had feared the worst. Had the wild dogs torn her to shreds and carried her off? He had tracked them but couldn't find their lair. The rain had washed away all trace of them.

He had found a dead dog under a tree branch by the pit filled with mud. In anguish, he had torn off a ten-foot branch and probed the depths of the slime. He'd been relieved not to locate a body. There had been signs of activity and footprints, but nothing clearly pointed him to Suzanna's presence.

The earthquake had caused serious damage to many of the buildings on Cyprus and Barnabas's house hadn't escaped the trouble. Masons and carpenters would have to be hired and repairs made.

At the home of a winemaker, Caleb was received with compassion.

"I think I saw your wife," the host declared. "She was covered in mud and being carried by a man. I think she was dead. I don't know where she went, but I think he probably buried her."

Caleb redoubled his efforts going door to door but no one else had any news. By the end of the day, he returned home in despair, sure that the winemaker had been right.

Itchy scabs pulled at Nabonidus's skin, but he resisted the urge to scratch at the healing wounds. Two weeks after his lashing he still wasn't fit for the arena; the physician had ruled him ineligible for the latest match. His quest for a mansion on the side of Mount Koressus would have to wait.

He saw Daphne, the innkeeper, walking slowly into the temple market with her face shielded by a head covering. Why was she hiding? She was scanning the stalls, not raising her eyes in his direction.

She passed a row of loud hawkers with clay figurines, amulets, and lamps. The glass bowls filled with floating eggs and onions didn't draw her attention. Even the ostrich in a pen surrounded by giggling children didn't warrant more than a momentary glance.

The cacophony of escalating voices, mixed with chicken squawks and dog barks, made it hard to hear anything specific. The smell of hot sausages, lentils, chickpeas, and fresh pastries mingled with the odor of donkey, camel, and human sweat. This all mixed with the incense drifting out of the temple. And the sun stood over it all, baking anything and anyone left uncovered.

Nabonidus backed into an alcove and continued his surveillance as Daphne stopped at the date vendor to purchase a handful of fruit. She made stops at the baker, the olive vendor, the cloth merchant, and the potter. The stops appeared to be deliberate and the conversations brief. To each she passed a leather pouch along with the required coin.

As the woman turned past the temple entrance, he noticed a turbaned Egyptian starting to shadow her. He sheltered a small dagger behind his back and didn't appear to be acting in a protective role. Nabonidus pushed his way down the stairs, keeping his eye on the man. He was still twenty feet away when Daphne stopped at a fountain and the man withdrew his weapon. Nabonidus pushed harder, ignoring the protesting shouts of shoppers.

The Egyptian noticed the angry screams, and so did Daphne. When the would-be assassin saw the volcanic fury in Nabonidus's focused eyes, he stepped away into a small garden dedicated to the goddess Diana. Daphne, not having noticed the man, stood open-mouthed as Nabonidus charged with a roar into the temple grove.

The small man scaled a stone barrier and vaulted over a canopy. Nabonidus wasn't so nimble as he rolled over the fence and fell through the canopy, breaking a vendor's cart.

"Stop," Nabonidus shouted as he scrambled to his feet and took up the chase again.

The Egyptian eluded him near a public bathhouse and Nabonidus spent the next hour scouring the neighborhood for his prey. Some passersby, danced in joy at witnessing the unguarded presence of their favorite warrior while others recoiled in horror at having an untethered killer loose among them. Nobody he spoke to could claim to have seen anything unusual.

As Nabonidus hunched over, catching his breath, he noticed droplets of blood dripping into a small puddle at his feet. Some of his wounds had reopened.

Chapter Eight

Nabonidus next saw Daphne as he exited the public baths. His wounds had scarred over and he was back in training. The hot and cold baths, followed by scraping and massages, had left him exhilarated. He soaked in the sun near a statue of the emperor, allowing the healing sunrays to reach deep inside him. For this one day, he had earned his freedom to walk about unattended.

The recent rains had cleansed the sewer ditches and washed the thicker dust off the cobblestones. The world had burst forth like a spring blossom, renewed and filled with hope. A gaggle of geese waddled near a pool of water and a cloud of flies hovered over it. A host of sparrows darted in and out of a grove made up of fig, walnut, and oak trees.

Daphne set her basket at the edge of a fountain, removed her head shawl, and lifted her face to the sun. She acted as though she hadn't even noticed his existence. A shiver raced up his spine as her beauty devoured him.

Nabonidus got up and took a few steps closer. He stooped to scoop up a pebble and tossed it playfully near her.

She didn't flinch or open her eyes. Her lips hardly moved. "Do you play with fire so close to water?" she asked.

He smirked. "Perhaps I stay near water precisely so that I *can* play with fire."

She turned toward the fountain. "The Way you seek rests in the fish's mouth. The footsteps you follow will lead to life."

"I don't know what kind of message you're trying to pass along to me," he mused as he stepped even closer. "But I can't get you out of my head."

"It's not me you need to know."

"Then who?"

"Yeshua, the Messiah, the Lord." She reached for her basket. "Search the minnow's mouth. If you want to know more, I'll see you there, with John."

Three women, draped stylishly in long flowing dark gowns, approached the fountain and joined Daphne. The innkeeper stepped into formation with them and marched off away.

Nabonidus, bewildered, pivoted and looked for some further clue as to what she had been talking about. He searched under a stone bench, in a nearby bush, and even in the fountain itself. What had she meant by telling him to look in the minnow's mouth? He recalled the etchings of fish he'd seen around the city… but those fish hadn't seemed to have anything in their mouths.

After a few minutes of frustration, he plopped down on the bench and surveyed his surroundings. Across the way stood a coppersmith, a wine merchant, a baker, a wool vendor, a fishmonger, and a carpenter. An old woman kept a dozen chickens tied up in a basket under an old olive tree. Customers milled around, bargaining for better prices.

He gave up and began walking back toward the ludus. In fact, he had already gotten to the gates before the obvious answer surfaced in his mind.

A minnow is a fish, he thought. *Perhaps she meant for me to visit the fishmonger…*

He stopped turned around, walking back into the market. When he reached the fishmonger's stall, he discovered a young girl playing with a doll. She appeared to be Assyrian.

"What is in the fish's mouth?" he asked in Aramaic.

The waif, with her dark tangled locks, tattered frock, and dark eyes, examined him with a puzzled expression on her face. Perhaps she didn't speak Aramaic, after all.

"What is in the fish's mouth?" he repeated in Hebrew, then Latin, and finally in Greek.

"A tongue," she replied in Greek, although she still looked puzzled.

"Show me the fish." His size and intensity clearly intimidated her and she appeared to want to run, so Nabonidus calmed himself. "Please, I'm looking for a fish left here for me by a beautiful woman."

The girl reached under the counter of the stall and took out a basket of pickled herring.

"No," he said. "The fish must be bigger. Something large enough to contain a message. Do you have a bass or tilapia?"

Her delicate hands scooped several handfuls of the herring onto a scale, despite his protests, and finally she withdrew a small bass from the bottom.

"The fish left by the lady," she announced. "Two denarii."

"Two denarii," he repeated. "Are you a fishmonger or a thief? Where is your father?"

The girl smiled sweetly at him. "I'm an orphan caring for my own needs. If you want the fish, this is the price."

His jaw clenched, his shoulders tensed, and his fists tightened. As he prepared to pound the counter, he noticed the look of fear in the child's eyes and it stilled his fire. Those eyes reminded him of his sister's when the bandits had struck their caravan so many years ago… He would not terrorize a child like they had.

As he regained his focus, he glanced toward the fountain. Selsus stood a dozen yards away, surveilling him.

"I'll take the fish," he said, laying down two denarii. "But what is the message?"

"Look inside," she said. "Did you know that if you think about the letters for fish in Greek, it stands for Jesus Christ, Son of God, Savior?"

With that, she handed him a woven basket large enough to carry the fish.

As he reached for it, he felt Selsus's large hand clamp onto his shoulder.

"So, Nabonidus, it has come to this," his handler said. "That you should join the spy network of the Nazarenes… to think, I have defended you up until now. Give me that fish."

The wide-eyed girl snatched up her doll and slipped away, running in her rags toward the market gate. Nabonidus released his hold on the basket.

Selsus grunted as he poked and prodded at the fish. "A tongue…"

"What?" Nabonidus replied as he turned to face the man.

"A tongue!" Selsus declared. "There's nothing in this fish's mouth but a tongue."

Titius urged Ananias's son, Stephen, to keep his sisters quiet as the cart rolled along Straight Street toward the main gate of Damascus. The former thespian assassin had fashioned a wooden box toward the front of the cart, covered it with blankets, and filled the rest of the space with ears of corn which he had removed from the governor's granary. Their donkey had been borrowed from a neighbor who had come along without protest.

The morning traffic in and out of the city was dense and the lineup for inspection long. Titius eyed the four sentries examining goods and targeted one of them, a young Roman who appeared unsure of what he was searching for. The young man thoroughly inspected one cart, then, recognizing he was behind, would let the next cart through with only a cursory check.

Titius manipulated his way into the anticipated easy inspection by allowing an oxcart to go ahead as he took time to inspect his donkey's hooves.

As he drew up to the legionnaire, the young man asked him, "Is there something wrong with your donkey?"

Titius adjusted his accent to match his costume and lowered his eyes toward the braying donkey's feet.

"Stupid beast," Titius said. "My neighbor told me he was good for the journey and now I'm late after having to care for his feet. Nothing but a load of corn and the dumb animal can barely pull it. Watch the one behind me, he's been known to bluff his way through these inspections."

The young man eyed the two bearded traders sitting innocently in their oxcart filled with brick.

"Best be moving on so I can get this taken care of," the legionnaire said. "It looks like we'll have some heavy lifting to do with all those bricks—if indeed they're not hiding anything under that load. There's been an escape, you know. But those prisoners won't get past this check point."

Titius gave his thanks and shooshed his donkey forward.

Around the corner and out of sight, he stopped to move the cobs of corn from off the hidden box. He lifted the blankets, waited until a caravan of camels had sauntered by, and then urged the woman and three children to climb out of the cart. He tied the donkey to a tree and led Ananias's family through a camp of traders and out the other side.

Only a mile later, a chariot charged down the road pulled by a pair of strong Arabian horses. Titius's heart raced as he saw six horsemen galloping along behind it.

Even worse, the man in the chariot was none other than Marcellus.

Abigail huddled in the bushes as bandits ambushed the convoy she'd joined. The warning for her to run had come only minutes before the sword-wielding robbers had swarmed over the hilltops and descended on the circled wagons. From her refuge, she couldn't see the carnage, but she could hear the blood-curdling yells of attackers and the panicked responses of defenders.

Within ten minutes, the chaos had quieted. The battle had been decided. She crouched quietly, waiting for some signal that all was well.

The birds resumed their song, an oxen bellowed, and the whinnying of horses added some testimony to life. A deer stepped tentatively into a clearing near her and flicked its ears up at the source of havoc.

Still she waited. The most beautiful wildflowers lined this small meadow. A raven floated overtop of the grass and landed in a tree. A gurgling waterfall splashed into a pool at the bottom of rocky crags nearby. A vulture circled overhead. A rabbit raced for cover.

It was dark before Abigail dared to move toward the top of the hill overlooking the scene of the ambush. Minutes seemed like hours as she inched her way forward. The sound of crickets and frogs interrupted the stillness, but she could hear nothing else.

Until she heard the moaning.

The rope around Suzanna's wrists and ankles cut into her skin and she kicked, kneed, elbowed, and head-butted her captors. They had been unnecessarily free in their handling of her, but she fought back just as freely.

One of the men slapped her across the face. It stung and paralyzed her into momentary submission. She felt her jaw being pried open and a potion being poured down her throat. She had no idea what was in the mix, but the men appeared determined to subdue her with it. She tried to spit out as much as she could.

It had taken two of the three men to wrestle her down while the third handled Hemera. The one who had tied up Hemera sat astride her, grabbing her hair and lifting her head while he forced her to drink, too. She hadn't resisted long.

Suzanna feigned unconsciousness and the men eased up, laying her down and laughing at their success.

"That medicine man was right," said the man getting off Hemera. "A little potion and they stop resisting."

One of the men who had tied Suzanna muttered his own thoughts. "The problem is, we were supposed to knock out that thief and get him to the creditors..."

The third man moved to opening cupboard doors and pilfering their contents. "Come on, let's get what we can. We need to think of another plan for these two and get out of here before someone comes after us for failing."

"What about the thief?" the first man asked. "We should lie low and wait for him to come back. Then we can get what we're owed and make a profit on these women at the slave market."

"What if he comes back with help?" the second argued. "We'll end up with nothing. I say we take these two and get on the next ship out of here."

———————————

As Nabonidus retold the tale of Selsus looking inside the fish's mouth and finding only its tongue, the group of twenty Christians chortled. They all huddled over a loaf of bread and cup of wine, laughing over the story.

"You should have seen his great blond beard shaking in confusion," Nabonidus said. "He used his dagger to slice that bass into tiny little pieces and screamed at the crowd who had gathered to watch him."

John stepped closer. "And what did you say?"

"I told him he owed me two denarii! In front of everyone, he told me no fish was worth two denarii and I was a fool for paying it. I'm sure we would have fought if his guardians hadn't intervened and shackled me up again."

"Dorcas was brilliant," Daphne said. "When she saw him coming, she hid that message in the bottom of the basket. Such a brave child to not run away from a brute like you…"

Nabonidus scowled playfully. "Me, a brute?" He turned toward the child Dorcas, standing near the apostle. "You, orphan. You robbed me of all the money I had to eat with!"

"So how did you find us?" John intervened.

The gladiator stood up and stretched. "It wasn't easy. Dorcas told me that when you spell fish, it stands for Jesus, Son of God, Savior. She was pointing at a small drawing of a fish carved into the counter. Only after Selsus dragged me away to the ludus did I have time to consider the fact that I'd seen small drawings of fish in different places around the city."

John carried a clay lamp to the table with the bread and wine. "Ah, so Jesus is also the light of our world and he leads us to be together. I trust others haven't connected the drawings with directions to where we meet. How did you figure it out?"

"After my training match, I went back and examined one of the drawings. I decided to look in the direction where the fish's mouth pointed. Sure enough, I found another fish within a few hundred yards, pointing me toward a path. I followed that path and almost gave up… but then I found another fish carved onto a tree branch. The directions were clear as long as I followed the fish."

"And what of the note in the basket?" Dorcas asked.

Nabonidus smiled. "Oh, so you do talk. It was from John, but I still don't understand it. It spoke of God loving the world and believing in his Son so I won't perish. It motivated me to find you so I could better understand."

John beckoned the group closer and prayed over the items on the table. "The body and blood of our Lord," he declared. "It is our life, our hope, our joy. Let us examine ourselves and eat together, looking forward to that day when we will see him face to face."

Chapter Nine

The chariot ride around the arena was Nabonidus's first. The gold and silver helmet he wore, along with the chest armor, long red cape, and special sword, marked him as the emperor's champion. It was like wearing a bullseye, and at the moment it was all for show.

He had finally been declared ready for the day's elimination match. There would be no referees today to accept an act of surrender.

Sixteen warriors had been fully equipped with individualized weaponry, and each was a champion fighting to live.

Nabonidus analyzed the strengths and weaknesses of each as they circled under the deafening roar of the quarter-million-strong vulture-like mob. The last four standing would advance to fight in Rome, or they could choose their freedom and retire to a life without glory, fame, honor, and wealth. Nabonidus planned to choose freedom.

Two Samnites, carrying swords and shields, formed an alliance and maneuvered in his direction. A lone Mongul retiarius moved confidently and defiantly with his net and trident, waving them in the direction of the nobility. A javelin-hurling velite was vulnerable and not too eager to join the fray. The essedarii, in their two-horse chariots, seemed destined to clash first with the two andabatae preparing to charge on their fearless warhorses.

Nabonidus was outfitted as a dimachaerus, with two sharp swords in his hands and a whip tucked into his belt.

A Thracian teamed up with a murmillo to torment a hoplomachus—a Greek fighter armed with a sword; the man sported a feathered helmet, round shield, and spear. A laquearius circled the trio, throwing his lasso with one arm and making stabbing motions with his dagger.

Three heavily armored legionnaires completed the field of fighters.

All the fighters did their part to hype up the crowd into fits of hysteria so their bets would be generous.

Horns blared as white-tunicked priests completed their sacrifices and oaths. Murmured incantations, prayers, and warrior self-talk echoed through the priests' dark, smoky rooms.

The sponsor of these games had spent lavishly for some reason. Perhaps a Roman senator or nobleman had come to scout for a gladiator worthy of the Coliseum in Rome. The fighters' training in the ludus had been intense for months and the variety of warriors from all over the Empire had been selected in order to satisfy more than just a local crowd.

Nabonidus ignored the reality of the arena as he rested. The day had been scripted to please the bloodlust of a debauched citizenry. Lions and wild dogs would shred human flesh. Criminals, and perhaps Christians, would be martyred on crosses. Animals would be hunted, battles staged, and camels raced… all to taunt the crowd into a fever pitch.

Abigail listened to the groans from the remains of her convoy. She'd been here for hours, and in the morning light she realized that the groans were coming from an older man who had been riding in a donkey cart. A spear protruded from his belly as he lay on his side clutching it.

The oxcart she had been riding in had been smashed and rendered useless on the side of the road. The oxen had been butchered, their heads, legs, and entrails discarded. A swarm of flies and a dozen vultures were working to strip the carcass bare. A pack of wild dogs howled in the distance, no doubt having sensed their next meal was nearby.

The dogs stimulated Abigail to walk away from the scene. She had never travelled this road before, but she was sure she would be able to find shelter and protection over the mountains in Tarsus—as long as the dogs didn't get distracted by her scent and forget about the easy meal waiting for them.

A few miles down the road, she climbed to the top of a hill to determine the best course forward. The illusion of peace permeated everywhere she searched. Birdsong rose like a chorus of wellbeing. A tumbling creek spoke of life, and she removed her sandals and dipped her feet into the cool water. Minnows darted around and nibbled at her toes. Grasshoppers flitted along the bank and a myriad of butterflies fluttered along under the clear blue sky.

No one was around, so she stripped down, washed the dirt from her clothing, and floated in the water. As she rested, she yearned for Titius.

Scrubbing herself down afterward with a handful of sand revitalized her skin and renewed her spirits. Thanking Yeshua for his mercy in sparing her, she got dressed again and examined her surroundings. The rugged mountains to the north promised protection from raiding barbarians.

The Taurus Mountains, she knew, had been named for a bull—a symbol of the storm gods whose numerous temples dotted the landscape. Small dark clouds hovered over the most distant peaks, promising more storms to come. From here, the Tigris and Euphrates rose to fertilize the land all the way to the distant sea.

Titius had spoken of this land, where Alexander the Great had defeated the Persian, Darius the Third. She knew the strategic pass she would come through had been the final resting place of many warriors far from home.

A small swarm of gnats descended on her and she engaged in her own battle swatting at the annoying insects. She covered her face and continued on her way, praying another convoy would pass before the dogs found her.

———————————

Caleb spent one last day surveying the island. Apart from disturbing herons in the shallow waters, Egyptian geese in the lakes, and swans in the river mouth, he found no sign of Suzanna anywhere.

When a dockworker said he was sure the woman he was searching for had gotten on board a cargo ship with a woman and three men, his hope surged for the first time.

"And where was the ship going?" he asked.

The man glanced toward the wharf, reflecting on what he had seen. "We had six set sail in the last two days..." He held out his hand expectantly and waited until Caleb had deposited a coin in his palm. He held it up to the sun and examined it, biting it. "I'm sure it wasn't the one to Britannia or the one to Gaul. It was either the three-master to Alexandria, the two-master to Caesarea, or the two-master to Tarsus. The military galley to Rome is unlikely."

Caleb eyed the man's open hand. He was still waiting for more, but Caleb decided he'd paid enough. If Suzanna had assumed he'd been killed by wild dogs, where else would she go but to her old home in Jerusalem? The obvious first stop was Caesarea.

As Caleb negotiated his fare with a ship captain, a young Greek woman stood nearby listening in. The sun glistened off her wavy auburn hair. Her short purple-lined toga marked her as nobility, and she made no effort to hide her interest in Caleb as she adjusted her clothing.

When the agreement was done, Caleb turned away to purchase a handful of dates. The Greek woman sidled up to stand beside him at the vendor's cart.

"It looks like we'll be sailing on the same ship," she said. "It'll be good to have someone with your strength there to protect women like me from all those rogue sailors who might take advantage."

"Do I know you?"

The woman smiled invitingly. "Are you hoping to get to know me?"

Heat rushed into Caleb's cheeks. His tongue grew twisted and unable to find the words to reply. He turned back to the date vendor, who held out his hand for payment.

The woman produced a coin and planted it firmly in the vendor's palm. "I don't want the man to think he has to pity me. Please add a few extra so we can eat together."

The vendor dropped in a few more of the brown chewy fruit, rolled up the purchase, and handed it to the woman. "May destiny multiply your pleasure."

The Greek had walked a dozen steps away from him before Caleb gave chase. "Hey, those are my dates!"

She ignored him and continued to walk away.

He quickened his pace. "Stop. Bring those back here."

Caleb jogged a dozen steps and was about to grab the woman when a broad-chested security guard stepped out from an alcove and struck him hard with a club. He made an effort to duck away from the ambusher, but the man's fist to his face brought him up short.

When Caleb regained consciousness some time later, he was aware of the gentle rocking motion underneath him. Sea spray drifted over his face and eased the powerful sun probing his face. Directly overhead, two gulls drifted against the clear blue sky.

"So, my hero returns from his journey," said the Greek woman, peering down at him. "You are so noble to sacrifice your face for me."

"I still don't even know you."

"Call me Aphrodite."

"Aphrodite is a goddess."

"Well, thank you. Now, what are we going to do with you?"

"Where are we going?"

"We're going to my home in Caeserea," Aphrodite said. "For now there's no one but you and me to enjoy these three days together. A storm is coming, though, so we might just have to go belowdecks. You probably haven't had much practice being a slave."

Suzanna heaved her stomach's contents over the ship's railing as the wind swirled and caught the sails in another lurching plunge. The ship dropped into the trough of the storm surge which rolled thirty feet above the bow of the freighter. She was completely soaked but didn't dare hide in the hold. The stench, combined with claustrophobia, had already overwhelmed her.

One of the passengers had warned the captain not to sail, but the men who had kidnapped Suzanna and Hemera had paid enough to encourage his effort in outrunning the angry black clouds which now blocked out the entire sky.

"Heave ho," yelled a sailor wrapping a rope around his waist. "Trim the sails. Secure the cargo. Fasten yourselves to the mast."

"How long before we reach Alexandria?" one of the swarthy kidnappers called to the captain. He had already tied Hemera to a mast and now was intent on securing Suzanna.

The captain turned over the rudder to another seaman. "We'll have to hide out in Ephesus… if we can make it that far. The waves will crush our hull if we try to keep on toward Alexandria. The storm could breach the ship. If we get rolled onto our side, we're all going down."

"You told me you could do this." The kidnapper pulled out a dagger from under his cloak and pointed it toward the captain. "I paid you good. Now, turn that prow toward Alexandria before I have to do it myself."

"The crew would finish you off before you took the rudder." The captain turned and motioned urgently toward some of the armed crewmen tethered to the deck. "If we don't keep the right angle and right speed into these waves, we'll shred the sail and end up helpless. These waves are higher than the ship! If we don't get enough momentum to ride up and catch the wind, we're doomed. Then we'll never reach Alexandria or anywhere else."

Two of the kidnappers pulled themselves along the railing until they reached Suzanna. One wrapped his arm around her and pulled out his dagger.

"Change course, Captain," one of them said, "or we start killing off the passengers and unloading cargo."

The captain braced himself as another wave crashed down onto the prow. The ship shuddered as it dropped into another trench and lurched as it drove the crest of the next wave.

"Furl the mainsails," the captain yelled. "Secure the yardarms."

Four men scaled the main mast and worked with the heavy, water-soaked sails. They had almost secured the sail when a breaking wave caught the sailor holding the rudder and knocked him off his feet. The ship lurched hard to the right and three of the sailors on the mast flew overboard. The fourth swung from a rope, holding on for dear life as he tried to swing back onto his former perch.

A yardarm on the mast cracked and crashed onto the bow. The man holding Suzanna was knocked off-balance by the sudden swing and fell. As they slid across the deck, he released his hold on the knife, and her. Suzanna slid into a bundled fishnet, but the man bowled over one of the armed men, skewering him with a sword as he fell.

The following wave caught the ship broadside and washed the dying man, his compatriots, and several sailors over the side. Suzanna held on to the fishnet with all her strength as the water retreated and pulled her toward certain death.

———

Nabonidus had never been so weary or so bloodied. Only one of the essedarii with their two-horse chariot, one of the andabatae on his warhorse, and the murmillo stood with him. Three horses and twelve men lay writhing or motionless on the bloodied sand. The roar of the crowd washed over them like the pounding surf of the ocean against a rocky shore.

The hypnotic wave of color and sound combined with Nabonidus's loss of blood to blur his vision. His legs weakened under him and he saw the essedarii accelerate in his direction. For a flash of a hummingbird's wing, he thought how freeing it would be to stay and enter the world of the dead.

Daphne's voice seemed to call to him, and without thinking he rolled away in time to avoid the slashing sword aimed at his head. The contest was over and still the determined gladiator in the chariot fought on. The champion on the warhorse chased the chariot down from behind and hurled a javelin into the driver's back. The chariot spun out of control and toppled, tossing the dying gladiator onto the ground with all the others.

The jubilant crowd roared, horns blasting again and again to announce the end of the match.

Physicians rushed out with stretchers to claim their living corpses for dissection. Trainers rushed out with stretchers and assistants to help the recoverable survivors back into the cool underground rooms where they could be stitched and coaxed back to life.

Neither freedom nor fighting were on Nabonidus's mind as Selsus urged him to wave to the crowd from his stretcher. His focus was on Daphne and the group of believers who had knelt and prayed for him the night before he'd entered the arena.

I wonder if any other gladiator has had Christians pray for him before he started to fight, he thought. *This prayer is a powerful thing.*

Chapter Ten

Dorcas raised the wooden sword Nabonidus had been given to declare his freedom from the arena.

"The champion is free," she said. "This rudis and that ivory pendant around your neck mean you never have to fight again. The Lord Jesus has had mercy on your soul. Now bow and declare him as your Lord."

Nabonidus grinned from where he lay on the stone bench. "One day I shall bow as every knee shall bow. Today I can hardly move. Perhaps you'll win believers through that sword."

The girl sprang back in horror. "Never. Rome may try to bring peace through the power of the sword, but I shall bring peace through the power of the Name and by prayer."

Daphne corralled her charge, took the wooden sword, and returned it to Nabonidus.

"Our visiting time is up," she announced as she steered Dorcas toward the exit. "We will return back to the inn and this fine man will get his rest. We have plenty of time to convert him."

As Daphne and Dorcas exited through the front door of Nabonidus's new manion in an elite neighborhood on the hillside, the old Persian Anoshiruvan and his daughters Adrina and Atossa stepped in through the garden entrance.

"Ah, my Persian prince," Anoshiruvan greeted. "May the mysteries and masteries of the magi rest on you. You have conquered in the arena of men, and now my daughters have brought you healing stews so you may conquer in the arenas of life."

Nabonidus struggled to sit up. "I'm honored to learn at the feet of the wise."

Anoshiruvan bowed to one knee before Nabonidus. "Honor me with a promise that you'll rise to protect the cause of our people. Promise me you'll raise your sword over the welfare of my daughters. Promise me you'll be who you were born to be."

Nabonidus put his hand on the shoulder of the old Persian. "Truly, I have much to learn about who I am and about what such a promise might mean. Come, sit and teach me."

"First, tell me how you obtained this mansion on the hillside of Ephesus," Anoshiruvan said.

"It is my reward as the Champion of Ephesus." Nabonidus pointed out the front window at the fine view of the city and the ocean beyond. "It was a blessing of God that it came available at the exact time I was retiring from the arena. My only regret is the fine view I also have of the Temple of Artemis."

Anoshiruvan peered across the waters. "It's a blessing to be given a view. With a big view comes a big vision. Come, let me share with you the vision of the Persian peoples…"

Selsus, kneeling before the status in the Temple of Artemis, stared up at the hills and made his vow. "By the power of your name, I will restore your honor to this city. I will cleanse the stench of the Way from the streets and alleys. I will fill the graves and slave markets with those who dare to oppose you."

Incense and smoke filled the temple courtyard. A raven arrived with a whir and settled onto the statue.

A handful of priestesses circled the gladiator, chanting and holding white doves over his head. A priest beat a drum in an ever-increasing cadence as the women whirled around the warrior. The very heavens seemed to answer with rolling thunder and flashes of lightning.

With a final flurry of ecstasy, the women twisted the heads off the doves and poured out small streams of blood over the head and shoulders of their anointed one.

A nearby raven flapped before finally lifting off and disappearing into the night.

A young girl watched from the shadows. As she prepared to turn away, Selsus glared through the darkness and transfixed her with his stare.

"Come!" he called. "Come. Artemis has chosen you. Shed your fears and prepare to meet the Queen of the Night. Together we will bring her power back to this great city."

Titius urged Ananias's wife, Hannah, to walk closer to him as Marcellus and his six horsemen dismounted and searched through the caravansary they had just left. The three children huddled close in fear.

Hannah prayed over and over. "Yeshua, have mercy. Yeshua, have mercy."

"Has anyone seen a Roman trying to hide among you?" Marcellus called out. "He's a criminal wanted by Rome and may be a danger to you. If we find you're hiding him, you'll face the same fate he faces. Stand aside while we search your belongings."

Titius backed up against a tree and crouched down. "Sit with me," he urged the family. "Act bored. They're trying to get someone to panic and run. Don't stare at them or they'll see the fear in your eyes."

One of the horsemen soon approached the family and interrogated them. Titius shrugged and responded in Arabic, risking that the young man didn't know the language. His hunch paid off and the soldier left in frustration.

So far Marcellus hadn't come close enough to recognize him.

The horsemen rifled through everyone's goods, despite significant protest. Several of the men were beaten for resisting too much and the chaos allowed Titius and the family to back away into the bushes.

When the abandoned oxcart, filled with corn and the hidden box, was discovered, the uproar urged them to run faster.

"We head for Ephesus," Titius said. "I have men loyal to me there, and we'll meet with other believers until we discover where your husband is."

"What if they catch us first?" Ananias's son asked.

"Just do as I ask and all will be well."

Titius pulled the family off the path into dense bush where he covered them with a blanket and threw leaves and earth on top. On his own, he climbed into the thick upper foliage and watched the scene from above.

Marcellus and his men, having finished interrogating the bystanders, backed out onto the road. After a few moments, Marcellus looked up into the trees, as if knowing exactly where Titius would be found. To avoid being seen, Titius pulled himself even tighter against the tree trunk, glad for the abundant foliage.

Below, Marcellus glanced down again and issued orders to his men. Some of them spread out into the forest to continue their search while others mounted and rode away with Marcellus.

As soon as Titius deemed it safe, he climbed down, dug out Ananias's family from their hiding place, and took them deeper into the bush.

They walked for a long distance before coming upon the edge of an estate that was surrounded by high walls. Titius guided them into the darkness of the forest, to wait until nightfall.

After the sun had set, Titius scaled the walls of the estate and borrowed two horses from the stables. He then set Ananias's wife on one of the animals with the youngest child; the two other children sat upon the second horse with himself.

By moonlight, they moved off through the brush.

As the sun rose again, they picked up speed and rode toward the Pharpar River, stopping to drink and get some rest.

It took two weeks of stealth and persistence before the small group circumnavigated Mount Hermon. On the other side, they borrowed a boat and sailed down the Leontes River until they reached the Great Sea. From there, they found a commercial ship at Tyre which set them on course for Ephesus.

The chariot and Roman horsemen who stopped to help Abigail in the road were in a hurry.

"We can only take you to the next village," the charioteer declared. "We've been assigned to catch the bandits. Have you seen them?"

Abigail couldn't help much, but she told her story in as much detail as she dared without giving up her own attempt at escape.

"This is the third convoy this month to be attacked," the charioteer informed her. "Twenty-three men, ten women, and six children have all perished. This road is an important trade route to the east. It must be kept open and safe."

The village where they dropped off Abigail an hour later wasn't much more than a few mud homes huddled around a small apple orchard. Her bones had been shaken to the core on the chariot ride and she was glad to dismount and rest.

An old woman with a stick for a cane hobbled out to greet her in Aramaic.

"Peace to you," the woman welcomed. "What brings you in such a fashion and why do you stop in a place so far from anywhere?"

Abigail, hands on hips, stretched her back. "My convoy was attacked by bandits yesterday. These men found me on the road this morning."

The woman smiled a toothless smile as she held out an apple. "My name is Barbatha. We are few in this place. The stream is a hundred yards in that direction. You can drink and wash there."

Abigail accepted the apple and walked toward the stream. But as she knelt to scoop up water in her hands, a sword flashed in front of her face.

By a miracle of God, the captain regained control of the rudder, the storm passed, and the ship on which Suzanna still clung to the fishnet returned to bobbing up and down under grey skies. Sailors scrambled like spiders over every surface of the boat as supplies and personnel were accounted for.

The captain turned over the wheel to another sailor and surveyed the damaged ship. After twenty minutes he declared, "We sail for Ephesus for repairs. Set the sails for Ephesus."

"Thank you, Yeshua," Suzanna prayed. "Thank you."

A young Greek sailor, also clinging to the fishnet, overheard her. "Who is this god you pray to?"

Suzanna was startled at the question. "Yeshua is the Messiah for all peoples. He's Lord over the oceans and over all living things."

"Who were those men threatening you?"

"They kidnapped me and my friend because her brother owed them a debt. He was intent on selling us as slaves in Alexandria."

"You're fortunate this Yeshua was watching you. And your kidnapper was unfortunate. Yeshua was also watching him. Why do you follow this Yeshua?"

Suzanna's teeth chattered as she hugged herself tight for warmth and tried to share her story. The sailor was soon called to duty and promised to find her upon arrival at Ephesus so he could learn more.

One question bothered her as she tried to stay warm: where was Hemera?

The ship carrying Titius and Ananias's family stopped in Cyprus to take on more passengers. Titius walked from the deck as the new arrivals boarded, including twenty-seven Roman legionnaires. The centurion, a man named

Quintus Ptolemy, was quick to build relationship with Titius, who introduced himself as a Roman general, and to boast of his exploits in Palestine.

On the second day at sea, the two men leaned against the ship's railing, watching a pod of dolphins.

"We hunted down twenty-three zealots and fourteen bandits in a single month," Quintus said. "The last three months have been peaceful, though, and I'll be glad to return these men to their base in Rome."

"Sounds like you have a good report ahead of you," Titius said. "But why are you on a ship bound for Ephesus if you're heading for Rome?"

Quintus winced. "The truth is, there have been complaints about a children's farm outside Ephesus where the daughters of a Roman nobleman have been taken. I've been given orders to stop and recover the girls."

"You've brought a lot of men to recover a few girls."

"That's my problem. I only need three men, but I don't trust the rest to control themselves in a new city without supervision."

"I'd be happy to take your men with me while I make my own brief stop in Ephesus," Titius suggested. "I'm delivering a family for protection and a small show of force will assist me in that."

"General, I'm grateful. If you need further assistance when you get to Rome someday, please call on me."

Titius turned aside to watch the children of Ananias and Hannah playing in the fishing nets. "What of the other children on this farm?"

"My duty is only to rescue two girls. The rest have a purpose beyond my concern. It seems that these other men's daughters must be groomed to serve our temples."

Titius nodded. "My friend Licanor in Ephesus is a righteous nobleman who might be interested in a cause like this."

Quintus noticed a scuffle among two of his men on the deck behind them. "You see what I have to deal with? Duty calls. Keep a close eye on these men while they're in your care. They're good soldiers as long as they have something to do."

Nabonidus hobbled with his cane toward the door of his mansion on Mount Koressus and welcomed the apostle John, Daphne, and Dorcas.

"I see you brought protection in case I might have other things on my mind," he said, smiling at Daphne. He was sure by now that his interest in her was becoming clear.

The innkeeper smiled and walked past him to place a basket on the table. "The more friends we have, the better the celebration."

"And what are we celebrating?"

Dorcas twirled in the middle of the tiled room. "We're celebrating your new home and the church being birthed here to feed the poor." I see you've removed all the frescoes of Greek goddesses."

"What is this about?" Nabonidus asked John as he settled onto a cushioned couch. "Not once do I remember talking with anyone about using my house as a church or a feeding station for the poor. Why can't they feed themselves?"

Daphne gathered her robe and seated herself gently next to Nabonidus. "Such deep questions from a warrior," she said. "What kind of answer would you like?"

Nabonidus reached for a fig from the plate Daphne had arranged. "I've had this home on Mount Koressus for less than a month. I haven't even hired servants yet. The place needs to be cleaned and furnished with new curtains and sculptures, and already you're taking over my life, Daphne. You're not even my wife."

Daphne rose and removed a roll from a small towel she had placed on the table. "Are you asking?"

Nabonidus sat wide-eyed and open-mouthed.

"Yes!" said Dorcas, spinning in the middle of the room again. "Turn on the fountains, sound the trumpets, run to the market. We're going to have a wedding."

Nabonidus waved both hands back and forth. "Wait! I said nothing about churches or feeding the poor or having a wedding."

"But we all know you want Daphne, and the apostle is here, and this house is begging for a celebration. Besides, Daphne is willing." The girl ran up to Daphne and took her hand, drawing her toward Nabonidus. "You are willing, aren't you, Daphne?"

Innkeeper and gladiator stared at each other, neither daring to speak.

The apostle finally stepped forward. "Thank you, Dorcas, for pulling us all together with your love. These two need to talk and we need to plan how we'll feed everyone in the city who's coming to know the Messiah."

John took the young girl's hand and pulled her out through the door.

The sun shone brightly over the sea as the massive Greek freighter Caleb had booked passage on finished loading its cargo and slowly unfurled its sails. The favorable winds promised a quick trip the rest of the way to Caesarea.

Aphrodite had overplayed her hand with Caleb, and he chose to spend his time on the deck rather than enjoy the companionship she offered in the cabin. She tried many different temptations to lure him, but he resisted. By the end of the second day, he saw her trying her wiles on another passenger.

Caleb examined the piles of timber secured on the deck. The stack of ebony logs caught his imagination. There was willow, pine, oak, fir, and olive bundles in the inventory.

He even engaged a fellow traveler in conversation about Yeshua.

"So we're going to the home of the new Messiah," Caleb said as he leaned against the ship's railing.

The man was clearly Jewish in facial features and in dress. "Am I supposed to know you or this Messiah you speak of?"

"My name is Caleb from Nazareth and Yeshua grew up in the same village as me."

"Nothing good comes from such a small place," the man said. "Yet I have heard of this Yeshua. They say he was crucified. So even if he did good while he lived, he can do no good while he's dead."

"Didn't you know he still lives?"

"How can the dead live? I don't believe it."

Caleb smiled. "Would you believe the word of someone who saw him die and then saw him alive again?"

"I'm not sure anyone could believe someone who said such things."

"I am one of many who saw it."

"You?"

"Yes. I was the cross maker who built the cross on which the Romans fastened him. He was my childhood friend and was innocent, but the religious leaders convinced Pilate to have him crucified because they didn't like how the people followed him. I too believed dead men cannot live again. But the proof of his empty tomb convinced me, and the others who saw him in the flesh."

The man still seemed skeptical. "So you didn't see him with your own eyes?"

"No."

"And you still believe?"

"Yes."

"Tell me, why shouldn't I think you're demon-possessed or a lunatic?"

As the day slipped by, Caleb told the man his story. It turned out the man's name was Zedekiah, and by the time the mainland came into view the two had agreed to search out some of the eyewitnesses who had seen and spoken with Yeshua after his resurrection.

They finished their dialogue while tying the ship to the wharf in Caesarea.

"Perhaps this all has something to do with the strange dreams I've been having," Zedekiah mused.

John rose to his feet and hushed the two dozen men and women gathered in Nabonidus's newly blessed home.

"Please gather in a circle in the triclinium and we will introduce ourselves," he bellowed as the excited voices hushed. "Tell us who you are, where you come from, and what you do. Daphne, please begin."

"Daphne. Alexandrian. Freeborn. Innkeeper." Daphne then nodded to the couple on her right.

"Pelonius. A new seeker from here in Ephesus."

"Adronicus and Junia. Jews. Followers of Yeshua. Merchants." They in turn glanced at the young man on their right.

"Hermes. Athenian. Glass maker and olive vendor."

A tall, broad-shouldered man, heavily scarred along one cheek, stepped forward. "Urbanus, humble servant of Yeshua and his people."

"Julia. Roman. Estate manager. Curious to hear about why a Persian gladiator I sponsored wants to follow a Jewish Messiah."

A rush of whispers filled the room like a sudden spring waterfall. Nabonidus shifted uncomfortably as all the people's eyes turned toward him.

John held up his hand and signaled for quiet again. "He will have his turn. Please, let's finish the introductions."

"Tertius. Syrian. Scribe. Also curious about a wedding. Has a certain former gladiator proposed his betrothal to a certain innkeeper, or is that still just a rumor?"

The rush of whispers this time turned into a roar of laughter.

Finally, Nabonidus rose to his feet and the room silenced. "I see it's safer to fight in the arena than to gather the followers of Yeshua for a meeting," he said to even more laughter. "I can only accomplish one thing at a time, and I was informed that the most important thing was to begin this church."

The men and women shouted questions at him, but the former gladiator merely sat down and clamped his mouth shut. The group then turned to Daphne, but she bowed her head and slowly backed out of the room.

When the introductions were complete, a prayer was shared along with a song. The apostle then delivered a message about the life, death, burial, and resurrection of the Messiah and the need for the group to focus their efforts on feeding the poor.

A Greek named Urbanus led the discussion. "For those of you who don't understand the Roman social order—or Greek culture and our traditions, for that matter—please be aware that Romans are recognized by their class, ordo, and status. But we here in Ephesus don't distinguish ourselves as clearly. Anyway, we must first finish what we came to do. In Rome, only the wealthiest own land. This city is dominated by equestrians and the decurionum, our governing body. These men have many slaves working their fields, and those slaves are turning to Jesus. When they fail to bow the knee to Caesar they're fed to the lions, crucified, or turned out on the streets with no support. We should fight for them."

Nabonidus nodded. "They need a champion."

As if in response, a huge roar from the arena down the hill reminded them that someone new had likely just perished—perhaps a brother or sister in Christ, perhaps a gladiator who had trained with Nabonidus.

Without instruction, everyone's heads bowed and eventually John led a prayer asking for God's mercy on those who were perishing physically and spiritually.

As the group finished their prayer, they heard a rustle at the doorway and three figures shuffled in. John approached the group, whispered with them, and then turned to address the whole gathering.

"Good news, my friends," he said. "We have our first newcomers, hungry for food and hungry for a Messiah. You can see that their feet are still white with chalk—marked for purchase at the slave market. Our sisters Tryphena and Tryphosa have been busy purchasing the lost, and these are the latest of them. They'll serve our church and learn about the one who has set all of us free."

Dorcas grabbed a wet rag to wipe the white chalk off the slaves' feet, declaring that they were welcome and free to eat.

Within minutes of the welcome, the sound of hobnailed sandals on the cobblestones outside reverberated through the open windows. In panic, one of the newcomers yelled, "Run!"

In the flap of a hummingbird's wing, the hall was emptied except for John, Daphne, Dorcas, Nabonidus, and Urbanus.

Titius Marcus Julianus, dressed in all the glory of a Roman general, led two dozen legionnaires up a cobblestoned pathway toward an Ephesian villa. Its marble pillars and numerous statues marked it as the home of a nobleman he had gone to often for support in the old days. Ten years had passed, and it was time to call up a favor.

As he passed the bougainvillea bushes, in full bloom, he called out to announce his arrival. "Licanor of Ephesus, Titius Marcus Julianus has arrived and begs your hospitality."

Instead of the jovial white-haired Ephesian nobleman, however, he was greeted by a broad-shouldered, heavily bearded Jew, a tall slender Greek, and a black-skinned Persian giant. Although there was a sense of tension in their stance, they didn't show any fear or awe at the man standing before them.

Titius removed his golden helmet with its ostrich feather and tucked it under his arm.

"If you be servants of Licanor, I call on you to announce my presence. I am General Titius Marcus Julianus, a friend and confidante."

The broad-shouldered Jew in the plain brown tunic stepped forward. "I am John ben Zebedee of Capernaum in the Galilee, follower of Yeshua and friend of the new owner of this villa. You're welcome to enjoy our hospitality with your men."

Titius glanced past the Jew toward the two men standing behind him. "What has become of Licanor? And who are these with you?"

John turned and extended his hand toward the two men with him. "This is Urbanus and Nabonidus. Urbanus is a friend and Nabonidus is a freeman who now owns this villa. The one you call Licanor passed on this past year from a fever."

"And what of Licanor's family? His wife and two sons?"

"His wife and oldest son also passed from the fever. The youngest son sold us this home and moved on to Rome. He was a great fan of the games, a sponsor of Nabonidus in the arena, and a man with ambitions to achieve greater status."

Titius scanned the former gladiator. "I can see you're a man of great power and wit to have won your freedom through the arena. Where is the ivory pendant all freemen wear to show their liberty?"

Nabonidus motioned to a girl behind him who fetched the wooden sword and displayed it.

"This is the rudis which belongs to the champion of the Ephesian games," the girl said. "He gave his life for this freedom."

Titius smiled. "I see a maiden with spunk in her loins and fire in her eyes. Are you, too, a part of this strange household? Perhaps a servant? And what of the pendant?"

Nabonidus stared Titius in the eye. "It is my most precious possession."

The former gladiator then pulled the pendant out from his tunic and displayed the carved ivory trophy.

Titius stepped forward and drew his gladius. "If you hadn't declared yourselves to be followers of Yeshua, I wouldn't believe you. The pendant is your declaration of identity and freedom. Without it, you are still a slave to Rome."

Nabonidus nodded and welcomed Titius to enter his home. The legionnaires with him spread out around the villa to ensure the safety of their commander as he rested.

During the exchanging of stories, Titius twigged to a potential connection with Nabonidus.

"You speak of time in Caesarea when Romans took you to be a galley slave, as an assurance that your master would build crosses," Titius said. "I was the guardian for such a cross maker. His name was Caleb ben Samson."

Nabonidus stood to his feet. "It is the same man. What has become of him?"

Titius drained his cup of wine and motioned for the girl to bring him more. "You probably don't know this, but he's the one who made the cross for this Yeshua whom you follow." He stood and snagged a date from a tray of food. He turned to John. "I, too, am a follower, since Yeshua freed me from a terrible demon. Caleb married and ran away from the persecution in Jerusalem. I don't know where he has gone."

John rose and hugged Titius without shame. "You are welcome to this fellowship. We're preparing to start a church in this very home, and you're welcome to join us anytime you're in town."

Titius motioned out the window to one of his men, who moved down the hill toward a horse cart where a woman and three children waited.

"It seems God has gone before me in ways I didn't imagine," Titius said. "This family was in danger in Damascus and I have rescued them, hoping my friend Licanor would shelter them. They are also followers of Yeshua and would make a great addition to your church."

Nabonidus opened his arms. "They're welcome in this church and in this home. We will care for all who need sanctuary."

One of the men motioned to Titius and whispered in his ear.

"I must go," said Titius. "But I leave these in your care until a brother named Ananias can find his way here. May the blessings of Yeshua guard you in this place. And brother Nabonidus, I must beg your forgiveness, for I am the one who chained you in the warehouse to be caught by the legionnaires." Titius let that sink in a moment. "I was the blind man, and you distrusted me for a reason."

Nabonidus hugged him. "You are forgiven, my friend."

"God has been gracious to us both. These men with me serve out of respect for my position without knowing me, just as I respect those who lead the church of Yeshua. I go now to return these soldiers to their centurion before checking in with the governor. Say a prayer for me and for my wife who is on her way here."

"May God bless you on your journey," John said.

Titius turned to go, but then pivoted back. "Do you know anything about a so-called children's farm where girls are taken and prepared to serve Artemis?"

John rubbed his bearded chin thoughtfully. "No, I don't know of it… but we're trying to free slaves, whoever they might be. Few of those we see are children."

Titius dug out his coin purse from inside his tunic. He tossed a gold coin to John. "For your next purchases."

"May God bless you."

Titius offered up a brief prayer and waved his farewells to everyone in the home.

In moments, his red cape flying behind him, Titius and his troop descended the hill and disappeared into the streets of Ephesus.

After General Titius's departure, when Daphne could breathe again, she set to work scrubbing down the kitchen. In the background, Dorcas's laughter bubbled through the home.

Nabonidus wandered into the kitchen and gently put his hand on hers to stop her from scrubbing. "You're a guest here, Daphne. This is not your place. Yet."

The sense of his presence overwhelmed her and she turned so her back was to the counter.

"What do you mean, *yet?*" she asked, looking deeply into his eyes.

The confusion in his expression was clear as he tried to look away. He stepped back. "Not that you're not welcome here, of course. But you're welcome as a friend, not a servant."

She reached out to touch his hand—the hand that had killed so many men in the arena. It trembled under her contact.

"Is that all you hope for?" she said. "A friend?"

"I have blood on my hands."

"And I have souls on my hands. My time in the temple did not pass without exacting a price."

He walked to the back door and peered outside at the garden. "With pasts like ours, how can we dare try to love?"

"We live in truth and we do it one day at a time."

"It will take time."

She crossed her arms. "It may be that now we have it. Thinking of love still taps into my fear…"

"This community of believers will have to help us."

"I have a feeling they will." She turned back toward the kitchen and reached again for the cloth.

"We have no other family to call on."

She continued to scrub the counter. "We have what we need."

"Who will I talk to about a betrothal?" he asked, leaning against the counter with a smile on his face.

"Well, the apostle is like a father to me."

"I hope he's ready for this."

She smiled. "I hope *we're* ready for this."

Chapter Eleven

Perspiration beaded Nabonidus's brow as he waited for John and Daphne to arrive. He leaned against one of the marble pillars in the main atrium of his home near a small fountain. The sun sat fixed just over the hilltops, in no hurry to cross the sky.

Urbanus plopped himself down on a cushioned bench alongside the nervous Persian and chuckled loudly.

"Relax, my friend," said Urbanus. "Perhaps I should tell Daphne to dress as a murmillo, to make you feel more comfortable. Perhaps she could swing at you with a sword…"

Nabonidus rose to his feet and reached for a handful of apricots from a nearby table. "She is worth more than I could imagine."

"I believe it." Urbanus rose to join him at the table. "Nabonidus, have you now come to believe Jesus is the Christ, the Son of the Living God?"

Nabonidus stopped pealing an orange and set it on the table. "Yes, he is my Lord, my God, my King… is there something else I'm supposed to add?"

Urbanus shook his head. "No, that's fine."

"What else should I do?" Nabonidus snatched up the orange and bit into it, spilling juice down his chin.

"You need to tell the apostle that you want to be baptized."

"Where should we do it? At the harbor? In the fountain by the arena? Surely not at the pool of cleansing at the Artemission!"

Urbanus gave in to a belly laugh. "Now that would be something, being immersed at the Artemission in front of all Satan's companions."

Nabonidus, wiping his juicy hands on his tunic, wandered to a window and searched down the hill for the expected guests. "Do you think that Roman general will come to the wedding?"

"You mean Titius? He's a man with money, and a man who knows how to fight."

"He could kill you without you even knowing he's there," Nabonidus said. "He told me he was trained as a thespian assassin. But you're right… he's a man with money. How much does a senator earn? Titius's father was a senator, you know."

"Augustus set the minimum at one million sesterces. That's two hundred fifty thousand times what a gladiator earns in a day of training. But forget money. Leave it to the bankers, the merchants, the road builders, the tax collectors… just enjoy your freedom. Money is only a burden."

"Having money doesn't seem like such a burden. I feel trapped without it."

"If you had as much as the wealthy, you would be expected to spend yourself into bankruptcy to please the masses," Urbanus said. "Maybe you could become one of the hundred decurion of Ephesus, but you'd have to sponsor the games and support the gladiators who kill each other and tear apart the martyrs."

Nabonidus sighed, giving the prospect some thought. "Maybe I could change the whole system."

"Only after you supplied the city with all its corn, paid for all the public projects, supported the temples, built better roads, secured the harbor, covered the city's tax bill, and hosted banquet after banquet until no one was in their right mind anymore."

Upon his arrival in Ephesus, Titius dismissed his legionnaires for a few days of freedom to enjoy the delights of the city. Disguised as a house servant, he did the same, loitering among the market stalls to pick up local gossip. Using his Greek personae, he joked with an olive vendor and told wild tales of his exploits in Alexandria, Rome, and the far-flung reaches of the Silk Road. All the while, his eyes and ears soaked in all they could.

As the day came to an end, he saw someone he hadn't expected: Marcellus, the prefect of Judea. Again. What was he doing in Ephesus?

Dismissing himself, Titius casually wandered from booth to booth until he slipped out of the market and doubled back, climbing up a sturdy trellis that had been designed for roses. Sure enough, there he spotted Marcellus, moving steadily in the direction Titius had just gone.

The day before, he'd received a summons from the governor and had been given sleeping quarters. He returned to those quarters today and set up a dummy under the blanket on his mat, suspecting Marcellus would come by looking for him. He hid himself in a corner of the room, wedged tightly against a wall.

He waited long after the torches had dimmed and flickered out. Hours went by, but he willed himself to stay in place.

An hour before dawn, as his eyes grew heavy with sleep and his muscles cramped, he detected a noise as soft as a cat's padded footstep. The door had opened and closed, but no presence had shown itself. Titius focused on the shadows, where a faint shaft of moonlight dulled the deepest darkness. Sure enough, something moved in the direction toward his mat.

Two somethings, in fact.

Seconds later, the attackers slashed at the dummy. A surprised sound came from one of them, and then the figures slipped out as quickly as they'd come. This time, Titius was sure he recognized Marcellus.

Governor Petronius had a long reach indeed if he would authorize Marcellus to blatantly attack the guest of another regional governor.

At the morning meal, nothing appeared amiss—and neither Petronius, Marcellus, nor the governor, Octavian, showed up.

Afterward he sought refuge in an orchard, where he sat under a tree and ate a tangy orange. Servants wandered in and out, but few others in the household seemed to use this space. He skipped the noon meal and by midafternoon he was convinced that Governor Octavian may just have invited him to the mansion as a courtesy.

While the household ate the evening meal, Titius slipped out of the mansion and rejoined his men in an inn where they had sheltered. The cheap wine and chewy chunks of goat were preferable to the delicacies offered at the governor's table.

For three days, he checked in with the servants of the young Ephesian church, but none of them had any message or word from Abigail. He'd had such confidence in his wife's ability to slip away from Damascus and get to Ephesus, but for the first time his hope flickered.

Once on shore in Caesarea, Zedekiah invited Caleb to join him in the newly built Roman baths.

"We're only now beginning to see the value of what Rome offers," he said as they stood outside the two-story structure surrounded by polished marble columns. "We Jews have always been modest about our bodies, but we agree that cleanliness and fitness are important."

Caleb ran his fingers over a mosaic built into the wall. It featured a tapestry of Roman gods and goddesses at play.

"These Romans think they're superior to all of us," Caleb said. "I don't usually enjoy the baths, but I know this is where everyone of all classes comes together and shares the news of the day. If I'm going to hear about Suzanna, it will probably be here."

The bath complex was surrounded by food vendors and had separate entrances for men and women. It turned out that Zedekiah had helped build the heating system under the floor of the baths, and he proudly explained the unseen intricacies which made it all work.

"Notice how the baths are situated to maximize the sunlight on the bathers who are resting?" he said. "There are heated furnaces built underneath the floors, and the slaves stoke the flames continuously. The floors of the baths are raised so the steam can be channelled through special chambers under the floors and in the walls."

In the Apodytrium, the dressing room, the men left their clothing in the care of an attendant. Ignoring his discomfort, Caleb moved to the palaestra, the gymnasium, where he stretched out from the stiffness of the journey. He lay down on a raised mat to have his body oiled by a slave who provided a soothing massage.

Upon rising, he followed Zedekiah into the frigidarium, the cold room, where he plunged into icy waters. The shock to his system was enough to help him forget the strain of his journey. It also made the visit to the tepidarium, the warm room, a season of pleasure.

It was impossible here to distinguish rich from poor, free from slave, senator from legionnaire.

"Alexander!" Zedekiah called across the room to a corpulent Greek who was chatting with a Syrian man. "Alexander, this friend of mine has just arrived from Cyprus. His wife was taken by bandits and put on a ship. You know everything that happens in the ports. Have you heard news of a woman brought here against her will?"

Alexander broke into a belly laugh. "Almost every woman brought here comes against her will," he chortled. "Slaves, whores, wives, even governesses. This is almost as far from civilization as you want to travel."

"That may be true, but this man has come far to take his wife back to civilization."

Alexander rose, patting his generous belly. "I just saw one of the port managers move into the caldarium. Come. We'll share the steam room and hot pool. This manager will have the information we need."

Inside the caldarium, several dozen men loitered on benches surrounded by steam. Others soaked in the hot pool. Still others lay on tables having the oil scraped off their skin by slaves with strigils. Alexander interviewed each of them and although there was plenty of gossip to fill the time, it seemed no one had heard about a woman matching Suzanna's description.

Zedekiah and Caleb then visited the rooms in reverse order before dressing and emerging back into the sunshine to walk the streets. None of the vendors, traders, or even beggars had seen Suzanna, either. One wily street urchin claimed he had seen men taking three women off a ship recently, though, and for a few denarii he would take them to the brothel where they were kept.

Caleb's gut twisted as he thought about his wife being forced to work as a whore. Yeshua had freed her from such a lifestyle! The nausea consuming him almost left him retching on the side of the alley.

Caleb paid the boy and followed him to a rundown shanty. This didn't feel right to Caleb.

When the boy opened the door, Zedekiah hesitated and put out his arm to hold Caleb back. At that same moment, two men rushed at them from inside; two others appeared around the corner of the building to attack from the back. Meanwhile, the street urchin ran.

While Zedekiah was no warrior, Caleb had been trained by Titius in the art of the thespian assassin. A kick to someone's knee, a punch to a throat, an elbow up into a jaw, and a roundhouse kick into a nose left all the men grounded and gasping.

Caleb took the largest in an armlock and interrogated him, but it was soon clear that none of these men knew anything about a kidnapped woman.

Caleb released his hold before backing away with Zedekiah wide-eyed at what he had witnessed.

"Who are you?" Zedekiah asked.

"Just a man looking for his wife."

———————

Suzanna found herself ignored as the captain and crew focused on unloading the remaining cargo from the ship into a warehouse. The dockhands and recruited slaves scurried back and forth with their burdens while several carpenters surveyed the damage and figured out what needed to be repaired.

The cool breeze off the water chilled Suzanna and she sought shelter behind a small storage shed. While her teeth chattered, she tucked her bare feet beneath her tunic and hugged herself for warmth. Her tangled hair hung limp and stringy and her facial wounds stung from sea salt.

As she bent her neck, wondering what to do, she noticed a nobleman being carried past on a litter by four Gauls. The rich man threw out a sesterce, which landed near her. As she reached for it, a young boy ran forward and grabbed hold of it. He raced off before she could react.

Anger flashed through her body as she sprang to her feet. A few steps across the rough ground, though, convinced her not to take up the chase.

A Phoenician sailor approached her as she stood watching the boy disappear. "I haven't seen you in this area before. Do you charge the same as the others?"

The anger she held back for the boy unleashed itself on the sailor.

"How dare you cheapen me like a common dog!" she said. "May the wrath of the Almighty curse your manhood and cover you with blisters. May you sink to the seabed, never to rise. May the arms of Hades wrap you in chains and never let you go."

The wide-eyed sailor back-pedaled from this invoker of curses. He finally turned and took refuge in an alley out of sight from his tormentor.

No one watching the interchange sought to intervene as Suzanna turned and made her way gingerly into the city of Ephesus.

———————

John found Nabonidus in the garden with two of the servant girls, Phoebe and Jumai. A young flautist played Hebrew psalms from a small dais. The trio were sorting an array of herbs and potions to titillate the senses. There were cloves of garlic, mounds of blackberries, heaps of purple cabbage, a basket of pomegranates, a dish of frankincense, an open pouch of myrrh, fennel, tarragon, sage, and hyssop.

"So, my friends, I see Urbanus might be right," John said. "We're planning to open a medicine shop instead of host a wedding! At least none of us will be sick another day in our lives. Our healing prayers can be spent on something more serious."

Nabonidus ignored the apostle and continued to peel garlic pods, his ivory pendant swinging freely from his neck.

"We need more blackberries and cabbage," he said to the servant girls. "The market never seems to have enough. What about those pomegranates? I don't think they're Persian. And where did we get those grapes? They look like they're already becoming raisins!"

John stepped into the space immediately in front of Nabonidus, refusing to be ignored. "Since when does the groom become a cook? Daphne will be here soon and you're dressed like a scullery maid."

Nabonidus sat back on his haunches with his hands raised. "I've never had to do an honest day's work as a free man. I've always been a slave and a gladiator. Today, I do a noble deed with noble women."

Phoebe and Jumai smiled at his gesture toward them.

"We are honored to be the sisters of our brother in Christ," said Phoebe. "We will celebrate your baptism with everyone else."

Nabonidus rose to his feet and extended his hands toward the two young women. "No, you must be baptized with me. We'll celebrate the greater family of God and our unity. Upon your baptism, I will declare you free."

Phoebe collapsed to her knees, sides shaking, sobs intensifying.

Nabonidus knelt, put his hand on her back, and peered inquiringly at Jumai. "What have I done?"

Jumai knelt with them. "From her childhood she has served to pay her parents' debt. Now they have died and she has no one to care for her. To free her is to abandon her. There is no one to protect or provide for her."

"Then she shall be as my daughter," Nabonidus said. "She's free to live here until she herself is married."

Phoebe sobbed harder, covering her face with her hands and lowering herself to the ground.

"She is grateful," Jumai said, interpreting.

John laid his hands on the servant girls' shoulders. "God is great, and our Lord Jesus called us to look after the orphan and the widow. Perhaps now you are ready to be baptized."

Chapter Twelve

As time passed, the responsibility of marriage began to weigh on Nabonidus. He had a home, a community, and enough money to keep a new bride happy. But could he love her? Could he even receive love?

And no matter how long he searched, he couldn't find his lost ivory pendant. The pendant that guaranteed his freedom.

He paced the Ephesian harbor front for hours, despite the rain that had begun to fall. The cold drizzle had turned into a torrential downpour. A handful of dockworkers, sheltering just inside a warehouse, made room for him around their fire. Not a gull or pelican floated in the dull grey skies. His tunic was so soaked, he might as well have been swimming in the sea.

The men boiled a mash of onion, garlic, and olives with milk and barley flour. Another man arrived with a freshly caught fish, and this was sliced up into the mix. Crudely carved wooden bowls rested at the feet of each man as they waited for the feast.

The waves in the harbor rocked the dock underfoot, and Roman warships swayed back and forth, straining at the ropes which held them.

Just two weeks ago, he'd been baptized here. It had been a far better day. He and the servants girls had been immersed at the harbor's edge, with onlookers either cheering or jeering their statements of faith. John and Daphne had both stood beside him as he acted out the death, burial, and resurrection of Yeshua.

The former gladiator crouched near the fire, warming his hands. He surveyed the merchandise stacked around the room. Tightly woven baskets filled with walnuts, figs, olives, dates, apricots, and cabbages sat destined for Rome. Crates of cabbages, pomegranates, grapes, pickled herring, and clay oil lamps had been designated for Alexandria. Brightly woven cloth lay nestled on pallets destined for Caesarea.

Caesarea, he thought, remembering that city. *That's where the Romans stole me from Caleb. In a warehouse just like this one.*

Sweat mixed with the raindrops falling off his beard. His heart raced in rhythm and his hands shook like an epileptic. Numbness swallowed him like the whale which had swallowed Jonah. The darkness and smoke intensified. The walls of the warehouse closed in on him.

One of the warehousemen rose and stood in front of him. "Persian, what's happening? Are you beguiled by demons? Look at me!"

The man placed a hand on Nabonidus and he fell writhing to the floor, bellowing fierce groans. The man reached down and took hold of the Persian man's ivory pendant.

"A gladiator," he said, laughing. "Took an extra clubbing to the head, did you?"

Nabonidus reached up, grappled the man like a wrestler, and hurled him onto a crate of onions. He then pounded his chest and hurled a roll of carpet at the man's limp body.

Two of the men around the fire backed away, but three others charged in to protect their comrade. Nabonidus dispatched them quickly with crushing blows. The fleeing warehousemen ran, screaming for help, their sandals flapping against the wharf and echoing through the streets and alleys.

Nabonidus shook himself and surveyed the destruction around him.

The carnage was enough to set him running. As he left, a fisherman tried to throw a net over him, but Nabonidus grabbed the flimsy trap and yanked it, tumbling the thrower onto his face. A sentry threw a club in his direction, but he dodged it and kept running up an alley. Soon he was far away from the shouts and drumbeats at the water's edge.

As he ran, he reached for his ivory pendant and realized it was gone.

Selsus stood in the shadows of the warehouse as Nabonidus fled.

"See that Persian," Selsus said to a young woman resting on a crate of apples nearby. "Find your way into his house and into his heart. Tell me every weakness you find. Artemis will no longer be mocked."

The woman slid her bare feet into her sandals, hitched up her robe, set the hood in place, and slipped through the crowd in the wake of her quarry. In her hand, she fingered the crescent-shaped amulet Selsus had given her. No longer an unwanted orphan, she was a woman with a mission. The German man would be waiting to reward her when the night was done.

She expected Nabonidus to run up the hill to his mansion, but instead he hurried into an alley toward the west. She tried to keep pace with him but soon found that people were staring at her. She slowed to a walk, and it wasn't long before he was out of sight.

For hours she combed the alleyways until a group of men intercepted her, and had their way with her like vultures with a corpse. She refused to scream despite the pain. When they had consumed her dignity and spent their lust, they tossed her into the middle of the street where the sewer ran full.

At dawn, she stumbled half-clothed back to the hovel to rendezvous with Selsus. When the German man arrived, he stepped over her and poured himself a flagon of wine.

"Perhaps this Persian isn't as virtuous as I was told," he said. "He prides himself on humiliating those who are weaker than he."

She lifted her head. Deep abrasions on her chin and forehead belied any previous beauty she'd boasted. Her dark eyes, black with bruising, stared from puffy folds.

"He's not the one who did this to me," she said.

"What?" He turned on her with fury. "What have you been doing to earn the gold I wasted on you? Selling yourself like a common whore? I think Artemis will need a sacrifice tonight more powerful than doves."

With one last disdainful glance, he set down the wine and left her alone.

Caleb spent two days in Caesarea, until he was certain Suzanna hadn't been brought there by her kidnappers. Throughout this time, Zedekiah had listened eagerly to his stories about Yeshua but hadn't been able to get past the depth of tradition which defined him as a Jew. The two had agreed that sometime in the future Caleb would return for a more in-depth walking tour of the sites where Yeshua had turned the world upside-down.

The former cross maker boarded the next ship to Alexandria and Ephesus, setting his mind back to finding his wife. The previous night, an owl had hooted near the inn where he'd been staying. He feared it might be an evil omen.

Yeshua, preserve me and save Suzanna.

Nabonidus hid for three weeks in the underground cavern across the street from Daphne's inn. He chewed on pickled herring, gnawed on day-old bread, and consumed market vegetables and fruit, washing it all down with diluted wine. In the evenings, he dined on puls, a mix of watery milk and red wheat flour filled with garlic, cheese, and onions.

In the waking hours, believers wandered in and out of the room above, bringing market goods. Daphne had cleaned out the passageway under the street and clay lamps regularly lit the way as Nabonidus walked back and forth to loosen his legs.

As time passed, the group of believers gradually dispersed to find alternate places of refuge. Ananias's wife Hannah, her three children, and Dorcas left to shelter with a group of believers setting up a new church in Smyrna.

"Go with God. May Yeshua protect you," John had prayed as they prepared to leave the city.

Nabonidus followed the apostle into the garden behind his home one evening and watched him kneel under an apple tree, praying.

"What is on your mind, my friend?" John asked, sensing the Persian man's presence.

Nabonidus knelt on one knee. "Will the church survive here?"

"What makes you wonder?"

"You're sending everyone away, and the food you've been buying is of poor quality. We haven't purchased any slaves in weeks."

John hung his head for a moment before rising to his feet. "Come, let's sit."

The two sat back against the trunk of the apple tree. Apart from the crickets and noise of neighbors conversing around fires, there was silence.

Finally, John spoke up. "We must protect the young believers first, as it will get more dangerous here with the followers of Artemis growing strong again." He scratched his beard thoughtfully. "I had to send most of our money with those who are travelling. We have nothing left to support the work here."

The former gladiator rubbed his knees. "I could go back to the arena to earn money."

"You've been away too long. We can't take the risk of sending you back to your death." John let out a long sigh. "Besides, Selsus has grown strong in his opposition to us. There's no guarantee your life would be spared. Those men kill for their own fortune."

"I could sell my home."

"Not unless you must. We must pray and trust the Lord's provision."

The sailors hadn't even secured the ship's mooring lines in Ephesus before Caleb jumped over the rail and onto the dock. He stumbled into the arms of a bulky warehouseman who swatted him to the ground like a fly. Caleb then slithered away, crablike, before grabbing a post and springing to his feet. His sea legs had left him wobbly.

"Stupid Jew," the sailor snarled. "Why don't you stay at home where the Romans can eliminate you like rats?"

Caleb stood tall but didn't reply.

"Don't mind him," a gruff voice said behind him. "It isn't personal. His brother was a leper in Jerusalem. He was taking him to get healed by the Messiah when the Jewish leaders betrayed the Galilean to the Romans and got him crucified."

Caleb swiveled to see a square-jawed tower of humanity, shirtless, bony-ribbed, and minus half his teeth. The dark-skinned man was clearly young in life but aged by the briny scouring of his years at sea.

"Name's Ptolemy," the man said with a genuine smile. "Egyptian. Welcome to Ephesus."

"I'm Caleb." He glanced back at the irate sailor who continued to glare. "What else is wrong with him?"

"Well, he survived that storm weeks ago, but some of his scrolls and gold coins washed overboard. He isn't happy about it."

Caleb's heart leapt at the prospect that this man might have some answers for him. "The ship that got caught in the storm... do you know where it came in from?"

"Cyprus. Why?"

"I think my wife was on that ship. She may have been kidnapped."

"By the beard of Neptune! That vixen was your wife?" Ptolemy stretched his neck to scan the crowds. Seeing nothing, he then stared Caleb in the eye. "She fought like a demon of Hades when they tried to take advantage of her. She survived the storm but left while we were trying to unload cargo."

Caleb climbed up on a crate and also scanned the wharf. There were warehousemen, slaves, sailors, merchants, traders, beggars, and scamps begging from the vendors, but no Suzanna.

"Have you seen her since you arrived?" Caleb asked.

Ptolemy coiled a rope and tossed it onto the dock. "This isn't a place where women survive on their own, my friend. If I see her, where should I tell her to meet you?"

"Tell her to wait right here at noon. I'll be back every day until I find her."

The Egyptian nodded. "There are a quarter-million souls in this city, and I wouldn't let half of them near my own mother. You better hope she found a friend."

———————

Over the next three afternoons, during the heat of the day, Nabonidus went back and forth between his home and the tunnel. John followed him, alternately teaching about Yeshua and listening to the erratic ramblings and musings tossed back at him. All the while, an unexplainable fear gnawed at Nabonidus's very bones.

"This fear..." John said. "Is it a result of all your battles in the arena?"

"No, it's more than that."

"Is it because of your days as a galley slave, beaten by the Romans? Your near-death at sea." Nabonidus shook his head. "Is it because of something which happened to you as a slave?" Nabonidus shrugged. "Is it something from your childhood?"

"I met a man who thinks I may be a lost prince," the Persian man said.

"Is that what you believe?"

"Is it possible to be a Persian prince and a slave of Yeshua at the same time?"

Rage, fear, doubt, hatred, panic, anxiety, hopelessness, and terror wove themselves like a boa constrictor around his heart and lungs. After several of these walks between the house and the tunnels, his sense of suffocation was so strong that he curled up as if a child, whimpering, refusing to be comforted. Finally, he refused to speak at all.

Only Daphne was able to nurture him back to peace. She sang to him day after day, gently feeding him broth, stroking his brow, and sharing the biblical stories of mighty men doing great exploits for God... stories she had only just learned from the apostle.

On a morning after a Sabbath celebration with the believers, Daphne returned from the market with a treasure trove of roasted meat. Every mouth watered as she set out the plates and described the delicacies.

Nabonidus was ready to eat all the duck, mouse, lamb, and pork, but John stopped him. The apostle took the time to instruct the believers on why certain things were prohibited under Jewish law. He told them a story of how a follower of Yeshua named Peter had seen a vision declaring that in Yeshua all foods were now clean. Still, everyone had to pay attention to their own conscience.

Daphne sliced the chunks of meat into strips. "I'm sure the man I got these from said he was Jewish," she said. "Certainly he wouldn't have sold them to me if we couldn't eat them."

"What was his name and where did he come from?" John asked.

"He said his name was Caleb from Nazareth. I was going to ask him if he knew Yeshua, but there were so many people pushing to buy his meat before it ran out..."

Nabonidus bounded to his feet. "Caleb! Did he say he was a cross maker?"

Daphne halted in her task and turned toward him. "A cross maker?"

"Yes. Did he say he worked for the Romans making their crosses?"

"Nabonidus, he was selling roasted meat."

"Didn't you ask him why he was here, in Ephesus, instead of back in his home country?"

Daphne wrinkled her brow. "We're in the Roman Empire, free to travel wherever we want. What else matters?"

Nabonidus walked over to the plate of meat and grabbed a chunk, stuffing it into his mouth. He moaned with pleasure.

"Hey!" Daphne said. "There are more of us than just you around here."

"Fine, I've had my share," Nabonidus muttered through the mass in his jowls. "This Caleb might have been looking for me."

"And why would he be looking for you? Did you once steal the meat off his cart without paying?"

Nabonidus shook his head and swallowed. "No, no, no! He was my owner. Maybe he's come to claim me back as his slave."

"But you've earned your freedom through the arena," she pointed out. "You have nothing more to fear."

"There *is* something to fear. I've lost my ivory pendant. I have nothing to prove my freedom."

Chapter Thirteen

By the time the moon crested above the hills of Ephesus, Nabonidus was running the roads leading past the Artemission and out of town. Despite the assurances of his fellow believers, the panic attacks that had consumed him lately wouldn't let him rest.

A gourd of diluted wine from John and a bundle of cheese, matza, and barley loaves from Daphne provided sustenance. Dorcas had cried as he backed away from the group in the shelter.

The appearance of loss in Daphne's eye had almost made him stay.

"I will not be a slave again," he'd told her.

The road was familiar under his feet because of his many years of training on it. Today, the terrain seemed darker and more ominous. When he reached the top of the first hill, he glanced back on the flickering torchlights of the Artemission, the few faint spots of light in isolated courtyards, and the bonfire surging in front of the arena where the gladiators gathered to share their stories and prepare for the next day of life-or-death struggle.

He hadn't been a follower of Yeshua long enough to figure out the signs and omens which Christians used to guide them. The voice of the Spirit was elusive to him, and there were many voices fighting for dominance in his mind.

The first harrowing experience of his journey came in the form of bats, diving into his hair from out of nowhere. He yanked the flying mammals out and threw them to the ground. A wild dog barked repeatedly as he ran by and he feared the pack would soon be on his trail.

Whatever came his way, he had to keep moving.

———————

Suzanna strolled along the harbor front, looking back at the sea which had nearly claimed her. A flock of pelicans glided over the bay as gulls scattered out of their path. Kingfishers dove for sardines and swallows darted in and out of the trees along the shoreline.

Losing Hemera had shaken Suzanna to the core. Now, nightmares kept her walking the floor of the inn where she'd found shelter. Every morning she haunted the docks and wharfs, hoping against hope that Hemera might somehow appear. But no, she had seen the woman get washed overboard during the storm.

If I hadn't of fallen into that pit and had to be rescued by Diogenes, I would have never met his sister, she thought. *If I had kept my mouth shut instead of mocking the men coming to collect that debt, if I had fought harder, I wouldn't have been on that ship and created all that trouble for the crew. I'd be safe with Caleb in Barnabas's house in Cyprus.*

She blamed herself for what had happened to them.

———————

It took Caleb three days of searching Ephesus in vain before he realized that he had to find a way to stay in one place and survive. He began to beg for work, and he eventually found himself helping the dockworkers as they loaded and unloaded the ships that came and went from the busy harbor.

The work was strenuous, so when a meat vendor whom he frequented offered to sell his business for a reasonable price, Caleb took him up on the offer and gave him the money.

The vendor stayed two days, teaching Caleb the business and introducing him to his suppliers. Parts of the business were clearly shady, but Caleb was too desperate to judge how others did their jobs.

From that time forward, rain or shine, he stood in place behind his booth next to the fountain outside the arena—selling, waiting, and watching for Suzanna.

Time went on and he began to feel anxious that all the leads he'd started with had dried up. His anger grew with his helplessness. What had happened to his wife?

As he worked one day, he grew careless, burning himself on the small charcoal fire. He kicked over the burner, then kicked at the young boys who ran in to snatch the meat off the ground.

Suddenly, a woman who'd been nearby came to his aid. She took a cloth from her bag, dipped it in a nearby fountain, and held it up to Caleb as she walked into the path of his fury. As he charged toward one of the boys, his fist caught her in the shoulder. She spun around, basket flying, and fell into some of the coals on the ground. She screamed in pain.

Caleb froze in the middle of his rant and looked at the woman. He realized that he knew her. She had bought meat from him before. She'd said her name was Daphne…

He scooped her up and took her to the fountain, where he laid her in the cool water along with his own burned hand. A minute later, her screaming had turned to whimpers.

Two legionnaires who had been standing guard at the arena suddenly grabbed hold of Caleb and twisted his arms behind his back. One held him as the other leveled him with blows to the head. When Caleb stopped responding, one of the soldiers picked him up and threw him in the fountain. He sprang up sputtering and choking only to be knocked down again. The soldier held his head under until Daphne screamed for the man to release him.

The two legionnaires dragged him out of the fountain and wrapped a cord around his wrists behind his back. One took out a whip and snapped at Caleb's legs as the other prodded him with a gladius.

"We'll see what a night in the dungeon does for that temper of yours," the legionnaire said. "Now walk."

As the weary Nabonidus stepped out of the bush onto the main thoroughfare that led to Philadelphia, he encountered an oxcart filled with bricks that had broken down on the side of the road. An old man and young woman sat on a delimbed log, staring at the cart's bent wheel while the oxen fed on grass nearby.

The elder lifted his white bearded face. "Shalom, my friend," he shouted with his arms raised high. "An angel sent by Yahweh himself."

Nabonidus glanced around and saw no one else in the vicinity. He slowed his pace and tried not to stare at the young woman. She looked so much like Daphne.

"Shalom, my friend," Nabonidus replied. "I'm no angel, but I see you need one. I know nothing about repairing a wagon wheel."

The man chortled loudly. "You do me good, friend. I have the knowledge and you have the strength. If you'll but hold up the cart, I'll brace it with a log, remove the wheel, and repair it. My daughter will feed you well—if you but take a moment of your time."

Nabonidus's gurgling stomach urged him forward and he bent his shoulder to the cart while the old man and the girl rolled the gnarled log under the axle. The heavy weight of the loaded cart strained his strength as the pair fussed over the exact placement of the timber.

"Hurry," Nabonidus chastened. "It's fine there…"

The old man rolled out from under the cart and took up a hammer to smash the pin out of the wheel. Nabonidus then let the cart down and rubbed at the fresh wounds on his shoulder.

The daughter plucked up a rag, poured a dash of water on it, and rubbed the cuts. It made him long for Daphne's touch even more

"Are you from around here?" the daughter asked. "I'm Elizabeth of Laodicea and this is my father Zedekiah. We're trying to get to Philadelphia before nightfall."

Nabonidus took the cloth from her hand and stretched his back. "You don't intend to stay camped on top of Mount Tmolus so the bandits can relieve you of that load of bricks?"

The white-bearded senior stepped forward. "It's more than bricks I'm worried about. This fertile plain is rich and peaceful, but only when the sun rules the sky. Even with the Romans parading through, these highways aren't as safe as they seem. There are mineral springs near those rocks. We should fill our gourds before going farther."

A fully loaded camel caravan heading for Ephesus lumbered up the hill and Nabonidus kept his head low as greetings were exchanged. Two donkey carts from a nearby village halted and the young men driving them stopped for longer than necessary to interact with Elizabeth and Zedekiah.

"We should get water before any other rascals come by," the old man urged when the men and their donkeys departed.

Before long, Elizabeth had laid out a blanket with clay dishes filled with dried raisins, dates, figs, cheeses, and a generous helping of flat bread.

"Eat up, before I can't hold off the birds anymore," Elisabeth said. Several curious ravens were hopping around on the ground nearby.

The older man led them in a brief prayer, then turned to Nabonidus as the meal got underway.

"You don't appear to be a local, so let me tell you about this place," the man said. "Two hundred years ago, the king of Pergamon, Eumenes the Second, named Philadelphia for the brother he loved. That's what the name means… 'the one who loves his brother.' But the king's nephew came to rule after him, and he had no heirs. So he willed the city to the Romans who had been his allies."

Nabonidus guzzled the fresh water. "Did no one object? Most often people fight to keep their land. They don't give it away."

The man smiled. "Ah. Well, the Romans were wise under Tiberius."

He went on to tell the rest of the story, about how twenty years ago a tremendous earthquake had devastated Philadelphia. Emperor Tiberius had released the city from its tax burden while the people rebuilt—and they were forever grateful. They continued to expand ever after, even to the modern day. They were in the process of building another theatre, as well as a temple on the northern edge of the city.

Once the wheel was repaired, Nabonidus bade farewell and jogged down the hill toward the city. The sun was just kissing the far horizon as he reached the market. Thoughts of Daphne and his promises to Anoshiruvan and John swirled like tumbleweeds in his mind.

Abigail tried to believe the best of humanity as she endured yet another day tied up in a mud hut. She'd heard enough from her captors to know that the small huts and poor apple orchard were a front for the gang of thieves who had attacked her convoy. The bandits had hidden the horses and looted treasure in a dense thicket not far from where they were keeping her.

No one would have suspected that old toothless hag who'd befriended Abigail as having been a spy for a notorious gang of killers, but that's exactly what had happened.

A young boy had been assigned to put a date in her mouth twice a day, but no one had been assigned to keep her from having to sit in her own filth. Her humiliation grew when the men who stopped nearby mocked her for her inability to control herself. They suggested all sorts of things they might do with a woman like her.

The hut was far enough from the road that her screams may not have been heard anyway, but a woman stopped by to stuff her mouth with a rag whenever a traveler showed up at the front of the property.

Abigail believed it was only a matter of time until the gang would dispose of her.

Yeshua, she prayed. *See me, hear me, save me.*

After a month, Abigail still hadn't arrived in Ephesus. Titius also had to remain on the lookout for possible assassins sent by Petronius. Emperor Caligula's demands to erect a statue in the Jerusalem temple had only softened a little, despite his slow deterioration in Rome.

But mostly he was concerned for Abigail. He'd sent messengers along the main road, but they'd turned up no sign of Abigail, despite the fact that she had to be on the way from Damascus. The main focus of their attention was on a spot where several bandit attacks had been wreaking havoc on convoys. The bandits had been disappearing into the wilderness without a trace.

In his prayers, these bandits kept rising in Titius's conscious. Finally, he determined to take a troop and ride the roads all the way to Damascus if necessary. He feared that Petronius might have apprehended her as blackmail to ensure his return.

Fresh horses were arranged and he sped away at dawn to cover as much territory as possible. The group exchanged horses tree times in order to keep pace until evening.

Three full days into the journey, the men were exhausted and asked to take a one-day break in Philadelphia. Signs of rebuilding were still underway from the earthquake which had destroyed the city some twenty years before.

They stopped overnight at an inn and Titius paced the path outside the building, feeling drawn to it. There had to be a reason why he had felt compelled to stop there.

Nabonidus saw the fish sign clearly etched on the stone pillar at the Philadelphian market. A young girl stood nearby, under a torch, holding out a loaf of fresh baked bread.

"Come, taste and see that the Lord is good," she called.

The former gladiator checked over his shoulder before stepping up to take the treat.

"He is good," the girl affirmed. "Find your rest in him."

"I have nowhere to rest," Nabonidus confessed. "Do you believe the truth of the fish?"

"The truth is always in the fish's mouth," replied the girl while holding out another loaf. A beggar took it, and she called after him. "Walk in the light and you will not walk in darkness."

Nabonidus moved westward, in the direction the fish had pointed. He soon discovered another fish, this time pointing to the northwest. He followed the pathway until the next sign.

As he ran his finger over the sixth fish etching, a robed figure stepped out of an alley and stood in his way.

"Do you walk in the light, my brother?" the man asked in a deep voice.

"I do," Nabonidus replied. "I do indeed, and I search for rest."

"Follow me."

Nabonidus found these fish etched in all the markets of the cities east of Ephesus, and they proved to be his salvation as he travelled. They'd led him to churches in Philadelphia, Laodicea, Colossae, Antioch of Pisidia, Derbe, and finally Tarsus. The followers of Yeshua lived hidden in plain sight. Each time he'd found an inn run by Christians—places of refuge where he could rest. The people fed him, prayed with him, and completed the visit with a time of remembrance over bread and wine.

During these prayer times, there had been no end of lament over all the children of God who had faced a hideous death for standing up for what they believed. At each stop, though, he was given words of encouragement.

The Christians always sought information about apostolic teachings or news of others. When they learned that Nabonidus had been with the apostle John, they all pressed him to remember every word he'd been taught. They longed for stories and laughed wholeheartedly as if he were a professional raconteur.

Little eased his own inner fear and turmoil, though. Regardless of how fast he traveled or how far he went, he kept seeing Daphne in his dreams, calling him to come home. Not far removed were the nightmares of Caleb calling out, "Nabonidus! Come back, come back…"

Chapter Fourteen

The road through Anatolia, under the scorching sun, offered little comfort to Nabonidus's blistered feet. All his time away from the rigorous training of the ludus had made him soft and weak for the task he had set for himself. After being devoured by bed bugs at the most recent inn, he'd chosen to sleep at the side of the road tonight, despite the chill.

Roman patrols marched along the road on a regular basis. Although Nabonidus sweated each time he heard their hobnailed boots thundering along the rough-hewn stones, no one stopped to hassle him. Because of the patrols, there were no more than a few thieves practicing their trade. The streams were plentiful and the towns and vendors hospitable.

On the fifth day, resting near a convoy of camels from Arabia, he noted about a dozen Jewish zealots among the traders enjoying an evening of music and dance. He was familiar with their ways; his former owner Caleb had worked with the Romans to combat them.

He slipped into the bushes near one of the resting camels and watched. The zealot plan was clear. Three had moved to one side as a distraction while the other ten crept toward the traders' saddlebags. The sentry assigned to watch the goods was well away from his post, watching the festivities.

As the first zealot reached in to open a saddlebag, Nabonidus rushed at him, yelling with all his might. The sight of the gigantic terror, arms raised and issuing a blood-curdling scream, set the zealot man back on his haunches. Before he could scramble away, Nabonidus hoisted him high and tossed him toward the Arab traders.

The other zealots tried to melt into the night but the Arabs, torches held high, were quick to give chase. Two Arabs had already dispatched the thief Nabonidus had found, and when the chase was abandoned the traders had returned to check their belongings. Nabonidus was hailed as a hero and welcomed to the feast.

In the morning, Nabonidus set his sights on Tarsus.

———————

Titius paced restlessly as his troop groomed their mounts and prepared for the next phase of their journey. The only reason for the latest stop had been to rest, something he hadn't had much of due to his anxiety over Abigail.

While he bent over a barrel, scooping up some water, an old man ambled over to him.

"What kind of protection are you good for?" the man asked. "Those of us trying to make a living are being killed and you all sit here like kings."

Titius glared at the man, noting the slash on his cheek and pronounced bruises on his face.

"What happened to you, old man?" Titius asked.

"Ambushed, I was. Not a Roman patrol in sight. Pax Romana, safe and peaceful. I spit on your peace."

"Where did this happen?"

"Day and a half from Damascus by oxcart. Just this side of Mount Amanus." The old man splashed water on his face, rinsed out his mouth, and spit it back into the barrel where Titius had just had a drink. "Left me for dead, they did. Slaughtered my oxen and left me lying right next to their heads. Made me so mad, I tracked them right to their village."

A quiver ran right up Titius's spine. "Did you happen to see a woman travelling on her own? Galilean. Face of an angel."

The man scrutinized him. "Come to think of it, I did. She was riding in the back of my cart a month ago. I told her to run when a messenger warned us the bandits were coming. She was hiding in the hills when they swooped down and ambushed us."

A stable boy approached, beckoning Titius to come for his mount. Titius waved him away.

"You said you tracked the gang to their village," Titius pressed. "Was it close to where they attacked? Could you have seen Parthians, or were they simply bandits? The Parthians once took their stand at Mount Amanus."

The old man surveyed the scene. "Feeling sorry for your poor efforts, are you? Think you can show them something they might not expect?"

Titius grabbed the old man by the tunic. "That woman was my wife. I need to find her. Tell me how to find their village."

"Your wife? What kind of man leaves his wife on her own these days?"

Titius shook him and almost lifted the man off his feet. "Tell me."

Terror filled the man's eyes. "I don't know if they have her. The village is hidden. There are many fighters in that place."

"How did you find them?"

"I came across the hills and thought I'd found help before I saw twenty mounted men with swords racing around our carts." He rubbed his beard and shook his head as if in disbelief. "I ran for the main road where I met a group of horsemen. They gave me a ride to Tarsus and I caught another convoy here. I've lost everything."

Titius ran toward his mount, calling for his men. In a moment, the troop was on the road at full gallop.

Suzanna turned away from the harbor in Ephesus and scanned the buzzing marketplace. Its noise washed over her like a tsunami and she fell to her knees, retching. Her hands were numb, her skull ready to explode. Her body didn't feel like her own; she felt trapped and unable to escape. It was hard to breathe...

When a woman came to her aid, it only accentuated Suzanna's terror. It almost felt like a tiger was loose inside, tearing at her very soul.

The wharf under her rocked and the warehouses swirled. Nothing made sense.

She gripped the woman in desperation, holding on so tight that the woman had to pry her hands off and back away. Suzanna crawled after her begging for help. This only made the woman turn and run.

Then another woman arrived, kneeling down and trying to enfold Suzanna in a hug. The woman's arms wrapped around her like chains. She struggled against them as the woman spoke powerful words through the darkness, words of light and healing: "Yeshua, Yeshua... mercy... Yeshua... peace."

Finally, Suzanna collapsed into a fetal position and cried like a baby.

"I've lost her," she whimpered, thinking of Hemera. "I lost her... it's all my fault... she's gone."

"Yeshua, Yeshua," her comforter continued to pray. "Yeshua, mercy... Yeahua, peace."

When Suzanna at last recovered, she found herself surrounded by a forest of legs. She didn't dare look up to examine their accompanying faces. Instead she buried her eyes into the folds of her comforter's tunic, refusing to move.

The woman spoke kindly to those around and eventually the shuffling of feet showed that the people had lost interest in this desperate soul.

"Thank you," Suzanna whispered to the woman as the cool evening breezes caressed her cheeks. "Thank you for staying with me, for whispering his name to me, for being my angel."

"My name is Jumai," the woman said. "I'm just a servant of Yeshua. Come with me. It's not safe here anymore. I have a place you should stay and people you should meet."

Suzanna sat up. "I'm Suzanna, a daughter of Yeshua. I've lost a good friend at sea. I need to go home."

"Where's your home?" Jumai asked. "Do you have a husband or family there?"

"I was on Cyprus. I think my husband was eaten by wild dogs." Suzanna bowed her head and allowed her tears to flow. "I was kidnapped and put on a ship... then the ship got caught in a storm. I nearly died."

Suzanna led the young woman to the inn where she'd been staying. From the look in Jumai's eyes, Suzanna could tell she was concerned. After all, rotting food lay in the corners and there were no extra clean clothes to change into, no clean bed to crawl into.

"I can take you to a safer place," Jumai said. "A warm place, a clean place."

———————————

A mile away, Daphne was arguing with a prison guard about Caleb's release. She ignored the guard's comments about the need for a trial, knowing she had to find the right price.

She had debated already with John about springing this hotheaded and violent jailbird from his cell. John had argued this could be the very man Nabonidus was running from, and that it risked everything to bring in someone who could re-enslave her future husband. He also hadn't wanted to use the church's meager offerings on a bribe.

"Didn't Yeshua tell us we must love our enemies and care for those who despise us?" she had reminded the apostle.

She held a dozen silver coins in her palm and held them out to the chief guard.

"Is this not the coin of the goddess?" Daphne asked. The guard stepped closer and visually examined the silver. She reached into her waist pouch and withdrew two more coins. "Surely your family hungers for the taste of meat. Is not Artemis the goddess of the wild boar, the bear, the wolf, the hare? Will she not celebrate with you if you satisfy yourself with such bounty?"

"My family has grown large during this season of trouble," the guard said. "Perhaps I could release this worthless vagrant and let you deal with the trouble he brings."

And so, Caleb's price was determined.

Caleb had been dropped naked into the lower depths of a damp hellhole beneath the governor's mansion. This section of the prison had circular walls, like a well. Its tufa stone blocks were ten feet thick and water seeped through the joints to gather in an icy pool. Rats occasionally fell from above, scurried momentarily, and finally died.

For the first hours, he howled for justice. For the next hours, he called out for mercy to God, to Rome, to anyone who would listen. The cell was so dark that he didn't know when night started or ended. His feet were numb from the cold and he hugged himself to get warm. Nothing worked.

It seemed forever before a rope was lowered. He grabbed hold of it and was dragged up, scraping his body against the rough walls. He didn't care. He hung on until the flickering torchlight above revealed two legionnaires.

When he reached the top, he grasped for the edges of the paving stones with numb fingers so he wouldn't fall back into the hole. He was almost too weak to hold on.

As the soldiers walked away, he noticed a Syrian woman standing nearby. She calmly walked up to him, holding her torch, wrapped the rope under his armpits and secured it to a post at the far side of the room. She took her own cloak and laid it over his naked body.

"Caleb, I am Daphne, a follower of Yeshua, a friend of the apostle John here in Ephesus." She knelt down and laid a hand on his head. "I've come to help you. You must be strong. I'll take you to a safe place where you can be warm and clean."

Caleb took heart and pulled himself over the edge of the hole. He wrapped himself in her cloak and gasped for air, rubbing his feet to restore circulation.

In Tarsus, Nabonidus spent the best part of an afternoon searching the marketplace for fish etchings. The city was an international mecca with Medes, Parthians, Phrygians, and Syrians mixing together with Alexandrians, Gauls, Greeks, Britons, and Ethiopians. He had examined stall counters, posts, benches, and walls. Even trees didn't escape his thorough check. Twice he had been run off by security guards, especially after he'd asked the fishmonger and fig vender if they "walked in the light" or "listened to the words from the fish's mouth."

That night was spent hungry, curled up in an empty stall meant for horses. The chilly wind still found him and prodded him every time he nodded off to sleep.

In his dreams, Daphne called to him, crying for him to return. Caleb laughed at him as legionnaires lashed at and bound him. The crowds called for his blood as he knelt at the mercy of a Thracian gladiator's sword.

The rooster crow was a welcome end to it all.

Nabonidus understood why followers of the Way were somewhat secretive; he had watched them die too often in the arena after being tortured and imprisoned. Some Christians looked for fellow converts at synagogues, but he didn't dare ask where the synagogue might be in such a large center like Tarsus.

So he sat.

It was while sitting at a city well, basking in the early morning sun near a wide gateway, that he spotted a woman staring at him. She was dark, like him, with distinct Persian features, and she held a basket. Her pantaloons were uniquely patterned and reminded him of something his mother had once worn to a festival. Her wide sleeveless tunic was clasped at the shoulders and drawn tight around the waist. A mantle, wrapped around her hair and shoulders, draped down over it all.

She stood directly behind a group of stoic philosophers pontificating on their beliefs. The men spoke with an air of superiority and arrogance, and the woman didn't pay attention to them. Instead she stared directly at Nabonidus.

As she moved nonchalantly ahead, he shouldered his way through the crowd to meet her.

He caught up to her at a fig vendor. She ignored him as she purchased a handful of figs. He then followed her to a bakery where she purchased several fruit loaves. At the fishmonger's booth, he finally decided to walk away.

Suddenly, she turned to him.

"I think I need another denarii for this purchase," she said. "Would you happen to have an extra?"

He pulled out the money pouch hanging around his neck under his tunic. He handed over the coin and she in turn gave him a piece of paper. As she turned back to speak with the fishmonger, he unfolded the paper and read:

At even's night, come look for light, right here.

With her purchase complete, she walked away and left him behind without another glance.

He munched on dried apricots, dates, and figs through the rest of the afternoon and wandered the market. Well after dusk, though, he returned to the fishmonger's booth and waited. Before long, a young man stopped next to him, kneeling in a small garden.

"Do you have the light?" he asked softly.

Nabonidus nodded. "I seek it."

"Follow me."

Chapter Fifteen

After following the young man to a home built of stone, much like the one he'd bought in Ephesus, Nabonidus came face to face with a balding middle-aged man studying at a table full of scrolls. The scholar glanced up from the scrolls and waved his hand over them.

"It's all right here, plain as day," the scholar said. "Yeshua is the Messiah. It's here in the Torah, the Psalms, the prophets… how could anyone be so blind?"

Nabonidus stood silently as the young man left him alone with this scholar.

"Are you the Persian scholar I was told about?" the man asked Nabonidus in Hebrew, then Greek, then Latin. When Nabonidus hesitated, he asked again in Aramaic and Persian.

Nabonidus glanced around the room since the man was still examining the scrolls. "I am only a former slave. A gladiator. A freedman, having won my own championship."

The scholar frowned, scrutinizing him. "A gladiator? Yes, of course. You have the size and marks of one."

"Are you a follower of Yeshua?" Nabonidus asked.

The man allowed a scroll to roll up on itself as he scratched his well-cropped beard. "Such a question!" The man smiled. "A few years ago, such a question would have had you put in a dungeon, and perhaps even had you stoned to death. But today, yes, I follow Yeshua ha Mashiach. He is the Son of God, Savior of all mankind."

"I am Nabonidus, and I too am a follower," Nabonidus declared. "I've been with his disciple John in Ephesus. I seek safety from one who would try to enslave me again."

"I am Saul of Tarsus, a Pharisee who studied under the great Gamaliel in Jerusalem. But that is of no account." The man stepped out from behind the table and extended his hands in greeting. "I know this John of whom you speak. He was a pillar of the church in Jerusalem. One well loved by Yeshua. Did he send you with a message for me?"

Nabonidus, even though he was a foot taller than Saul, felt small in his presence. "I am still new to the faith. I didn't know I was coming here specifically, so the message I carry is only what I've learned from him. He writes messages for the world about God's love and the love of Yeshua, who gave his life to forgive our sins and bring us new life."

Saul walked to the back of the room and returned with a tray of cheeses, bread, figs, and dates. "You must be hungry, my friend. Have some nourishment. I'll get you some wine. I must hear your story and you must hear mine."

It took a full day of riding for Titius and his men to reach Laodicea, but they had to switch out the horses halfway, at the twenty-mile mark. The mountainous terrain had been hard on horse and rider alike. Two of the soldiers sought medical attention with eye salve for trouble with dust or bugs. The medical center in town was famous and the physicians were expert in their care.

But regardless of how hard Titius pressed them, none of the stable boys, legionnaires, or local merchants knew more about the bandit hideout. Titius wanted to ride another eleven miles to reach Colossae, but the men concluded that the darkness would put their horses at risk and subject them to ambush by the very bandits they hoped to capture. In the end, Titius relented, but he was up and ready at first light.

The hard ride to Colossae was uneventful and frustrating. The road was thick with caravans and convoys all vying for space with their camels, donkeys, oxen and flocks of sheep. The smell of spices, sweat, droppings, and food filtered over everything in a grey haze.

Rain poured down on the outskirts of Colossae and again the men urged Titius to delay until the storm was done.

Years of training had kept Titius alert, and each night he set up a false figure in his sleeping quarters and kept himself semi-conscious within sight of the mat. On this night, he lay in a balcony alcove overlooking the stables. As he watched, six shadowy figures crept across the square toward his quarters; on this moonless night, they would have been invisible to any untrained eye.

One of his own men met them and led them inside. Titius swung down on the outside of the balcony and hid in a bush. He put on the garb and disguise of an old drunkard and curled up on the edge of the square.

The invaders soon crept out into the open and spread out.

"He's got to be here," said Titius's own soldier. "Governor Petronius wants him at all costs."

One of the newcomers spotted Titius just then, but mistook him for a drunk. He prodded Titius with his foot.

"Stupid drunk," said the man. "Why can't you be sober enough to tell us where he escaped?"

The betrayer from Titius's own troop decided to leave with the ambushers, recognizing that his identity might have been compromised.

Soon after, Titius crept inside and woke a man he could trust. He left the man instructions and then slipped away into the night. He waited miles down the road for the rest of his legionnaires to meet him. Before sunrise, all those still with him had joined him and acquired new horses.

It took two more weeks galloping through Antioch, Lystra, and Derbe before they came to the home stretch to Tarsus and Mount Amanus.

Walking next to Jumai, took every bit of energy Suzanna had. It was like stepping into knee-deep mud, pulling your foot out, and stepping down into that same mud, only to do it over and over all the way up the hill toward the villa.

Jumai was patient, encouraging her when she couldn't seem to take another step. The world had become a dark and dangerous place, and it seemed ludicrous to Suzanna that she should put her life in the hands of a stranger. Yet she didn't have the will to resist.

By the time the pair reached the villa, the sun was high overhead and Suzanna was dripping with sweat. A servant girl met her and led her to a room where she could bathe and dress in a clean tunic. She sunk into the familiar smell of lavender, dreaming of her childhood before a lewd uncle had stolen her innocence, before the gang of soldiers had caught her unawares while picking flowers in a field, before she'd found the only reliable way of surviving on the streets night after night…

She shook off the terrors of the past and shuddered for Caleb. He had sacrificed everything for her. Now she was alone again. Their true love had lasted so short a time, and she had no offspring to show for it.

Tears ran freely down her face. Jumai hugged her and rocked her back and forth like a little child.

Daphne and John supported a wobbly Caleb into another part of Nabonidus' home. John brought warm water and laid out a clean tunic for him. The apostle set down his own sandals beside the tunic and went barefoot.

Pelonius, now in charge of all the animals, stepped into the house to snatch a few apples for his charges. He gave a wave and then wandered outside again.

The house servants set about making a special lamb stew with trays of dates, figs, olives, cheeses, and breads. Soon Dorcas returned from the market with eggs and fruit and Phoebe hustled to set up the beds for the new guests.

As Caleb attempted to surface from his despair, Urbanus arrived with yet more white-footed slaves he had purchased at the market.

"Phoebe and Jumai! Wash that chalk off their feet," Urbanus ordered. "This Arab is named Seti and this Gaul is Asturex. See that they receive our best."

Dorcas took the tall Greek man aside. "Urbanus, this is the sixth person we've taken in these past three days. We've already given away the last of the tunics. We need more clothing and sandals."

Urbanus patted the girl's head. "Don't you worry, my little one. I'll head right back to the market. Serve everyone in their own room, and when I come back we can bring them all together for a service of praise in the triclinium."

Six weeks into her captivity, Abigail had almost stopped watching for Titius to rescue her. She'd recently begun to cooperate, and so they'd dragged her out to the orchards and set her to work picking apples. She was roped together with a Nabatean girl, Gamilat, who had been taken from the same convoy.

Gamilat had claimed to be a princess on her way to get married, but the bandits had destroyed any sense of nobility she might have had by taking advantage of her night after night. Dressed in rags, smelling of her own filth, unwashed and unattended, she was now no different from any other girl on the streets. Her glazed eyes were those of the dead.

One day Abigail noticed her looking up at the cloud formations. She sat beside the destitute girl and hummed one of her favorite Jewish songs. The girl listened and laid her head on Abigail's shoulder.

"I miss my mother," Gamilat said.

Abigail put her arm around the girl. "When I missed my mother, I used to survey the clouds and imagine all the things I was seeing. Dragons and horses and flowers. And I would make up stories of all that God was doing to send me a message from my mother."

"What kind of stories do you see in the clouds today?"

Abigail encouraged her with stories of the great heroes and celebrations. She spoke of the armies and parades. She even shared secret promises that her husband, the great Roman general, would soon be there to rescue them. They had both watched expectantly, though, and now they meekly went about picking apples.

When the stories no longer had their hoped-for effect, Abigail told Gamilat stories of Yeshua. The healings and miracles caught the girl's attention and she gained energy and strength from the God who cared enough to enter into human suffering. She loved the story of the little girl who had been raised from the dead. She even talked and sang at times with Abigail. The first few times they sang, the old toothless hag, Barbatha, tried to intimidate them into silence. When that didn't work, she gave up and even started listening.

Through Abigail's interactions with Gamilat in different areas of the bandits' hideaway, they eventually heard cries from a group of people who had been locked in a cave. Having heard this, Gamilat mentioned that in the early days of her captivity she had been tasked with taking crusts of bread to an old shed deep in the forest. She had been sure children were kept there, and now she wondered if those children were still confined—only in a cave this time.

Abigail woke up one night with an idea. When she and Gamilat were picking apples, she deliberately walked some distance from the girl and began to speak loudly.

"Gamilat, there are so many good apples in this orchard. If we only had two more sets of hands, we could keep them from spoiling and help feed these people during the months to come."

Two days later, three of the hidden captives from the cave were brought to the hut—a woman and her two daughters. This time, no one was tied down, but the door was secured shut. The inevitable tears lasted for days, but none of the women were molested and the lone man with a sword assigned to guard them only whipped them moderately when they slowed their work.

"Tell them the stories of Yeshua," Gamilat urged.

So it came to be that Abigail nurtured her own small group with stories of storms quieted, fish multiplied, and people healed.

"It's sad we have no men who could dig a cooler place to store the apples so they wouldn't spoil so quickly," said Abigail a few days later while walking through the orchard. "There are so many things the people could do with apples if we could only get them to last."

A week later, three boys and a young man were dropped off—more captives from the cave. Their first task was to build a room for themselves. Their second task was to build a room underground with a peat moss roof over it.

And so Abigail grew her church little by little, pondering aloud how she could benefit the camp. At times, she would draw her group in close and talk more softly. During those moments, Barbatha crept closer to listen in.

As Saul walked Nabonidus around Tarsus, he pointed out the different sights of the city. There were palaces, bridges, roads, baths, fountains, aqueducts, and gymnasiums. He noted the Taurus Mountains inland, the Cydnus River feeding the green plain, and the Mediterranean just ten miles away.

"Some people think we're growing bigger than Ephesus," Saul said. "We're a learning center equal with Alexandria and Athens. We have Stoic philosophers like Zeno, Nestor, Antipater, and Athenodorus. I look forward to debating these scholars."

Nabonidus watched dozens of slaves unloading carts, hauling goods to the market, teaching, cleaning, purchasing, and creating new products. Surely the slaves were the real lifeblood of the Empire.

"The Romans have cleared away the pirates who used to ravage this area," Saul added. "We're now at peace with the rest of the world."

The scholar stopped at a bookdealer and examined the merchandise, asking learned questions and getting tepid answers.

"Listen, my Persian friend," Saul said as they walked away. He led the way toward another area of the market. "We have the best market, fully stocked with all things Persian. Do you desire pistachios, almonds, pomegranates, oranges, mint, grapes, saffron, walnuts, lamb… anything, we have it here for you." He opened his hands, palms up, and turned toward a colorful row of canopied booths. "Tell me your desires and I'll send my servants by to pick it up for your dinner. My Persian cook makes a pomegranate walnut stew with duck which cannot be beaten. She also makes an eggplant and tomato stew with just the right amount of turmeric. The rice with fava beans is heavenly."

"You make me hunger for foods I hardly even know," Nabonidus said. "I was captured when I was five and haven't been free to choose my meals."

"Then choose you must."

"I've lost the ivory pendant which declares my freedom to choose," Nabonidus admitted.

"Nonsense," Saul declared. "You are my brother. Slaves, nobles, men, women, we are all one in Yeshua. There is no difference. We're all free."

The two men moved from the foods on display to a section featuring carpets, trinkets, sculptures, and artwork. A painting of twelve royally robed magi astride camels in the desert beneath a bright star sat on its side in a frame at the back of the shop.

Nabonidus tilted his head and examined it. "What is this about?" he asked the shopkeeper.

The man set it right-side up and pondered it. "This, my friend, has just arrived from the courts of Herod. Legend speaks of wise astrologers from Persia who traveled for months following a star in search of a new king for the Jews. It seems they came in vain, for no word of their discovery was ever heard."

Nabonidus reached for the painting and pulled it closer. "I remember the Jew who owned me saying that the mother of his friend Yeshua had spoken of Persian wise men coming in a great caravan to visit him when he was young. If the great Herod dismissed the legend, perhaps it was only a story spun by his followers."

The shopkeeper swept over the painting with a feather duster. "It's strange the courts of Herod would produce such a masterpiece if there was no truth to it. Perhaps these wise men came simply for trade."

Nabonidus stepped back and examined the figures from a distance.

"These clothes of the magi bring back memories. When I was five, my family's caravan was attacked by bandits." Nabonidus stepped forward and ran his fingers over the jeweled camel harnesses and richly embroidered coverings. "Some of those who rode with us had camels dressed like this. Perhaps my family once sought to find and worship the newborn king."

The shopkeeper set the painting back on its side. "You can make the story say anything you want," he said. "If you'd like it, I can give you a special price. That's the beauty of being a free man. You can make any story into a great story."

"Come," Saul urged Nabonidus. "We can ask Mary, mother of Yeshua, once we see her. Perhaps you're a Persian prince who's now free to discover your destiny."

The life of this freedmen caught Nabonidus off-guard. He walked around with a complete lack of anxiety. Legionnaires marched by at regular intervals and Saul hardly gave them notice. Slaves served and paid deference and no one seemed to even see them as long as they were doing what was expected.

"What is that gate over there?" Nabonidus asked as they approached a wide archway.

"We call it the Sea Gate, or Cleopatra's Gate. My grandfather said the Queen of Egypt herself sailed up this river disguised as Aphrodite on her way to meet Mark Anthony." He paused, then pointed out a flock of shaggy black goats grazing nearby. "My family has a long heritage in this place. As you saw from my home, we're tentmakers. We use goat hides to make special leather materials. Our work is highly valued all over this area."

As Saul turned toward home, one of his servants ran to him. "Master, come quick, you're needed at home!"

Chapter Sixteen

The skies were unseasonably clear as Nabonidus stood by Saul, musing about what to do about General Titius, who had sent word of his upcoming visit. The stables had been prepared and the meal set out. The Persian now watched the large pen of chickens, each pecking at newly scattered seed while pigeons and doves dove to steal what they could. A large rooster strutted among the hens asserting his turf.

Saul sharpened a hatchet and eyed some of the plumper hens.

"Why would this general choose to come here?" He tested the edge of the blade with his thumb. "We always get larger caravans here because we've got the best tents and leather goods in the area, but why would the general come here instead of the governor's mansion? We better go find us a fat sheep and leave the chickens as a backup."

Nabonidus trailed the energetic scholar toward the sheep pens.

Titius rode hard into the outskirts of Tarsus, the horses having been pushed and their chests heaving in the cool air as they finished their journey in the military stables near the governor's mansion.

He released the reins of his mount into the hands of a stable boy and called for a replacement horse. He flexed his hands and rubbed hard against his thighs to get the circulation going.

An aide hurried over. "General, I thought we would rest overnight in the city."

Titius beckoned the boy to hurry with the Arabian stallion being pulled in his direction. "You and the men will stay here at the mansion, but I have business to attend to. Eat well, and warn me if any of the governor's men come searching for me. Tomorrow we'll find those bandits and deal with this injustice once and for all."

———————

Saul was still skinning the sheep when Titius arrived on his mount. Nabonidus was genuinely surprised to recognize the Roman general dressed in all his finery. Titius seemed equally as surprised to see him.

"I thought you were getting married in Ephesus," Titius said.

"The wedding has been delayed," Nabonidus replied. "What brings you here? If you've come to enslave me, I claim sanctuary in this place."

Saul drew in his chin and chuckled. "I see you and the general know each other. The ways of the Lord are amazing and amusing. Mysterious indeed. Perhaps we can find out more over dinner."

The general released his hold on the sheepskin and called over a servant to finish the work.

As the men washed up, Titius ignored Nabonidus and focused his attention on Saul.

"I understand you're familiar with all the caravans which come through this town." Titius waited until the scholar nodded. "I served under Governor Petronius in the legions tasked with ensuring the emperor's statue be placed in the temple in Jerusalem."

Saul smirked. "It seems you and the governor met your match with the Galilean peasants."

Titius nodded. "Indeed, they bared their necks and were as willing as any gladiator or legionnaire to give their lives. The statue remains in Sidon."

"Don't expect me to help you change their mind," Saul declared.

"That's not why I came," Titius said. "I encouraged the governor to plead with the emperor for another option, and this put me out of his favor. I've been on the run ever since."

Saul handed the towel to Nabonidus and turned back to Titius. "So why are you choosing to hide here?"

"I'm not hiding. Three months ago, my wife was taken by bandits near Mount Amanus and I've come to rescue her."

Nabonidus stepped forward. "You don't think she's still alive, do you?"

Titius rinsed his hands over the bowl of water and wrung them dry. "I have no choice but to believe. Either way, these bandits must be cleared off the roads. Perhaps I can win favor from the governor again if I succeed."

Nabonidus turned to Saul. "This man is a follower of Yeshua as well. You must help him if you can."

Saul moved toward the dining room. "First we eat, and then we talk. There have definitely been many caravans impacted by those bandits."

Jumai, Dorcas, Urbanus, and Daphne finished preparations for the meal in Ephesus and gathered their guests. The two recently purchased slaves had scrubbed the floors, cut up vegetables, and relished in their baths and clean clothes. Tryphena and Tryphosa had set flowers in clay vases and put out plates of flat bread, cheese, olives, oil, and leeks. John placed a dish of roasted lamb in the center of the table, filling the room with a pleasing aroma.

Suzanna flopped down on a cushion between Jumai and Dorcas as the apostle John stood and led the group in a prayer of grace.

The dinner conversation was brisk, although Suzanna kept her head bowed and hardly even looked up except to pick up the food in front of her.

When most of the food had been devoured, Urbanus rose and clapped for attention. "It's time for the news of the day," he announced. "We'll start with Jumai. Who did you bring home to our church today?"

Jumai stood to her feet. "Today, I have a new friend named Suzanna from Cyprus. Her husband was killed by dogs and then she was kidnapped, almost washed overboard on a ship, and left on her own in this city. I'm pleased to say she is a sister whom Yeshua has brought to us."

On the other side of the table, a man suddenly sprang to his feet. "Her husband didn't get eaten by dogs!"

Suzanna stood up quickly, examining him. Her mouth hung open in shock and joy as she recognized her husband.

"Caleb!" she shouted as she ran around the table to give him a hug. Everyone else in the room stared at the display in amazement. "How did you get here? Where have you been?"

"And this is Caleb, who didn't get eaten by dogs," Daphne said, smiling. "He was searching for his wife and became imprisoned here in the city. We were able to convince the guards to let us care for him. It seems God has again done something more amazing then we could have asked for or imagined."

It took two days to decide on the plan, but Titius rallied his group early in the morning for the last phase of their journey. They had compiled the intelligence gained from several convoys and Saul had confirmed some of Titius's suspicions with reports he had been given.

Nabonidus had insisted he be included in the mission, and he was tasked with sitting at the reins of an old carriage apparently filled with grain. In reality, its false bottom concealed two legionnaires. A dozen other wagons and oxcarts made up the convoy, each hiding a pair of legionnaires.

He watched as Titius dismounted and took ten men across the fields to approach the bandits' village from the back side. Another six men, riding on horseback behind the convoy, were dressed in large brown tunics to cover their swords. Riding just out of sight were a dozen cavalrymen, bows ready for the signal when it was given.

Nabonidus sat on a bench, glancing down every few minutes at the sword lying at his feet. It was his own sword, given to him again by Tititus. He assured himself that he could use it if he had to.

Grey clouds tumbled into the valley and began to drizzle as the convoy entered the valley of the anticipated attack. The apple orchards had reached the end of their season, and only a few small offerings still hung on the branches. Birds happily pecked at what they could reach. A deer darted across the road, followed by her fawn.

A few tattered huts sat back from the throughway. An old woman ignored them.

Half an hour past the village, Nabonidus adjusted the breastplate he'd been given. The protective covering was the largest Titius had been able to find, but it had still been an effort to squeeze the big Persian man into it. Nabonidus had to take short, shallow breaths, but there was no way to find comfort.

As he stopped to ask the others what else they should do, an arrow lodged into the seat right behind him. Instincts kicking in, he rolled off the carriage onto the opposite side of the road. The bloodcurdling yells coming down from the hills spurred the horsemen to throw off their capes and draw their swords.

The men in the wagons, carriages, and carts all flung back the wooden panels hiding them. They withdrew their bows as they rolled, taking cover behind the carriage. Within seconds, they were unleashing a barrage of arrows. Two wounded ambushers fell as they hurtled down the hill on horseback. A dozen others continued with spears and swords. Three bandit archers stood on top of the hill and shot down at the convoy.

Instead of running, the legionnaires on horseback flanked the wagons and waited. Another flurry of arrows took out another three bandits plus a horse.

That's the moment when the hidden cavalry charged onto the road, flanking the bandits and unleashing death. One of the Romans took an arrow in the back and fell to the road, dead..

Three of the attackers peeled off and headed down the road at full gallop. The cavalry followed in full chase mode.

Titius and six legionnaires dressed in dull brown clothing reached a half-dozen makeshift huts hidden among the trees, and among them he saw three armed bandits herding a group of bedraggled men and women toward the entrance of a cave. The captives were clothed in little more than rags.

He was sure Abigail was among them. And if the bandits were successful in moving the group into the cave, there would be no way to launch a surprise attack and rescue her.

The three bandits seemed to sense something, and they surrounded themselves with the hostages. They kept moving, slowly, toward the refuge of the cave.

Titius signaled four of his men to flank the group and cut off their escape. Then he stepped out in full regalia to draw attention while the others moved quickly through the trees.

"In the name of Rome, stop!" he yelled.

The bandits stood erect to get a view of him but then huddled down again. They ignored his warnings and kept moving, their swords trained on the necks of the hostages.

Titius strolled toward the group. "Stop. This is your last warning. If you've done nothing wrong, you have nothing to fear."

The three bandits spread out the hostages in front and huddled behind them, backing toward the cave. In doing so, they opened themselves up to the legionnaires' arrows.

It was still too risky to attack without harming the hostages, so Titius jogged forward. The men raised their swords just as one of the young boys broke away from the other captives, taking them by surprise. A bandit took a few running steps in pursuit, but he was quickly skewered by a pair of arrows. He dropped to the ground, writhing.

The remaining pair turned in alarm at the attack which had come from behind. Two other hostages ran, and one of the bandits raised a spear to try to stop them. He, too, was pierced with an arrow. He dropped to his knees.

The final bandit grabbed hold of a woman who'd been huddled near the back and held a dagger to her throat.

Titius's heart lurched. It was Abigail!

"Back away or I kill her now," the bandit yelled.

Titius kept coming as his men moved to gather the escaping hostages.

"Stop. One more step and she dies."

Titius finally came to a stop. "Whether she dies or not is no issue of mine," he said. "The only thing I want to know is whether you want to die quick and painless or slow and painful."

The man laughed. "You don't know what you've stumbled into. Right now, a dozen of my friends are destroying the convoy you were meant to protect. Some general you are!"

Titius laughed right back in his face. "The surprise is on you. Twenty legionnaires are hidden in that convoy. By now, your comrades are all dead."

"I don't believe you," the bandit shouted. He continued to back toward the cave. "Back off, or she dies."

Titius flanked him, causing the bandit to rotate to keep Abigail between them. He was sidestepping now, his footing uncertain in the muddy field.

One of the Roman archers shot an arrow into the ground near the bandit's feet and the hostage-taker turned again to protect himself. The archer dropped to the ground, maneuvering himself to block the entrance to the cave.

"There's nowhere to go," Titius said. "Quick or slow, your choice."

As the bandit glanced around, Abigail slowly reached up and grabbed the man's wrist, holding the knife. She bit down hard. The dagger fell, and in that same moment Titius threw his dagger right into the man's heart. He reached for his chest, coughed, and sank to the ground.

With quick strides, Titius reached Abigail and swung her up into his arms.

Within minutes, the sobs and expressions of gratitude mingled as rescuers and rescued relished their victory. Together, they walked back toward the roadway.

There, they came upon an old woman near a hut. She held a spear in their direction.

Titius drew his gladius and motioned for his men to flank her. "Woman, lay down your weapon and live to see another sunset."

"Kill my people and I live only to kill you," the woman spat back.

Abigail laid a hand on Titius's shoulder. "Let me talk to her."

Titius stepped aside for Abigail, but he motioned his men forward.

"Barbatha," Abigail said gently. "Enough people have died today. Put down that spear. You've heard us speak of love, sing of love, dream of love. You don't have to die here."

The old woman hesitated a moment and allowed her spear to lower. "Your love is for everyone but me."

Abigail took another step forward. "No, Yeshua's love is for even you."

Barbatha lowered her spear as she took two steps toward Abigail. "Do you really think so?"

"Yes."

"Then, I guess I don't need this…" Barbatha took two steps forward and drove the spear toward Abigail's stomach.

Titius threw himself forward and deflected the spear as it pierced through the rags Abigail was wearing. In a moment, another legionnaire struck the old woman through. She was dead.

Abigail fell to the ground and sobbed.

Nabonidus walked among the bodies of the bandits, examining them for signs of life. There was none. Several stared up in open-eyed surprise. They were all so young. Two of the men had only tufts of hair on their chins. Others had none. One was clearly old enough to have been the father of the others, though; the scars along his cheek and chin showed evidence of past battles.

He helped drag the bodies of the bandits into the back of his carriage.

Soon the rest of the legionnaires returned with the bodies of the last three fugitives. The gladiator hadn't seen so many corpses since his final elimination match in Ephesus.

Chapter Seventeen

Nabonidus stretched out in the morning sun, relishing the chance to be free of the adrenaline that had so often coursed through his body in the past few years. The sunlight reflected off a brass vase by the doorway of Saul's home and illuminated a sword propped up on a bench. The sword had been left to Nabonidus by Titius, and he pondered the difference he felt toward the killing tool now that he was no longer a gladiator bound to use it.

Titius had given him much to think about. As a slave and gladiator, Nabonidus had assumed he was bound by the fates to live as he lived.

But fate was a funny thing. When Emperor Tiberius had hesitated to name a successor, though, everyone had known it would be his nephew and adopted son, the great general Germanicus. Nabonidus didn't bother his mind with such great decisions. But Germanicus had mysteriously died and the whole empire had mourned. Then Tiberius's sons Nero and Drusus had been groomed for succession, and it had become clear that Nabonidus's fate would be determined by them.

Yet those two sons had mysteriously died, and Caligula, son of Germanicus, had been next in line. Suddenly, even Tiberius had died under mysterious circumstances.

Emperor Caligula appeared to be enamored with death in all forms, and Nabonidus wondered if that came from having grown up on the battlefield with his father. The mad emperor seemingly now grew drunk with power, using it on those near and far alike if they didn't immediately and unquestioningly obey his every whim.

It was because of Caligula's fascination with death that the arenas of the Empire had been filled lately with extra gladiators trained to entertain the unruly mobs. Nabonidus cared little about this new emperor, though. He cared little that Caligula had adopted a son and then had him killed. He cared little that the emperor's horse had been made a high priest. He cared little that the emperor planned to invade Germania and Britannia and take over the world... after all, as a gladiator his role had been to either kill or be killed.

But now the paranoia of the most powerful man in the world suddenly found space in Nabonidus's consideration. Having tasted freedom, he didn't want to become enslaved to Caleb or anyone else who might see that he no longer had an ivory pendent hanging around his neck.

In the middle of all this pondering, a visitor called out from Saul's gate. Nabonidus knew the servants had gone to the market and that Saul and Titius had left to make sure Abigail and the others were settled and cared for, so he got to his feet and walked to the gate.

The visitor was immediately energetic and friendly.

"Hello, my friend," the man called even before Nabonidus reached him. "My name is Barnabas from Cyprus. Please call your master and let him know of my arrival. It's been a long journey. Perhaps you could wash my feet and set me something good to eat before you trouble Saul."

Nabonidus was taken aback by the newcomer's enthusiasm. But even as a gladiator or galley slave, he had never had to reduce himself to foot-washing.

"My good man," Nabonidus said, "I am neither a servant nor the son of a servant. I am a freeman, sheltered here as a guest. All the servants are at market, so you'll have to wash your own feet and bide your own time until Saul returns."

The rebuke didn't faze Barnabas at all. "Very well. As a follower of Yeshua, I have learned to embrace humility. Show me the basin and I'll care for my own needs."

Nabonidus sat and watched with amusement as the man filled the basin at the pump, washed his own feet, and reclined on the bench beside his sword to let them dry.

"Strange place for a sword," Barnabas declared.

"It's mine."

"Appears Roman." Barnabas picked it up and let it flash back and forth in the sun. "And you look Persian or Parthian."

Nabonidus stood to his feet. "I was a gladiator, but I earned my freedom. That sword was given to me by a Roman general who was visiting here as he wiped out a group of bandits."

"So are you or the general also followers of Yeshua?"

Nabonidus nodded. "We are. Brothers for the cause."

"Praise the Almighty for his grace," Barnabas said, beaming. "Only months ago, on Cyprus, I chanced upon two followers of Yeshua who were keen to spread the good news of Yeshua. Unfortunately, they met a lot of misfortune."

Out of politeness, Nabonidus chose to engage the man in conversation. "And who were these followers of Yeshua?"

Barnabas wandered into the dining hall and picked up an orange. "The man was named Caleb and the woman, Suzanna. He said he had been a cross maker before following Yeshua."

Nabonidus stopped, frozen in his steps. "What was his name?"

"Caleb of Nazareth. He said he had even grown up as a carpenter in the very same village as Yeshua. But his wife was kidnapped and he became desolate."

"Did he send you for me?" Nabonidus asked.

"No. Why? Do you know him?"

"He was my master until I was kidnapped by the Romans and forced to be a galley slave so he would keep making crosses for them."

"I thought you said you weren't a slave," Barnabas noted.

"I *was* a slave."

"And now you are free."

"And now I am free," agreed Nabonidus. "And I am going to stay free."

———————————

Caleb walked with his wife through gardens outside Nabonidus's home, his previous despair giving way to anger as he listened to Suzanna's account of her kidnapping.

"But why did you draw attention to yourself?" Caleb asked.

"Diogenes rescued me," Suzanna said. "What was I supposed to do when you were nowhere to be found? How was I supposed to know these crazy people would kidnap me, put me on a ship, and nearly drown me?"

"But what did you do to draw attention to yourself on the ship?" Caleb shot back. "Why didn't they put a knife to the throat of the other woman?"

Suzanna crossed her arms over her chest. She jutted out her chin and stared hard at her husband. "Are you serious? I'm seasick, someone puts a knife at my throat, and it's my fault? You might as well go right back to prison, because I'm not putting up with this."

Caleb hesitated and then began to walk faster. "This is what I get? I nearly get eaten by dogs, travel all over the world searching for you, nearly get killed by soldiers, almost die in a hole… and you want me to forget it all and go back?"

He crossed his arms in frustration and was about to say more when he heard someone clear their throat. He turned to find Daphne at the entrance to the garden.

"Looks like your journeys were a lot harder on both of you than you thought," Daphne said. "Maybe you need someone to listen while you work this out."

Suzanna furrowed her eyebrows. "What are you talking about?"

Daphne took her place between the two. "It looks like a lot of hard things have happened which you're having trouble communicating. Why don't I stand in the middle and you can tell me? I'll interpret what you say and repeat it to the person you love in a way in which they can receive it."

Caleb faced Daphne and Suzanna. "I think this is between me and my wife. I don't need someone to stand between us and change my words!"

Suzanna moved to a nearby stone bench and sat. "I'm okay if she tries to talk some sense into you. The Almighty knows I sure can't seem to do it."

"Oh, and you've tried?" Caleb asked. "You just told me I might as well go back to prison!"

Suzanna didn't say anything, and Caleb walked over to the fountain. He scooped a handful of water and dumped it on the back of his neck.

"And I thought the Romans were out of control," he mused.

Daphne flexed her shoulders and adjusted the collar of her wrap. "It seems to me Suzanna is saying she's afraid that you, Caleb, might abandon her when she really needs you. And it seems to me, Suzanna, that he's saying he's afraid that you might not want him because you don't think he'll be able to protect you when you need it."

Caleb glared up from the fountain. "Who put that kind of nonsense into your head?" He moved toward Suzanna, extending both hands toward her. "I'm just angry those men took advantage of my wife and there's nothing I could do about it."

"I wanted nothing more than for you to come and save me, but you didn't." Suzanna raised her eyes to meet his. "I'm scared something like this will happen again. I can't tell you the terror I felt when the ground opened up and swallowed me. I thought I would die alone. I thought you were being eaten by dogs!"

Tears streamed down her face and she wiped them away. Caleb watched her, paralyzed.

Daphne went to her and gave her a hug. Together, the women shared tears.

Behind Saul's home in Tarsus, Titius and Abigail got reacquainted. Abigail had soaked in a warm bath, accepted a massage, and dressed in a new robe bought by her husband from a Tarsus dealer. She sat in the sun, running an ebony comb through her long tresses.

"I've dreamed of doing this for so long," Abigail said.

Titius smiled at her. "I've dreamed of watching you do this for so long!"

"Do you think the nightmares will ever go away?" she asked, pausing midstroke. She watched a sparrow hopping along the pathway.

"I hope so, but sometimes these things take on a life of their own." Titius walked across the courtyard to dip his hands in a fountain. The sparrow flitted away into a small tree.

"Are you talking about that demon you had in your head so long?"

"You mean Cleopas?"

"No… I mean the spirit who imitated Cleopas."

"It all seemed so real."

"It is real in its own way." Abigail ran the brush through her hair one last time and laid the brush aside on the bench. "But what about my nightmares?"

"Tell me again how you kept hoping for so long."

She walked to him and laid her head on his chest. "I almost stopped hoping to see you. I knew Yeshua was with me, with all of us. We were his church in that place."

He ran his fingers through her hair and cradled her head. "You are a hero to those people you rescued."

"I prayed God would spare those who he wanted to be in our group. Horrendous things have happened, things we can't undo. We can only move forward from here."

"I can't imagine how hard it was for you to endure," he said. "How did you keep them from harming you?"

"When they came for me, I told them I had my menstruation and was unclean." Abigail stepped back and stared into his eyes. "I regret that some days."

"Why?"

"When they brought Gamilat, they used her over and over, sometimes in front of me as I was tied up and unable to stop them. She was so young, an Arabian princess on her way to get married." Abigail walked back to the bench and picked up her brush. "They destroyed her spirit and her soul. Her eyes were so dead... until I told her stories and sang her songs of Yeshua." Abigail walked toward the house. "She would go to a far-off place and imagine Yeshua had come for her. I gave up searching for you before she did."

"Those men and that old hag deserved to die."

"The men, yes. Barbatha, though... I only wish we could have given her time." Abigail surveyed the sky and examined the clouds. "She used to listen to the stories and songs. At first she would try to stop me, but then she would come close and listen." She sighed. "I think she wanted to believe, but she couldn't deny her family at the end. I weep for her still."

Titius put his hands on her shoulders. "We'll wait here another week, but then we need to go on to Ephesus."

Abigail furrowed her brows. "What about Governor Petronius? He must still be looking for you. The emperor will be wanting that statue installed in the temple."

"Yes, we need to figure out what comes next. I met one of the original followers of Yeshua in Ephesus, the apostle John. I need his wisdom about what to do."

"Then we must go."

"We must. And there are others here who will go with us."

———

Nabonidus and Saul talked long into the night as the final preparations were completed by others to undertake the sea voyage back to Ephesus. Saul stood in the atrium, one foot resting on a stool, the other on the marble floor. He kneaded his chin through his beard, thoughtfully.

"I understand your fear of being enslaved," Saul said. "I believe one day all men will understand the importance of being brothers, equal before the Almighty. My word to you is to be strong and courageous as you face this man who was once your master."

Nabonidus paced back and forth, hands clasped behind his back. "I've earned my right to be free, but I lost the ivory pendent declaring that. What if he won't accept my word?"

"You will have Titius and Abigail to vouch for you. And you'll have Daphne. Surely, all these witnesses will be enough."

Nabonidus plucked a cluster of grapes from off a tray and nibbled off a single grape, chewing it slowly. "There's something wrong with me, something deeper than this. I never let fear master me in the arena, yet one man now makes me tremble to my core."

Saul walked to Nabonidus with hands outstretched. "Kneel, my brother. I've seen men gripped by terror like this and I've seen men freed through prayer. The Almighty is powerful and gracious. I'll pray for his healing as you return and trust him with your future."

Chapter Eighteen

When Nabonidus awakened at the rooster's crow, he shifted onto his back and stared upward at the wood grain in the ceiling beams. Something was different. His breathing was calm and even. No perspiration soaked his forehead or body. His neck and back muscles were pain-free.

A goat bleated from the yard and was answered by another. A second rooster crowed. A young man called to a dog, which answered with a short bark. The first songbirds sounded off with tentative notes welcoming the dawn.

Lurching to a sitting position, he listened to life as it woke up around him. Someone walked on sandaled feet by his room and lit the clay lamps on the stands outside the door. Another door opened, farther away, and one of the kitchen staff greeted another. Dishes slid across counters. It was such a miracle to enjoy such simple life.

The evening before had been intense, with the prayers of Saul and the others continuing long into the darkness. Visions of violence and terror had shaken him to the core—the faces of his mother, father, sister, and brother disappearing before his outstretched arms, the eyes of dozens of gladiators staring as he sent them on their way to hades.

Shaking, sweating, screaming, sobbing… he had screamed and wept.

The endless torment had consumed him as he curled up, arms across his chest, knees bent up, holding on for another breath, another heartbeat.

And then it had been over—the fear, guilt, and shame swept away like a cleansing river had come and taken everything that had defined him.

Now the long fingers of soft morning light confirmed that reality. He was safe. He was free. He was loved.

He brushed aside the thin blanket covering him and rose up to peer out the window. Shadowy figures walked briskly along the pathway toward the street. Two men jabbered freely to each other, laughing and drinking in the freshness of new life on a new day. A donkey brayed from the home next door.

A presence entered the room behind him and he turned to face his host.

"Tell me you slept," Saul said.

"Like a chick under a hen's wing," Nabonidus replied. "I don't know what you prayed for, but sign me up for another round."

Saul wrapped up the former gladiator in a bear hug and backed off to thump him firmly on both shoulders. "Hopefully you'll only need one treatment. The Almighty knows how to protect his own."

Nabonidus walked to the washing bowl in the corner of the room, bent his head over the basin, and scooped up handfuls of water to pour over his bald head. Was this the way a Persian prince should greet a new day? He snuffed the water into his nose and splashed it all over his face.

"Once is good," he said. "Once is good."

As the pair sat through breakfast, munching on dates, figs, cheeses, and other fare, Saul taught the core of what he'd learned from Yeshua.

"I spent three years with Yeshua in the wilderness, unlearning and relearning everything I thought I knew," Saul said. "If I were to sum it up in one sentence, I would say we're supposed to love each other in the same way Yeshua loved us."

"That's it?" Nabonidus asked, incredulous. "Caleb talked about hundreds of laws and traditions to follow if God were to accept us."

Saul motioned the Persian man over to a table where numerous scrolls lay rolled up. "See these? They are the laws I once lived by. I considered myself better than others because I followed them." He picked one up, opened it briefly, then laid it down and let it roll up on itself. "None of those laws changed my heart. I was proud, arrogant, conceited. But when Yeshua met me and showed me his love, I changed."

"Why are you here in Tarsus?"

"The family business needed attention, I needed time to study and learn, and the people of the church needed time to get over their fear."

Nabonidus stepped back to the window and glanced at the gardens. The flowers were dancing in the breezes of a glorious sunny day.

"I suppose I need to return to my home and help the church find its strength and courage," Nabonidus said. "I have a woman waiting for me to take her as my wife. I think I've been running long enough."

Titius, Abigail, Nabonidus, and the others in their group prepared to sail back to Ephesus. When they walked down to the harbor, Abigail noted a trading ship bound for Alexandria. Approaching Titius, she leaned against him and mused, "One day I'd like to visit my sister in Alexandria. We haven't seen each other since we were teens at your villa in Rome. So much has happened since then."

Titius gently cupped her hand in his. "When things settle down with our emperor, perhaps it will be safe to send you to her. Perhaps you could send her a message on that ship to find out the latest news."

"Good idea!" Abigail said. "I shall prepare that message immediately and send it with the ship's captain. Perhaps you could make the arrangements with the captain as I write it?"

The ship's captain willingly accepted the message when Titius emptied several gold coins into his hands.

For Titius, having his wife back and happy was worth any price.

By noon, the group had purchased their supplies, found their cabins aboard ship, and settled in for the trip.

The ship captain hugged the coastline all the way from Tarsus to Ephesus, putting into port every time the waves grew treacherous. With the port of calls, the journey took three weeks. On the rare sunny days, the passengers gloried in the snowcapped mountains, the sea spray in their face.

One morning, Poseidon unleashed a roiling mass of wrestling whitecaps under an avalanche of charcoal thunderclouds. A pod of dolphins skipped across the surface as a flotilla of small fishing vessels chased them, harpoons ready. Abigail and Gamilat silently cheered on the sea creatures in their flight.

Titius had insisted on disguising himself as a scholar, fashioning his appearance after Saul. He carried scrolls and engaged in philosophical discussions with others on board. Nabonidus often stood at his side, looking up at the sails as they strained under westerly winds.

After their last port of call, the group received news that changed everything. Six legionnaires had joined the crew and shared the latest report from Rome: the emperor was dead.

Titius positioned himself closer to the legionnaires, picking up snatches of their conversation.

"Caligula is dead."

"How?"

"Assassinated."

"He who murdered others has been murdered by a tribune from the Praetorian Guard. Those supposedly loyal to him stabbed him thirty times."

"The emperor's wife and daughter were also murdered."

"The line of the Caesars is broken."

The chains of Titius's own terrors lifted like the gulls in the air around him. Surely the edict to erect the statue of Caligula would be rescinded. No longer would Titius need to run from Petronius or Marcellus.

The news spread quickly among the passengers. The celebration was subdued, in case the reports were false, or in case one of Caligula's loyalists stood ready to carry on a mission of terror even now.

"I stood guard for the emperor in his early days," a legionnaire boasted as Titius overheard nearby. These two legionnaires were lounging on the fishing net amidst the ship's cargo. "He used to dance around in a wig and robe, singing and acting like a savage animal. He fancied himself as a god who could end the life of anyone he wanted with just a word—and he did."

"I heard almost two hundred thousand victims were put to death to ensure his power," the other soldier said. "There must be no one left who would dare speak up against him."

But the first was not to be outdone. "I was with him back in Tarsus when he put on the gladiator shows there. At first he brought out the champion boxers from Africa and Rome—the black against the white. Stage plays were performed all over the city and the lights never seemed to go out. The feasts were enough to make your belly burst! There were panthers and clowns, and of course Christians were martyred in the most diabolical ways."

The second man stood to his feet and positioned himself along the ship's railing. "Who would be a Christian these days? No matter who is emperor, it is a death sentence."

At Nabonidus's mansion, Caleb and Suzanna sat glumly through talks by Urbanus and the apostle. The former cross maker sat on a stone bench to one side of the room near some potted plants while Suzanna sat with Dorcas and Daphne on blankets near the back. The room was full and neither husband nor wife took the time to glance in each other's direction.

It had been a painful few days of discussions and interventions.

"Let me remind you of the conversation our Lord had with a Pharisee named Nicodemus," John preached. "Yeshua told him that unless he would be born again, he could not see the kingdom of God."

"What is the kingdom of God?" Dorcas asked.

"Good question," John said. "The kingdom of God is talking about the heart of a person where the Almighty has been given full control. God is working out his plan on earth through the people he has chosen. You and I are in God's kingdom and he is ruling over us to bring people from darkness into light."

Dorcas whispered to Daphne, "Do you know what he means?"

"I'll tell you later," Daphne whispered back. "Let's keep listening. I want to hear more about Nicodemus."

The group of worshippers completed the message, a hymn, the Lord's supper, and then were casually enjoying a meal when a young messenger boy burst into the room.

"They're here!" said the messenger. "The master has returned. They're down at the docks."

Servants scattered quickly, scrubbing down fixtures, fountains, and floors. Caleb, sitting on a bench, pulled up his feet as a male servant on hands and knees washed the floor underneath him.

"The owner here must be a terror," Caleb quipped.

The servant paused a moment. "Champion gladiator, he was. Killed forty-five men to get his ivory pendant. Earned his way, yes, he did."

Caleb stood on the newly washed floor. "A gladiator? The church is meeting in a gladiator's house? I thought the followers of the Way were a people of peace."

Daphne stood in the doorway listening to the exchange. "I can assure you," she said, "Nabonidus is a man of peace and a true follower of the way."

Caleb walked to the window and surveyed the harbor below. "I used to have a slave named Nabonidus. He was a huge Persian. The Romans took him from me to make sure I would build their crosses for them. I would love to have him back."

Overhearing Caleb, Daphne ducked out the door and headed down the pathway toward the dockyards.

———————————

On the wharf, Nabonidus helped Titius and Abigail unload their luggage. Wharf boys and alley rats, wearing only loin cloths, scampered among the ships and offered to tie up ropes, carry baggage, and take passengers to the nearest baths or massage houses. Gulls called overhead, watching for dropped fish or other delicacies.

Warehouses stretched the length of the horseshoe-shaped harbor. Ships jockeyed for position and weighed anchor as they awaited the signal that dock space was available. The combined chatter of sailors, warehousemen, legionnaires, and hawkers generated a pleasing hum to anyone arriving safely home after weeks at sea.

The legionnaires formed rank and marched into the heart of the mass of humanity flowing like a river into the harbor. A trail of carts and horses formed behind the soldiers, carrying their equipment and supplies.

Auctioneers offered up naked male and female slaves of all ages as buyers gawked, made bids, and moved on if they weren't successful. Off of one galley, a chained group of six gladiators were prodded by a legionnaire. Nabonidus recognized the men's clamped jaws, curled fists, and the slow shuffle as they faced the end of their hopes of ever seeing family or homeland again. He had been one of those men—and never would be again.

Nabonidus tracked his view along the hill toward his own villa and breathed deeply when he saw the roofline standing proud above the shrubbery. The imposing Artemission, Roman administrative buildings, hippodrome stadium, arena, Odeum theatre, Library of Celsus, agora, and two new aqueducts accentuated the myriad of lower businesses and homes.

A continuous line of burden-bearing slaves snaked across the square into the large marketplace. Warehouses surrounded it like a large warm cloak, and along the outskirts camels, donkeys, horses, oxen, and carts crowded together as owners and traders carried on their business.

Wishing to avoid the chaos, Nabonidus led his group away, past the arena and down the streets which would fork toward the road leading to his home.

Daphne, eager to get to Nabonidus as soon as possible, forged through the heart of the agora and strained to push her way through the shoulder-to-shoulder consumers. When she emerged on the far side of the lines entering and exiting the market, she spotted a three-masted freighter docking. Slaves unloaded crates, baskets, and containers from the cargo hold. but Nabonidus was nowhere to be seen. Frantic, she approached two of the sailors arranging the rigging on the foresail. They appeared to be Gauls.

"Did you see a large black man on this ship?" she asked. She tried Greek, Latin, and Aramaic while the pair glared down at her.

They only shrugged and continued on with their work.

Turning toward the warehouses, she then saw several sailors lounging about, playing knucklebones.

"Did you sail on that ship?" she asked in Aramaic, pointing at the freighter.

One of the men smirked. "If you're looking for a sailor, we might be available later."

She ignored his lustful glare. "Did you see a large black man get off the ship?"

The sailor shook his head. "Maybe he went into the market. If you want a slave, you can get one right over there."

He pointed toward the group of naked slaves chained in the middle of the square.

Daphne was about to rush into the marketplace when she noticed two young girls among the slaves. They hung their heads and attempted to cover themselves with crossed arms. Something drew her to them.

As she approached, a slave trader stepped in front of her. "This is your lucky day, my lady. The goddess of Fortune has smiled on you. I have Gauls, Britons, Persians, and Ethiopians. Large or small. The price will be right."

The man's hardened Roman face was scarred from many a skirmish. His golden earrings and generous row of necklaces displayed his wealth. The sword in one hand and the whip in the other showed his power.

Daphne had dealt with slave traders before. She knew if she wanted the girls, she would have to express interest in anyone but them.

"The Persian," she said, indicating a man she had never seen before. "How much?"

The trader smiled. "This one has the strength of the gods in him. Look at those arms and legs. He can carry you and an ox at the same time. Twenty sesterces gets you a closer look."

Daphne reached for her change pouch and stopped as if noticing the two Ethiopian men standing at the end of the line.

"Perhaps I need two," she mused. "What about those Ethiopians?"

The trader raised his whip and brought it down on the legs of the men. They quickly jumped and danced around. "See, full of life. Well worth the thirty sesterces if you take them both."

Daphne reached into her pouch and pulled out a few coins. She could see the hunger in the trader's eyes. Instead of giving him the money, though, she put it back, removed her hand, and shrugged.

"Maybe I'll come back another day to see if you have anything better," she said.

The trader put on a mournful expression. "This is my last chance to feed my family." Daphne backed away. "I'll give you a special price. Just take one." Daphne turned away. "I'll give you two for the price of one."

She turned back. "I'll give you ten for the girls."

The trader inspected the scrawny specimens. "Fifteen for both," he said.

Daphne nodded. "Only because you need to feed your family. Cover them and I'll take them with me."

Their chains were taken off as old brown tunics were thrown over their heads. Daphne then put an arm around each girl and urged them through the crowd. By the time she reached the villa with her two purchases, though, she heard loud voices emanating from inside..

Chapter Nineteen

It had taken all the diplomatic skills John had to negotiate the renewal of the relationship between Nabonidus and Caleb. Caleb, still wounded from his emasculating conversation with Suzanna, had attempted to reassert himself as a master. Nabonidus, fearful of what Roman power could do, had called upon his gladiator skills to push his power. Both men were skilled warriors and the surprise meeting had only heightened their temptation to rely on survival skills.

A week of chaperoned conversations saw them grudgingly forge a new relationship as brothers in Christ. And yet the tension continued. They shared the tale of their respective adventures, and those around them added details to flesh out the reality.

Nabonidus lived with pounding headaches as he was forced to relive memories he had worked hard to erase. The daily church services were thus welcome breaks from the questions which came not only from Caleb but from Daphne and the others. Fortunately, Daphne was occupied with trying to win the trust and hope of the two young Britons she had purchased at the slave market.

He took daily walks alone in the early afternoon to breathe in the fresh sea air and gain a new appreciation for the metropolis where he walked as a freeman. Many of the citizens still honored him, but their passions had switched to new gladiators who were proving themselves in the arena.

Walking by the Artemission one afternoon, Nabonidus chanced upon a large booth erected by a silversmith. The man's images of Artemis were sleek and finely detailed, and their beauty drew him in. They were so much like the woman who had helped with his healing.

As if by chance, as he admired the works of art, his thigh—the part of his body that had been wounded in the arena, throbbed.

A man in rich purple robes embroidered with silver stepped out from behind the booth holding a magnificent statue of Artemis.

"Ah, my friend," said the silversmith, "I see you have known the healing power of the goddess."

Nabonidus focused on the silver image being held in front of him. "She helped me many years ago," he admitted.

"And you, gratefully, have come to pay your respects."

"I was just out walking."

The elegant silversmith smiled and held out the statue. "Here, take her. My name is Demetrius and this is my finest work." He pushed the statue into Nabonidus's hand. "She belongs with you. If she took time to heal you in person, it would be good to remember her when you are apart."

Dozens of customers suddenly thronged the booth, purchasing images and pendants and tokens of the goddess. Among them was Selsus, who now reigned as a gladiator in his own right, with seventeen kills and counting. Several young women draped themselves on his muscular arms, eyeing him with desire.

Demetrius was as silver-tongued as his works of art and his inventory slowly disappeared as the hours passed.

The sun descended over the harbor, but Nabonidus stood transfixed, holding the silver image of the erotic goddess as if it had become a part of him.

Suddenly, there she was—a huntress in her white tunic and bow. Of course, she wasn't a real huntress, but as a priestess in the temple she had dressed as one in honor of the goddess Artemis. Her appearance struck him, since her costume was exactly what Daphne had worn during their first encounter at the temple—when she'd healed him.

This new woman stood beside Demetrius, watching Nabonidus. In slow, seductive steps, she approached Nabonidus and knelt. She placed her hand where his wound had been and chanted.

A crowd quickly formed around them and Nabonidus could do nothing about it.

As the sun touched the horizon, she rose and took hold of the statue in his hand. Warmth raced through him, followed by an icy chill.

"Come with me," she urged. "Celebrate the beauty of the goddess. She has protected you for this moment."

Selsus, led by two priestesses, then disappeared into the interior of the temple.

"Don't allow another to steal your place or your pleasure," the priestess whispered.

Trancelike, he followed her lead toward the Artemission steps, where the sick and lame huddled. Snakes lay coiled along the dark edges of the courtyard as torchlight danced hypnotically in the evening breeze. The sacred priestesses stopped to watch the spectacle.

On the top of the thirteenth step, Nabonidus felt a powerful pull toward the interior of the massive temple. However, another force inside him held back.

"My Persian prince, champion of the people, warrior of Artemis, slave of Rome… welcome to my throne," said the priestess. "Welcome to the Temple of Artemis, daughter of Zeus, sister of Apollo, mother goddess of earth. This is the Artemission for all Ephesians. How now can I bring you joy?"

The cry of a child sounded from inside as he reached the temple's entry. He froze.

"Come," the goddess whispered, tugging his arm.

Another voice sounded behind him: "Nabonidus!"

The call pierced his hypnotic daze and he pivoted to look backward. There stood Daphne and Urbanus.

"Nabonidus!" Daphne called again, walking toward him across the plaza.

Six of the temple guards stepped in front of her and pushed her back.

"Come," the goddess urged. "Pleasure and joy await you. It is time to show your gratitude."

Daphne and Urbanus fell to their knees.

"Yeshua!" Daphne called out. "Yeshua!"

In an instant, the priestess released her hold on him as if he had been transformed into hot iron. With a hiss, she stepped through the door into the darkness and disappeared.

Nabonidus looked down at the silver image in his hand. As if seeing it for the first time, he lifted it, saw it for what it was, and hurled it down the steps.

With long strides, he jumped down the stairs and rushed at the guards. They had their backs to him and didn't see him coming. He threw them onto the ground, and by the time they were getting to their feet again he had taken Daphne by the hand and was running away, with Urbanus close behind.

Demetrius crouched and picked up the damaged silver image of Artemis thrown down by Nabonidus. It had been one of his finest works. The face of the masterpiece was crushed, the arm fractured, the base bent.

"So, you are a follower of the Way are you?" Demetrius said to himself as he watched the disappearing form of the Persian gladiator whom the priestess had almost wooed into her temple. "Maybe there will still be another day for you in the Ephesus arena."

Titius scouted around Ephesus for any news he could unearth about the new emperor. There was a sense of relief among the people that Caligula was gone, but they were also suspicious that Claudius wouldn't be any better.

One day, at the shipyards, he inquired about news from Alexandria. A ship captain recognized him and handed over a scroll which had been inserted into a sheepskin tube. Inside was a message from Abigail's sister Lydia, informing them that she was pregnant and would soon be giving birth. Lydia's message said she'd love to have a visit from her younger sister.

Apart from a brief visit the month after Abigail's wedding, the two sisters hadn't seen each other much—not since they'd served as slaves for Titius's family in Rome.

When Titius brought the scroll back to the house, Abigail was beside herself with joy to read the full message. Her only concern was a brief allusion to the fact that Lydia's husband, as a leader in the local Jewish community, was being pressured by the local authorities.

Caleb reclined with satisfaction as he listened to the small orchestra of people getting ready for the next gathering of believers. One of the Britons was producing a deep tone from a four-foot bronze tube with a bone mouthpiece. The other Briton had a G-shaped bronze tube that had also been fitted with a bone mouthpiece. Tryphena played a silver set of double-tubed reed pipes and Tryphosa played the panpipes as Dorcas danced alongside her. Seti played a seven-stringed wooden lyre and Asturex played a Greek kithara. John played a lute for several pieces before putting down his instrument and leaving for the market.

During one rhythmic selection, Asturex lay down her instrument and danced seductively, moving closer and closer to Caleb. He displayed clear discomfort, but this only encouraged her to express herself more boldly.

Dorcas tried to emulate her moves for a minute, but soon quit and waved at the orchestra to stop.

"Asturex, that dance is from the Artemission," the girl declared judgmentally. "I've seen it in the bathhouses. It's something the priestesses use in the worship of Artemis."

Asturex continued to move in her slow dance. "Come, little one, we will dance for the Almighty who teaches us to move like the waves, sway like the trees, flow like a river. What is beauty for the goddess is beauty for all gods."

Dorcas planted her fists on hips and faced the dancer. "It's not the way of our people for a woman to display herself like a priestess before a man."

Asturex moved closer to Caleb and smiled down on him. "I don't see Caleb objecting. Surely, as a man, he appreciates the beauty of a woman in motion."

"Tell her to stop," Dorcas said to Caleb. "Yeshua is not a God who calls us to draw out our evil desires."

Caleb sat up, red rushing into his cheeks. "I'm sorry, Asturex." He stood and moved across the room to the fountain. "It's true that the way of Yeshua is not the way of Artemis. I'm a married man and should keep my eyes to my own wife."

Asturex in turn reddened, pivoted, and left the room.

Seti stepped away from her lyre and hugged Dorcas. "You must forgive us, little dove. We've only just been welcomed into this way of life and we don't yet know all that is acceptable and all that is not. When we were slaves, this form of dance and much more was required of us."

Dorcas buried herself into the hug and stepped into the middle of the floor. "Dance is a form of the Almighty's grace to his people, but not all men can bear it when their passions are unleashed."

Caleb nodded. "How did you get so smart at such a young age? Asturex has only known the life of a slave, though, and she meant no ill. I'm sure she will learn in time."

Seti moved toward the kitchen, speaking as she walked. "It may take her longer if she continues to visit the Artemission."

Gamilat strolled into the room holding a handful of jewelry. She held the strands up and watched the light reflections dance around the room as the necklaces spun in her hand.

"Did someone forget these behind the fountain in my room?" Gamilat asked.

Seti stopped and peered at the lot. "That carnelian with the golden swirl looks like one Asturex bought at the market. I think it's an amulet to invoke the blessing of the goddess when you're searching for love."

"I hope she doesn't think something like this will work with Caleb," Dorcas said.

"You better return that to the silversmith," Seti said. "That amulet can bring a curse from an owner who gets angry."

At that moment, Suzanna skipped into the room. "So the concert is over. Did I miss anything? I saw Asturex pouting in the garden."

Caleb and Dorcas exchanged glances.

"Nothing much," Caleb said. "We were discussing the differences between our lives with Yeshua and our lives prior to Yeshua."

Suzanna walked to the kitchen counter and accepted a tray of fruit from Seti.

"Sit, my man," Suzanna said to her husband. "It's been a while since I've been able to play the wife to you."

Caleb returned to reclining on the couch. He stepped out of his sandals and stretched his legs. "This is the life."

Suzanna playfully dangled a cluster of green grapes over Caleb's mouth and laughed as he tried to snatch them, resembling a gasping fish.

"It's good to feel close again," she whispered.

Caleb reached up and squeezed her wrist. "Yes, you tease. But I wonder what's taking Urbanus and Abigail so long to find Nabonidus. I hope there hasn't been any trouble."

Titius, disguised as a nobleman, settled himself in the governor's atrium with a scroll and pen, busying himself with what appeared to be important matters. None of the servants dared ask the reason for his presence, even though several had inquired if he had any needs.

Others waiting to see the governor were seated nearby, and Titius welcomed them as if he were part of the governor's household staff. The visitors had no reason to doubt him. When he casually inquired whether they had news regarding the previous emperor, they freely told him.

An Egyptian aristocrat, eager to set up a trade mission, bubbled his response like a fountain unplugged. "Caligula pushed hard to take over Mauretania and Britannia. We had no idea he would invite Ptolemy, our ruler, to Rome and have him executed. Ptolemy was his cousin!" The man finished his wine and looked around for more. "Caligula was all about fear and jealousy. Now our kingdom is divided. Hopefully, the new emperor will unite us again."

A house servant who had waited on Titius many times, flitted in and out. Eventually he decided to engage the woman directly to allay the suspicions she seemed to have about him.

Titius waved her over. "Has the governor run out of wine for those who await his hospitality?"

The woman glanced into his eyes, bowed, and backed out of the room. In moments, she returned with two flagons of fine wine which she poured for the men.

"Things aren't always as they appear to be," she said, smiling. "Perhaps there are more appointments than we had planned for."

Titius lifted his glass to her and returned the smile. "The ability to see beyond appearances is a gift the governor should cherish. For now, there will be no need for you to trouble the governor." He turned back to the Egyptian. "Why were the Jews so unsettled?"

The aristocrat pivoted and pulled in close. "Caligula didn't trust his governor in Egypt, and he tried to force him to set up statues of himself in all the synagogues. The Jews rebelled and the emperor recalled the governor and had him executed for insurrection."

"Didn't he order the same thing for the temple in Jerusalem?" Titius asked.

"It's a good thing King Agrippa, king of the Jews, delayed him long enough so others could stop him."

"How did the emperor die?"

"He threatened to move to Alexandria and proclaim himself as their sun god. The guard stabbed him thirty times, just like they did his grandfather Julius Caesar. It was his destiny."

Titius thought about this for a moment. "What happened to his wife and family?"

"The assassins killed them when the military refused to restore the Republic. They tried to get to Claudius, too, but the Praetorian Guard took him out of the city and protected him. Now Claudius is emperor and we're at his mercy."

"Do you think it's safe for Jews to travel to Alexandria?"

The man stared out toward the harbor. "With proper accompaniment, yes."

Titius rose. "My wife needs to travel there in safety, for her sister is having a baby there. May I count on you to protect and provide for her? I'll pay you well."

The arrangement was made and Abigail's passage to Alexandria was secured.

Toward noon, the Egyptian left and a Gaul took his place. The new arrival wandered nervously around the room, caressing statues, examining trinkets, and opening his palm to feel the cool flow of the fountains. On his second tour of the room, Titius offered him a tray of fruit that the house servant had delivered.

"You must be hungry after your long journey," Titius said after he learned where the man was from.

The man nodded politely and took several dates. "I've only just come from Rome. Such a mockery for us Gauls!"

"Did something happen to you in Rome?"

"Didn't you hear? Last year, the emperor dressed us up like German chieftains and had us parade through the streets as if we had fallen to his campaigns, chanting 'There is only one lord, one king, one god… Caesar.'" The Gaul took a few more figs. "He's dead now anyway."

Titius nodded. "Is it true he dressed as if he were a god himself?"

The Gaul harrumphed. "Gods, not god. One day he was Hercules, then Apollo, then Mercury. He even dressed as Venus at times. Whenever the politicians met him, they had to address him as Jupiter. I truly think he thought he might be more than a man. He even put his own head on the coins of Egypt, declaring himself to be their sun god."

"Do we have need to fear our new emperor?"

The man quickly turned away. "I hope not. Although I fear the tribune and legionnaires gathering inside. I fear they're here to bring justice to one of us."

"Then perhaps it's time for me to leave," Titius said. "Enjoy your visit with the governor."

Chapter Twenty

Nabonidus stretched lazily on the boat as it rocked under cloudy skies, lifting his head occasionally to watch Titius and the apostle John huddle over a fishing net. The two were carefully sorting the morning catch, an assortment of goby, bream, mullet, and mackerel. Gulls hovered overhead, hoping for a discarded treat, and John threw them a small rockfish from time to time. They all laughed at the flurry of wings as they rushed to their prey.

John raised his chin toward Nabonidus. "It seems the church is becoming too large for your home, my friend. Mary, mother of Yeshua, will be back soon from visiting her sister in Galilee, and she's bringing others. Perhaps we should think of starting another work elsewhere."

"Perhaps it's time for Abigail and myself to move on," Titius said. "I know Caleb and Suzanna wish to travel to Germania. With so many converted slaves, you already have enough witnesses to reach out."

"I'm surprised you let Abigail go to Alexandria," Nabonidus said to him. "Surely her sister's baby has been born by now."

"She'll be back soon," Titius replied. "The situation for the Jewish community there is delicate at the moment and she wanted to do what she could to support her sister, Lydia. It's been ten years since the two sisters were together. Lydia's husband is a leader among the Jews and his life is at risk if he's found."

Nabonidus glanced toward the docks, where dozens of vessels rested alongside the wharfs as they unloaded and loaded cargo. The shore was as busy as a beehive and gave little sign of the danger.

"This city isn't going to be an easy place for any of us to stay," Nabonidus said. "Since my run-in with Demetrius, I've heard he is working hard to blame every sort of trouble on the followers of Yeshua. He wants revenge. There's been more pressure lately to see followers of the Way crucified in the arena again."

John struck a large mullet on the head and gutted it with his flint knife. "The Temple of Artemis is losing some of its followers, and even some priestesses, to the grace of Yeshua. Demetrius and his group don't care about these people's spiritual lives. They only care that their own pockets be filled with coin."

Nabonidus scratched at his generous black beard and nodded. "You and I know that, and the city officials know it, too. As long as the officials know what's true and right, we are safe. But the games no longer draw the same crowds."

Titius shifted his weight and stood to pull a section of the net toward the boat's bow.

"The death of Caligula has given space to the rulers to find their hope elsewhere," said Titius. "If Rome starts to lose her glory with the new emperor, it won't be long until the emperor looks to distract the restless mobs again. Nothing does that like blood."

The apostle threw the fish guts into the water and unleashed another flurry of wings. "All they need is one big distraction to keep them occupied."

Titius reached into the mass of fish still in the net and pulled out a wriggling shark twice the size of his arm.

"Let's see the gulls get this one," he said, laughing as he tossed it overboard and watched it sink slowly into the water.

———————————

Dawn slithered across the Egyptian sky like a chimera of snakes, the endless waves of sandy dunes undulating their way toward the great sea. The imposing pyramids poked arrogantly at the few quickly retreating clouds.

The rumbles of a camel caravan helped chase away the remnants of Abigail's restless night. The herders' singsong voices echoed softly over the desert.

The peace was an illusion. A lie.

Abigail hurried toward a mud-brick hut. When she slipped through the doorway, she saw two half-robed women propping up her sister, all the while whispering urgent words of encouragement.

"Lydia, push harder, now!"

Abigail walked up to them, out of breath. "They're coming. Hurry."

One of the robed assistants, Shiphrah, shook her head and tried to flick a long strand of hair back over her shoulder. "Stall them, Abigail. We can't have them nearby if the baby cries."

Abigail hesitated, unsure of what to do.

The second woman, Leah, nodded and moved away from the birthing scene to wash her hands. "You take care of it, Abigail. This boy has got to be born."

Abigail stepped back, perturbed. What could she do to keep the men from discovering Lydia's baby? She needed a distraction. Perhaps if she had a child, somewhat older, someone who might attract attention but not retribution… after all, these men would only have been tasked with finding newborns…

She stepped into a pair of leather sandals, ran a brush through her hair, and stepped outside the hut again. Thinking quickly, she set her eyes on a second hut nearby. She wrestled back its flap, crawled inside, and moments later emerged with a two-year old child. The child's mother had only given up her little one after Abigail's assurance that she would protect him at all costs.

She walked a hundred paces and came face to face with a troop of eight legionnaires.

"What have you there?" barked the leader of the men. "It looks like a young boy. A rebel to be fed to the crocodiles. You people breed like rabbits."

Abigail covered the child and got down on her haunches. "Children come when children come. Our God knows the way of life and we trust in him."

The leader stepped back and spat on the ground. "Your faceless god is no match for the power of Rome. You spit out lies like cobra venom, but you don't fool me. The firstborn son of all your leaders will be shipped to the slave markets in Rome."

As Abigail stepped back with the child, she marveled that he didn't even whimper. She watched as the men began to search the huts for newborns. They pounded on doors and poked their heads inside, but no newborns were discovered this day.

Once they were gone, Abigail returned the child to its mother and took a roundabout path to the hut where she found Shiphrah and Leah washing down Lydia and her newborn son.

"Lydia, you have a fine son," whispered Shiphrah. She adjusted the garments and continued to clean up the afterbirth. "Now, we must keep him quiet and hidden. Your husband is sought after by the Romans. His position as a leader of the Jews here puts your own son at risk. The legionnaires aim to feed him to the crocodiles or ship him as a slave to Rome."

Leah examined the placenta in the growing light. "This will be a fine child. A strong child. Abigail, you must guard your sister while she rests."

Abigail bent over the little one and rubbed her finger along his cheek. "What if we're discovered? What will I say? Must I be honest in declaring who he is?"

Leah wrapped Abigail in a hug. "You must trust God to guide your words and thoughts. We have no messengers to guide us in what God expects. Perhaps your nephew will rise to greatness and teach us all."

Abigail crouched again by the child, picked up a cloth, and rubbed away the fluid nestling in his tiny black curls.

"What can someone so little do in a place like Egypt?" Abigail asked. "We hide, we lie, we creep around in the shadows pretending someday we will all be free. Roman power extends even into the darkest shadows."

Lydia cradled her newborn son. "That's where we have to bring the greatest light. Abigail, you've shared the truth of Yeshua with me. The truth you carry will be born in others as it was born in me." She suckled the hungry little one and smiled with satisfaction. "Remember long ago? There was another little boy born in Egypt who delivered his people. If Yeshua also spent his early years here, this may be the perfect place to raise up a new leader of the Jews."

Abigail moved to the door and looked out across the sands. "It has been my greatest joy to witness the birth of your son," she said to her sister. "But now I need to return to my own place and nurture my own love."

Seti, Asturex, and Dorcas walked through the market perusing spices and sorting through the stacks of fabric. Seti draped herself in colorful Arab garb and paraded before the other two. Once her choices were made, Asturex wrapped herself in plainer garments resembling her Gaulish background. Dorcas twirled with glee and dropped coins into the merchants' hands.

As they passed the silversmith's canopied display, Demetrius stepped forward with a smile and held out one of his prized images of Artemis.

"The goddess lives and cherishes all who bless her in this place," Demetrius said. "Today there is a special price for worshippers who share her beauty and grace."

Dorcas continued to walk by, but she stopped when she realized the two former slaves had stopped to examine the shining statue.

"Ignore that idol," Dorcas urged them. "The Almighty God considers these works of men to be abominations."

Demetrius gently laid his hand on Asturex's wrist. "Is this young girl your master?" he asked.

Asturex gazed at Dorcas, then back at the suave businessman. "I am a free woman."

"Clearly, the daughter of a king or a prince," crooned Demetrius. "You have a keen eye for items of value and worth. As a woman of nobility, beware the whims of foolish maidens who would sway you from what you know is your hope."

Seti backed away. "We were sent with limited coins to purchase specific goods for our household." She shifted the garments and spices she held in her basket. "We can't afford anything else today."

"Fear not," Demetrius replied as he placed the figurine into the basket. "Just tell me the name of your household and I'll trust you to bring the payment when you can. The usury is small if you pay me soon."

"I'm from the household of Nabonidus," Asturex replied. "I shall return when I can."

Demetrius stepped back. "Nabonidus, the Persian gladiator?"

"*Former* gladiator," Dorcas corrected.

"The follower of the Way?" Demetrius probed.

Dorcas stepped in front of the two women. "He is a true baptized believer in Yeshua. The church at his home is growing and we are witnesses of the true God."

Demetrius gave a small bow. "I shall double my joy when you bring me what you owe," he said to Asturex. "May the goddess of the heavens give you the blessings others cannot."

Upon her return home, Asturex slipped away from the others and stepped into Gamilat's room, where she reached into the place where she had hidden her precious amulet. Despite fishing around for a while, she came up with nothing. She searched the entire room without success.

Returning to her own room she rechecked all her belongings. Nothing.

She soon found Gamilat stooped over in the front garden collecting flowers for the vases.

"Where did you put it?" Asturex asked.

Gamilat straightened up and stretched her back. "What are you talking about?"

Asturex gripped Gamilat by the wrist and shook her. "You know very well what I mean," she snarled. "The amulet. Where is it?"

"I was told to take it back, so I did."

"What?! It wasn't yours to take back. I needed it to pay for my icon." She glared at the Arab woman, hands on her hip, chin jutting out. "Now what am I going to do? That was the only thing I owned."

Gamilat lowered her gaze. "The others said the amulet could bring a curse upon the household."

Asturex kicked over a bucket of flowers. "A curse? You'll see who gets cursed."

Tulips swayed in the breeze as Suzanna and Daphne strolled through the gardens of Nabonidus's villa. White, pink, and purple petals invited the eye. In another corner of the garden, colorful wildflowers fought for people's attention. The paths were also lined with roses and a selection of crocus flowers held onto their wilting petals near a hedge.

"What assured you that you should pursue your relationship with Caleb?" Daphne asked her new friend.

Suzanna smiled. "I sense this question isn't about me."

"Wisdom is found in a multitude of wise counselors, and you've just proven you are keen of mind and insight."

"I think it was his flute playing," Suzanna offered. "He carved the best flutes, and when he played I couldn't help but dance. When he offered to teach me to play, one thing led to another."

"How did you let him know you were interested? You had no mother or father, no uncle or family member to negotiate the relationship. Did he think it improper?"

Suzanna sat on a stone bench and patted the seat beside her. Daphne adjusted her robe and settled in place.

"When Caleb worked for the Romans, he was an angry and troubled man," Suzanna said. "The guilt of building crosses to kill his own countrymen shrouded his soul. His mind was tormented, trapped."

"What do you mean?"

"He'd been persuaded that peace could only come to Palestine, Galilee, and Syria through the power of the cross. His own father had been killed and he was determined to avenge it by killing his father's murderer, Barabbas. When Barabbas was captured and sentenced for execution, Caleb built a special cross. But the Romans killed Yeshua on that cross instead. Caleb's own people chose to kill an innocent man! A man Caleb had befriended as a child. It took a miracle to restore his mind, help him to embrace forgiveness, and to make room for me."

Daphne rose and paced back and forth in front of the bench she had been sitting on.

"Nabonidus, too, has much in his heart and mind to clear up, and to forgive, if he is to make room for me," Daphne said. "He thinks he has room, but the closer I try to get, the more walls I sense being erected. Although he's been freed from the arena, he hasn't been freed from the death masks which haunt him."

"What will you do?" Suzanna asked.

"I will pray for his mind, love his soul, and fill his stomach. The men should be back soon. What shall we prepare to go with their fish?"

"Dorcas, Asturex, and Seti are at the market," Suzanna said. "Once they're back, we'll mix onion, garlic, and olives with milk and barley flour, then set up a vegetable platter and some fruit bowls."

Daphne ran her fingers through her tresses and pulled her long hair over her shoulder. "With blue sky and love in the air, what could possibly go wrong?"

Chapter Twenty-One

Urbanus shook Nabonidus and ducked the blow that erupted from the sleeping Persian. "Whoa, Nabonidus, it's a dream, the haunting of spirits."

Nabonidus wrestled through the darkness of his mind and finally forced himself to sit up on the edge of his mat. He briskly rubbed his black curly beard with both hands and shook his bald head. The torch held by Urbanus flickered dimly.

"The darkest devils of the Artemission were dragging me toward the arena," Nabonidus said. "Selsus and Demetrius stood with swords ready to kill Daphne in the cruelest of ways."

"It's a dream. But dreams can be warnings, or they can be images of anxiety reminding us of work left undone."

Nabonidus knelt in place and stared down at the twisted blankets and mat where he had lain. "I sense a growing evil in this place. The people of Yeshua are at risk. The goddess is gathering her power to assert her authority here."

Urbanus chuckled. "So, now you're a prophet? A gladiator turned oracle to guide us all. Perhaps you should talk to the apostle when morning arrives."

Nabonidus rose and walked toward a small basin on a stand in the corner. "The apostle already knows my mind is deeply troubled. I don't need to give him more cause for concern." He cupped the water in his hands and poured it slowly over his bowed head. "Let's keep this between us and trust the Almighty to deliver us."

At the crow of the rooster, Nabonidus paced the pier, stooping to pick up smooth stones and skip them across the waves. For weeks, the death masks of those he had killed gathered in haunting dances to mock him and woo him to join them.

Abigail had arrived safely back from Egypt and she and Titius were even now renewing their vows of love. Now Daphne deserved his own full attention—and affection—yet he still wrestled with something deep inside.

The apostle John had recently told them about a prophet named Jonah who had boarded a ship and run from the God who'd prodded him to face the enemies of his people. The thought of running had gained power in Nabonidus's mind again, like it had when he'd fled to Tarsus.

Perhaps the recent holidays were contributing to his trauma. The roars from the arena over the weeklong festivals had brought back his yearning for glory, adrenaline, and the terror which erupted in involuntary whimpers. When he was out of control like this, he made for poor company for Daphne and the others who continued to gather in his house for church. While they sang, he wandered the gardens. While they ate and prayed and shared their lives, he roamed the hills. And everywhere he went, the imposing presence of the Artemission loomed over him.

He rested on a boulder that jutted out over the harbor. He dropped small tree branches and watched them drift on the current. As he prepared to drop the last branch, someone startled him by calling his name.

"Nabonidus!"

The sensation of falling enveloped him briefly, but he gripped the edge of the boulder and tried to settle the panic arising within.

"Nabonidus!"

He turned and discovered the priestess from the temple approaching him. Today, she was dressed in a plain blue robe with a white palin over her shoulder. She carried a basket, and the scent of frankincense was strong.

"Nabonidus, I come in peace." She laid a hand on his shoulder and rubbed it gently. "Twice you have rejected me now. Your will is strong. Yet here you rest alone."

"I'm here alone to think."

"I can see your dreams terrify you. The masks of death overwhelm your spirit. Your past is filled with loss and the future seems empty of hope."

Nabonidus shrugged off her hand and stood to his feet, facing her. "You should return to your temple and pleasure those who desire you."

She lowered her basket and held out a pomegranate. "I bring you a peace offering. Today I'm not on duty. I come with curiosity about this God you serve. How could he be worth your loyalty when he denies you the pleasures of the most beautiful of women?"

He stared into her eyes, swallowed up in her entrancing gaze.

"You cannot help who you are," he said, shaking his head and glancing away. "I cannot help who I am. There are forces greater than us at work in the universe. We are trapped by their whims and desires."

She sighed. "Since I was first taken from my family, I've known nothing but the demands of Artemis. Sometimes it feels like chains, and other times it feels like an energy I want to fill myself with. With Demetrius here, the culture and chaos is changing."

"What do you mean?"

"Demetrius seems to pleasure in the pain he causes," she replied. "The evil no longer feels like it lives around me. Now it feels like it wants to live *in* me."

"Then why don't you leave?"

"Where would I go?"

"You could come to join us in my home," Nabonidus said. "We've purchased dozens of slaves from the market. They're free now. People from all over are joining Yeshua's family."

She stopped and examined him longingly. "That name has a strange power to it. The thought of being part of a family pulls on my spirit. I've known a thousand men, yet I've never felt like I belonged to any."

"Come now," Nabonidus urged. "We can give you all you need."

The priestess watched a flock of pelicans skimming the waves out past a flotilla of Roman warships. "I may not see you again," she said. "Demetrius, with Selsus, have wrested control of the temple worship away from the old priest, and they've determined that I should be transferred to serve as a matron at the nearby children's farm. It seems I'm too old now to pleasure men the way he wants me to."

Nabonidus followed her gaze out to sea. "What is this children's farm and why would you go there?"

She slumped down onto a boulder next to him. "The farm is outside the city. It's where us temple matrons take orphans to train them in the ways of Artemis. The children then work in the bathhouses, the arena, the Artemission, and in other pleasure centers." She reached into her basket and retrieved the pomegranate. "When they become older, like me, they're sent to train the younger ones. Some days I feel like no child should know these things."

"And you're right," Nabonidus said. "I too had to experience things no child should have to know. Demetrius has no right to destroy the innocence of children like that."

"It's not just Demetrius. Selsus now has his men combing the streets for unaccompanied children. At first I assumed his purpose was to practice the charity of the goddess, but then I saw the money handed over to the kidnappers for each child. And then I knew—we weren't just comforting orphans, we were creating them." The priestess clutched her head as if in pain. "Last week, Selsus brought in two young Persian girls. He said the father had gotten in front of his chariot wheels and died. It happens too often for me to believe they're all accidents."

Nabonidus put his hand on her shoulder. "How old are these Persian girls? What are their names?"

The priestess recoiled in surprise at his touch. "What's your interest? Surely you wouldn't reject me because of your lust for such little—"

"No! No! No!" Nabonidus sprang to his feet. "I know two Persian girls, Adrina and Atossa. Their father is a friend of mine. If they're the girls taken by Selsus, I'll do everything in my power to free them."

The distressed woman clasped her hands over her mouth. "Perhaps my senses are right. This may be a trap for you."

"I don't care. Come with me, live free, and show me where I can find this children's farm. I will free them all."

"First I must go back to the Artemission," she said. "There's something I must have if I am to live free."

"I'll wait at the road leading up to my villa," Nabonidus assured her.

Two hours later, Nabonidus remained hidden on the roof of a shoemaker's empty shop. Traffic along the Sacred Way coming from the Artemission had slowed to a trickle and the torches at the temple flickered. The churning in his stomach turned from anxiety to disappointment.

He was about to leave when he noted Selsus arrive at the temple through a side entrance. Within a few minutes, the German giant had emerged down the front stairs with Demetrius and six of the temple guards. They moved quickly out of the grounds and scoured the dark streets. Nabonidus knew they were searching for him and swallowed his anger at being betrayed by the priestess. Surely she had been the one to tell them his plan…

How gullible am I to believe people can change so easily? he asked himself.

Before they could reach his hiding place, he slipped down the stairs and looked for a chance to get away and return home.

Daphne stepped into her sandals and washed her face in a bowl of water. The fresh towel next to it smelled of lavender and she breathed in its delicate fragrance as she rubbed her neck and chin. She then sorted through her colored fabrics and set out her wardrobe for the day. When the decision had been made, she dressed and joined Asturex and Seti in the kitchen.

"Have either of you seen Nabonidus?" she asked.

"No," they said in unison.

"Urbanus was already asking about him," Asturex added.

"That's odd," Daphne said. "Surely if Nabonidus returned last night, Urbanus would know about it."

The two servants set out flatbreads, cheeses, olives, dates, and fruit for the household while Abigail retrieved fresh goat's milk from the cool house. Flowers from the garden adorned the tables and the morning breeze off the ocean produced a promising aura of new life and hope for the day.

Urbanus met Daphne as she entered the dining area with the milk.

"I hope all is okay with Nabonidus," Urbanus said. "He didn't talk to you about traveling somewhere, did he?"

"No," Daphne replied. "He's been uptight lately, though. I sure hope he didn't go back to the Artemission. That place is a trap for someone in his weakened state of mind."

"I'll take a few of the servants and go out searching. When does Mary arrive?"

"Either tomorrow or the day after," Daphne said. "It wouldn't be good to have more trouble than we can deal with when the mother of our Lord arrives."

Caleb and Suzanna wandered in and helped themselves to the platters on the table.

"It feels like there's something wrong," Suzanna noted. "Has something happened while we were asleep?"

"Nabonidus didn't come home last night," Daphne said.

"He's missing, and we're worried the Artemission might have something to do with it." Urbanus tightened the belt around his robe and reached into a container to pull out a dagger. "This weapon is the last thing I expect to have to use, but I want to be prepared for any surprises."

"I'll come with you," Caleb chimed in. "I'm not about to lose that man after finally finding him again. With all he went through, I owe him."

Titius and John stood side by side on the balcony of the governor's mansion, scrutinizing the harbor. They had arrived outside the estate at first light and waited to be welcomed by the official guarding the entrance. Titius wore a centurion's dress uniform, which often opened such doors.

By now, the fishing fleet was starting to drift back toward the shore. The chatter of warehousemen and workers combined with merchants, shoppers, legionnaires, and devout worshippers. Gulls circled overhead, anticipating the scraps about to be discarded when the catch was cleaned by the fishermen.

"It isn't the Galilee," John said, "but I do love to see fishermen at work. There's something about feeling the tug of a full net that still gets my heart thumping."

"Are you sure Mary is coming this morning?" Titus asked. "I've heard so much about her, and I know Caleb is eager to connect again. He was almost like another son to her, you know. At least that's what he told me."

"I'm sure he did. Their home was always open. She's my aunt, so I know her habits well."

Titius turned to step back inside when John caught him by the arm. "Isn't that Nabonidus crouching behind those crates by the first warehouse?"

Titius followed the direction where John pointed and recognized the Persian man right away. "That's him all right. Looks like he's watching those people load their ship. What trouble is he getting into now?"

"We should go down and see if he needs help," John suggested.

"Not dressed like this." Titius gestured to his armored vest and red cloak. "I'll change into something else."

The apostle watched from the balcony as Nabonidus crept closer to the ship, crouching behind a stack of crated nuts, then crawling to sit behind a pile of abandoned baskets. Meanwhile, the ship's loading was almost complete. The leader, a big man with blond hair, made his assistants carry a roll of carpet onto the bow. He then gave the captain some coins and started to untie the ropes holding the ship to the dock.

John then searched for Titius, knowing that the man had changed into one of his disguises. There was a crippled shepherd boy hobbling while he drove his sheep onto the dock. Could that be him? Behind the shepherd was a slave owner with a couple of withered slaves. There was also a wide selection of sailors and warehousemen lounging about as fishermen cleaned out their nets.

Titius could be any one of them.

The shepherd boy absentmindedly drove his sheep into an area which had no place to pen them in, so several of the sheep wandered over to the blond-haired leader, who towered over all the other sailors and dockmen. The animals seemed to irritate the leader and he turned to chastise the shepherd. The boy bowed humbly, nodding and apologizing while he walked to the dock's edge to get his sheep. As the last mooring line was untied, the boy stumbled and fell over the dock and landed on the ship. Several sailors rushed to his side while the leader just laughed and mocked the clumsy boy.

With the sail catching and pulling the ship away, confusion reigned on the vessel. Meanwhile, the shepherd boy crawled along the deck toward the carpet still lying on the bow where it had been dropped. As John watched, the boy unrolled the carpet to reveal a young woman wrapped inside.

One of the sailors rushed to the bow and ended up overboard after being accidently tripped by the shepherd's staff. John had trouble believing his eyes. It had to be Titius.

As the ship turned to pick up the man who'd fallen overboard, another sailor found himself in the water on the other side of the ship. The crowd on the pier grew quickly as the entertainment in the water drew their attention.

"Nothing but fools," shouted the blond-haired leader. "Finish your work or you won't get paid the rest."

John kept watch as the shepherd boy gently slapped the cheeks of the woman who'd been rolled up in the carpet. By this time, Nabonidus had moved across the wharf to watch the proceedings. When the leader noticed him, he gave orders to the five men around him to grab the Persian. Nabonidus fought like a bear, but the leader tossed a fishing net over him while the others hit him with clubs. Only with a massive effort did Nabonidus struggle toward the edge of the pier and hurl himself and three of the men into the water.

The shepherd boy raced from bow to stern like a wild boar, bowling sailors overboard as he went. The ship's navigator was too preoccupied with the ship to take notice of all the chaos—and he, too, ended up in the water.

Yes, John was certain that shepherd boy was Titius. It had to be. As he watched, Titius steered the vessel toward the dock and pulled up alongside it just as Nabonidus's bald skull bobbed out from the depths of the water. The Persian man grabbed hold of a dangling rope and hoisted himself up onto the ship's deck.

In a moment, the ship spun and headed back out to sea. Curses could be heard echoing all over the harbor.

Chapter Twenty-Two

Titius, at the wheel on the ship in his shepherd boy disguise, noticed the apostle John leaving the governor's mansion. Quickly his attention returned to the several sailors still floundering in the water as blond-haired Selsus and the others screamed curses down on him from the dock.

Nabonidus knelt, heaving for breath.

Titius directed him to check the woman still lying across the bow. "She's either been drugged or poisoned. See if you can wake her."

Nabonidus pushed his way up to a standing position and wobbled toward the woman's prone figure. She appeared lifeless, and her chest wasn't moving—and he recognized her: she was the priestess he had invited to leave the Artemission and join him as part of Yeshua's family.

Perhaps she hadn't betrayed him, after all.

"Wake up, priestess," he urged. "I don't even know your name."

He bent low, putting his ear to her nose and listening for breath sounds. Gently, he turned her on her side and pounded on her back. A groan.

"She's alive," he called to Titius.

"I'm going to need your help," Titius called back. "That German friend of yours seems to be commandeering another ship, and they're rigging it to come after us. We need to set the sails on this racehorse and get moving."

"What do you need me to do?" Nabonidus asked as he picked up the priestess's limp body and carried it toward the stern. "The two of us aren't going to be able to do much without help."

"You take the wheel and I'll set the sails. We'll slip over the edge and swim for shore once we get around the bend of the harbor."

"What about the woman?" Nabonidus laid her gently in a bundle of fishing net, brushed the hair out of her face, and took his place at the helm.

Titius placed his fingers on the woman's wrist, checking for a pulse. "She'll go over the edge with you. Meanwhile, I'll turn the ship out to sea and join you as soon as I can. Get her to your place and hide. Get the apostle to pray for her… and find a doctor!"

As Titius set the sails, the wind caught hold and grabbed the ship in a powerful thrust.

"Turn us alongside the shoreline now," Titius yelled. "We're going to run aground if we get any closer."

Nabonidus swung the ship and it responded as easily as a chariot tied to racehorses.

Titius soon worked his way toward the helm and took over the wheel. "Now, take her and jump overboard. Keep her head above the water line." He glanced behind toward the harbor. "When you get ashore, don't stop moving until you're out of sight. They'll be rounding the corner in a few minutes. They can't see you."

The Persian man lifted the priestess, walked to the edge of the ship, and prepared to jump.

How am I going to do this without breaking her neck? he asked himself. *And what's Daphne going to think when I bring another woman home? Especially when I've been gone all night…*

"Jump now!" Titius ordered.

Without hesitating, Nabonidus tightened his grip, cradled the woman's head against his shoulder, and hurtled them both into the sea. The icy waters enveloped them, and he kicked hard to return to the surface.

For a moment, he appeared to be weighed down. Then he wrapped an arm around the woman's waist and with his free arm paddled hard. When he broke the surface, gasping for air, he didn't have time to worry about his charge; he simply cradled her head and kicked for shore.

It took several minutes to reach land and carry the woman into the nearest strand of bushes. Nearby, a group of curious children loitered in fascination at the ship which had come so close and discharged two people.

"Hide yourselves," Nabonidus told them. "There's another ship on the way, and we can't be seen. Tell me when you see it coming out of the harbor."

Most of the children gathered close and crouched on their haunches as he rolled the woman on her side and patted her back.

"Is she dead?" one child asked.

"I hope not," Nabonidus said. "Give her some space. I need to get her breathing."

Suddenly, the priestess coughed up water and gasped for breath. No sooner had she resumed breathing than a small boy came running toward them.

"I saw the ship," said the boy. "It's chasing the one that dropped you off. But then someone jumped off your boat and they haven't come up out of the water yet!"

John met Urbanus and Caleb when he reached the halfway point up the hill toward Nabonidus's estate. The three of them then turned toward the warehouses and walked quickly to the place where John had seen Nabonidus fall into the sea.

"Titius took over a ship, threw everyone overboard, and attempted to rescue a woman who was wrapped up in a carpet," John explained. "Nabonidus was captured and thrown into the sea. We need to pray—and hurry."

It wasn't hard to find the scene of the action, since hundreds of people had gathered there and were chattering excitedly about what they had witnessed. John led his companions toward a rabbi who was waxing eloquent with his six disciples.

"The curse of the Almighty is on all thieves and charlatans," the rabbi was saying. "The wrath of the Almighty rests on this den of iniquity. Guard your heart, for it is the wellspring of life—thus saith the prophet."

"Excuse me, rabbi," John interrupted. "Did you witness what happened here? Have they found the Persian man who went overboard or the shepherd boy who took the boat out to sea?"

The rabbi stood, mouth agape for a moment before staring harder at the apostle. "John? Is that you?"

"Rabbi Schmuli?"

"Yes! What are you doing so far from the Galilee?"

"We're bringing light into the heart of darkness," John answered. "But right now we're searching for some friends."

The rabbi turned and peered out to sea. "Were they on the first boat or the second?"

"What do you mean?"

"Well, the first boat carried a big Persian fellow who was half-drowned, a lunatic shepherd boy, and a woman who seemed dead." He turned back to John. "The second boat was filled with a lot of angry men out for revenge."

"My friends were on the first boat, but I don't think this is a good time to admit that," John said, pivoting around. "Did the second boat catch them?"

"We're not sure," Rabbi Schmuli admitted. "They sailed out of sight around the corner of the harbor. We're waiting to see what happened. And while we wait, we'll learn a little history and theology. Redeem the time, you know."

"I thought you were in Alexandria," John noted.

"Yes, I was sent on a mission from Alexandria to Emperor Caligula to protest the Greek harassment against us. Unfortunately, he died and now Emperor Claudius is making threats against us all."

"Do you think the threats will reach beyond Rome and Alexandria?"

"The emperor has set his sights on attacking Britannia first, but then he's made it clear we aren't welcome anywhere near him. Warn your friends not to agitate any political figures or they'll be targets. If you have time to join us, I'm teaching at the school of Tyrannus, and at the synagogue."

John smiled. "Thanks for the warning, but we need to go find our friends."

As the trio moved on away from the harbor, Caleb tapped the apostle on the shoulder. "Who was that?"

"My old rabbi in Bethsaida, before I met Yeshua. He became a leading teacher in Alexandria and helped them establish one of the Empire's great libraries."

"He's got a good memory to remember you from so long ago. Is he a follower of Yeshua?"

"Unfortunately, no. One of these days I need to sit down and have a long talk with him."

Urbanus and Caleb had just exited the house when Tryphena announced that they had a visitor. Abigail and Suzanna both went to the door as a tall and athletic Greek man dressed in a white toga appeared at the door.

"Peace to our visitor," Abigail said.

"And peace to those who live in this home," their Greek visitor replied. "I am Apollos, newly arrived from Rome. I bring news to the believers who follow the apostle here."

Abigail nodded at him. "You are welcome, Apollos. We follow Yeshua along with John and the whole church that meets in this home. What is your news?"

"The Emperor Claudius has declared that all Jews must leave Rome. We'll need places to stay until all this is over."

"You're welcome to stay here," Suzanna said. "Although the space is tight with all those who have already joined us…"

Apollos half-bowed. "I am grateful, but I'm only the messenger and need to continue my journey to warn others. It would be wise if no one travelled to Rome for the near future."

"We hear and appreciate the warning," Abigail said. "We'll tell the men when they get back."

Later that afternoon, Abigail and Suzanna sat on the estate wall, their legs dangling among the gladioli, oleanders, and poppies. Their clear view of the harbor gave them a front-row seat of the ship being chased down.

"What do you think is going on down there?" Suzanna asked.

"Maybe the Romans are practicing catching pirates," Abigail mused. "I just wish our husbands would get back home so I don't have to worry about them."

Suzanna hoisted herself up and stood. "They're probably distracted by something down there. I just hope it isn't some woman taking up their time."

Abigail chuckled. "Surely you aren't serious. Maybe you don't know your husband well, but I sure know mine. He's committed to me." She hopped down off the wall onto the marble patio. "I guess I'm worried after that messenger arrived to give us the new emperor's warning against Jews."

"Surely we don't have to worry about being sent to the arena again. I've always known we might have to give up our lives, but I thought it might be in Germania. Caleb and I always planned to go there next."

"I'm not sure why you think you need to go to Germania," Abigail said. "Have you seen the pagan magicians and soothsayers and idolaters in this city? You can reach the whole world from here."

Suzanna motioned for Abigail to follow and started walking down a cobblestone path toward the rose gardens at the rear of the home. A flock of chickadees flitted out of their way and into the surrounding trees.

"The Almighty has blessed me," Suzanna said.

"How so?"

Suzanna patted her abdomen and smiled. "I've missed the way of women for three months, and I know without a doubt my sickness is for a reason."

Abigail stopped and embraced her friend. "I too have news of pregnancy, but I don't cherish it the same as you."

"What do you mean? Surely you would be pleased. Our husbands will celebrate God's blessing together."

"This child inside me cannot belong to my husband," Abigail said. "When I was captured, one of the men had his way with me, and this child is his. I've been waiting to figure out how I can tell Titius, but I can't bear to see his disappointment. I've already lost three of his since we married, and in some ways I hope this one, too, will choose not to be born."

Suzanna embraced Abigail tighter. "Your fear is so much like mine."

"How?"

"Caleb has questioned me many times since our reunion about whether the sailors had their way with me. I assured him I was spared, but he hardly believes me. He doesn't reach for me as he used to, and now I don't know how to tell him this child is from our last union in Cyprus before we were separated."

"Oh, how can the blessing of a child mean such misery?" Abigail wondered. "We must pray for wisdom, as our time to hide will soon be done. We must guard these secrets and be there for each other."

As they stood embracing, neither of them noticed the shadowed figure slip away from behind the hedges and hurry toward the kitchen.

Demetrius rubbed his hands together with joy as he watched Asturex slip away from his booth outside the Artemission. Her inability to pay for the silver figurine of Diana meant she would now have to pay in other ways. Such as sharing the inmost secrets of the home where a small church was growing.

He set aside the disappointment of losing the priestess at sea. Drugging her had been a necessary act to assure Selsus he meant business. He had intended to dump her overboard himself anyway.

But it was odd how Nabonidus and that shepherd boy had managed to disappear as well.

An oxcart arrived with his latest stock and he carefully unloaded the figurines, polishing and placing them carefully on display.

"The goddess of the heavens is smiling on me," Demetrius said to no one in particular. "It won't be long until the greatness of Artemis fills the heavens and the blasphemy of Yeshua is wiped from the face of the earth."

———————

Having returned home, Nabonidus lay the priestess on a mat in the main living area, next to the fountain. Seti picked up a rag and washed the woman's face while Abigail shooed the men out of the house so she could arrange to change the woman's clothing.

Before the trek up the hill, Nabonidus and Titius had taken her to a trusted medicine shop. The resident doctor had poured a potion down the woman's throat, inducing involuntary vomiting. Although her pulse had continued to race, Nabonidus had lifted her up and walked home.

The streets had filled in behind them with curiosity seekers. The news of this moment would soon be out for all to hear.

"I know one man who isn't going to be happy," Nabonidus muttered.

"There will be more than one," Titius said.

Out in the gardens, the men shared their adventures with the others. Titius and Nabonidus dramatized their escape on the ship as Selsus and his crew had given chase. John then filled in the details of his encounter with the rabbi, offering his own take on the caper in the harbor. Caleb and Urbanus replayed the moments they'd witnessed, such as Selsus's henchmen throwing the net over Nabonidus and being pulled into the sea.

Their raucous laughter bubbled and boiled through the windows of the home, where the young priestess fluttered her eyelids open. Jasmine and frankincense filled the air as the women of the house wrapped her in warm blankets.

Asturex left the woman's side for a moment and stepped onto the garden pathway with a tray of fruits. She approached Caleb first.

"A gift from your wife to celebrate the life of your new little one," she said.

Caleb stood with his mouth gaping open as Asturex released the tray into his hands.

"What did you say?" he asked.

Asturex bowed low. "I'm sorry, I didn't know it was a secret. I assumed your wife told you about her baby, and about Abigail's illegitimate child as well. This is a good time to practice forgiveness."

Caleb set the tray down on the stone bench and ran into the house, where he saw Abigail draping a robe over the priestess.

"Suzanna!" Caleb's shouts reverberated through the house. "Suzanna, come here. Right now!"

Abigail tried to intercept Caleb as he moved toward the bedrooms. "Caleb, Suzanna has gone to the market. She'll be back soon."

Caleb whirled on her. "You lying whore. How do I know she's not seeing her lover? How do I know the two of you haven't been off cheating on us?"

"What are you talking about?" Abigail asked. "No one has cheated on you."

Titius stepped into the room. "What am I hearing about a baby?"

"Our wives have been cheating on us," Caleb said. "They're pregnant with other men's children. I can't believe I was such a fool to believe that lying wench."

Titius stepped toward his wife. "Abigail. What is he saying?"

Abigail lowered her eyes. "I think we need to go for a walk."

Instead, Titius merely spun on his heel and walked back out into the garden. Abigail followed.

Asturex stood calmly in the doorway, watching the disintegration of these two marriages. Demetrius had been right about the fallout a little word could have. Perhaps her debt had now been paid.

———————

As Selsus and his crew finished unloading and tying up their boats, he turned to look up toward the market—just in time to see Caleb pushing his way through the crowded aisles, ignoring the cries of protest from the disgruntled humanity left in his wake. He soon emerged from the market and came onto the dock. The man was so focused on finding Suzanna, though, that he didn't notice Selsus.

But Selsus certainly took notice of him.

Selsus walked quickly to the unsuspecting Caleb and wrenched his arms behind his back. One of his henchmen gut-punched the helpless Jew and knuckle-punched him in the jaw.

Caleb sagged to the ground without knowing what had hit him.

The German watched with satisfaction as his men hoisted Caleb over their heads and marched him toward the water's edge. The Jewish man gasped for air as he hit the water.

———————

Suzanna dawdled through the market stalls, sampling passionfruit and dreaming about what it would be like to cuddle her little one. She couldn't help smiling as she wrapped different fabrics around herself and wasn't even surprised when the merchant engaged her with a question as to when her child would be born.

Tea and a small cake took the edge off of her hunger. The gulls were especially glorious in their swooping flights around the harbor. The tantalizing sun and breeze caressed her skin until it glowed.

When she was finished her shopping, Suzanna made her way calmly back through the market, hurrying her step a little, when she heard coarse shouting from the docks. The flow of the human river suddenly changed direction, almost pulling Suzanna into the current of arms and legs.

She sidestepped into an alcove and waited for the excitement to be over. Perhaps this had something to do with the two ships that had been chasing each other earlier. People found all kinds of things to get excited over. It kept the boredom at bay.

She breathed in the scent of her handful of gladiolas and embraced the wonder of being alive. A bit of movement in her abdomen caught her attention, and she rubbed her belly and smiled. Life was good.

Chapter Twenty-Three

Nabonidus and Daphne sat with Seti, watching as the priestess sipped a goblet of wine held to her lips.

"Priestess, it is the grace of Yeshua which has saved your life," Nabonidus said.

The woman, weary from her adventure, her hair in tangles and recovering from poisoning, hardly seemed like the enticing temptress who had once roamed the Temple of Artemis. She scanned the room, taking in the horse fountain, the fish symbols on the wall, and the row of crystal vases filled with tulips on the marble counter.

"My name is Daphne," Daphne said. "This is Nabonidus and Seti. By what name should we call you?"

The woman glanced at Daphne through squinting eyes. "The name I've known is no longer the name I wish to be called. If Yeshua has saved me and brought me to life again, his priests should call me by a new name."

Nabonidus rose and carried a plate of cheese, cakes, and olives to the priestess. "We have no priests among us. We are only brothers and sisters who follow a teacher. You're welcomed as a sister and follower of Yeshua."

The woman stared at Seti. "If you're my sister, tell me the name you wish to call me."

Seti knelt, then crawled to place her hands on the woman's shoulders. "I will call you Ruth," she said. "You are leaving your people to join with our people. You are leaving your God to join our God. This is the story of Ruth, which you will learn and love."

The priestess smiled and set down her goblet. She accepted the embrace of Seti and Daphne.

"I am Ruth," the woman said. "How strange to sit in the home of the man who once refused my favors. If you can transform from an assassin to a brother, I can change from a priestess to a sister."

Suzanna walked inside from the courtyard, holding a handful of gladiolas. "Has anyone seen Caleb?"

Nabonidus walked past her and peered out the front door. "He went to find you in the marketplace. Perhaps it's a good thing he didn't find you, though. We need to talk."

The fisherman who dove into the water to rescue Caleb endured the jeers and taunts of Selsus and his glowering thugs along the edge of the dock. One of those thugs picked up a small chunk of wood and tossed it at the would-be rescuer struggling in the water.

"Here, grab onto that if you want to save something," the man called, laughing.

Another thug grabbed a fishing net that had been left out to dry. He hurled it in a swirling circle overtop of the pair in the water. The sinking weights wrapped around the fisherman's legs. He dove under the surface and freed himself, all the while fighting to recapture Caleb as he sank.

The thrashing in the water drew even more verbal abuse from the crowd and more debris dropped into the water around them. Two men picked up a crate of olives and hurled it into the harbor. The edge of the crate caught the fisherman's shoulder and elicited a bloodcurdling cry of pain. He released Caleb and thrashed with one arm before finally slipping below the surface.

As Caleb sank out of sight, another man hurtled himself off the dock and jumped after him. When none of the men emerged after a full minute, some of the crowd cheered.

Titius and Abigail sat quietly side by side on the marble garden bench. A pair of rabbits munching the garden produce didn't draw their ire. A hawk circling overhead didn't draw their attention, either.

"I chose to love you even when I knew those sailors had taken advantage of you," Titius said. "I grieve that this child will not be mine, but it will grow up being loved."

Abigail cradled his hand in hers. "My only wish is someday I will carry a son who will make you proud to be mine."

Just then, Suzanna stepped into the garden and saw them sitting head to head.

"Abigail," Suzanna called. "I'm so sorry. Something terrible is happening."

Urbanus gasped for breath as he wrestled Caleb's limp body onto a beam bracing up the dock's main piling. The roar of the crowd, mixed with the pounding of hundreds of feet, reverberated like thunder in his ears.

He had hurled himself into the water amid all the projectiles, catching the edge of Caleb's robe as he sank. Now, having tugged Caleb to safety under the wharf, he propped him up and attempted to dive after the fisherman who had also drowned in the first rescue attempt. That man's foot had snagged and Urbanus was breathless by the time he had freed the man's body and surfaced again.

Caleb was slipping under the water again and Urbanus had to make a difficult decision. He could only save one of these two men. At last, he made his choice and worked to get Caleb breathing again.

The crowd quieted overhead, and the silence now was almost deafening in its contrast to the thunderous stomping and yelling earlier.

One man's voice stood out, though.

"Who do we honor?" demanded Selsus.

"Artemis! Artemis! Artemis!"

"What do we do with those who dishonor our goddess?"

At first Urbanus couldn't understand the response, but when he finally did a chill ran down his spine. The words overlapped in a jumble: "Arena! Death by gladiator! Crucify them! Arena! Death by gladiator! Crucify them!"

Caleb's chest had begun to rise and fall again. Urbanus laid his head down and tried to ride out the panic rising from the depths of his soul.

"Yeshua, please," he prayed.

At that moment, a hand clamped down on his elbow and pulled him off the dock beam and back into the water. Two hands pushed him under and attempted to hold him down. Instead of struggling for the surface, he dove deeper and away from the attacker. He surfaced dozens of feet away, took a quick breath, and changed course to disguise where he would come up again.

When he finally arose and glanced back toward the point of his attack, Urbanus saw two men pulling Caleb and the fisherman's body through the water toward shore. On the dock, Selsus urged them on.

There was nothing more to do but get back and warn the others.

Ruth, former priestess of Artemis, sat on a wooden stool observing Seti, Abigail, and Daphne as they attempted to calm Suzanna. Nabonidus and Titius had gone to find the apostle John and others in the community who could help find Caleb.

Asturex busied herself in the kitchen with several of the other women, trying to quell the terror and guilt rising like a storm inside her. She had no doubt the roar of the crowd arising from the seaside had something very much to do with Suzanna's missing husband.

Ruth eventually recovered enough to rise and walk into the kitchen where she encountered Asturex. It didn't take her long to remember the last time she'd seen the woman from Gaul.

"Didn't I see you with Demetrius picking up one of his figurines?" Ruth asked.

Asturex gasped and blushed profusely. "Do I know you?"

Ruth peered over her shoulder and motioned to Daphne and Abigail. Daphne rose and joined her.

"This servant of yours is a regular customer at the silversmith by the temple," Ruth said. "I'm sure she's the one who has been giving information to Demetrius and those who wish to harm you."

Daphne scanned Asturex's dropping features. "Is that true?"

Asturex backed away but remained silent.

"Asturex, we freed you from the slave market. How could you betray us?"

Asturex wilted and teared up. "I just needed to pay for my statue. I didn't have any money of my own. I didn't know what else to do!"

Daphne took the girl by the arm and steered her out the front door. "We offered you shelter and peace in Yeshua's name. If you needed anything, all you had to do was ask. Since you've chosen Artemis, to Artemis you need to go."

Asturex collapsed in a heap just outside the house, sobbing. "No, no. I don't want to go back to that lifestyle. Please, I'll destroy the idol. I'll repay you for everything."

Ruth crouched beside her and placed her hand on Asturex's shoulder. "I've only just arrived here, but I can tell you that your worth as a woman, and your dignity as a human, will be far higher in this place than where you're choosing to go. Being at the mercy of men every night is no life worth living."

Suzanna strode quickly into the room and headed directly toward Asturex. "You're the one who did this? I hate you. I hate you!" She pounded on the woman and Daphne had to pull the hysterical attacker away.

Asturex crawled down the path away from the house before rising to her feet.

"He's going to send you all to the arena," Asturex yelled. "Don't you see? Choosing anything but Artemis is a choice for death. I don't want to die."

Daphne, Suzanna, and Abigail embraced and hugged as Asturex walked away.

Ruth stepped up beside them. "If we're going to rescue the children from the farm, we need to go soon—before Asturex warns them that we know their plan."

"Shouldn't we wait for the men?" Suzanna asked.

"There's no time," Ruth said. "The guards at the farm won't know yet about my leaving the Artemission. I can convince them to send all the children with us for the upcoming festival."

"How many wagons will we need?" Abigail asked.

"Four will be fine. We'll each have to drive one, and we can get the wagons from the farm, but we need to hurry."

"But someone needs to tell the men," Abigail said. "We won't be able to stay in the city if word gets out."

Nabonidus and John led their ragtag group of rescuers down the alleyway toward the marketplace. There, they encountered merchants, residents, and loiterers who glanced up to see the determined look on their faces. Everyone stepped aside to avoid being bumped over. A small parade of curiosity seekers jogged along behind the posse.

The wailing in the market square ahead alerted them to trouble. When they broke into the market, they came upon a circle of women kneeling around a prone body lying facedown on the ground. A group of men stood passively behind the women.

Nabonidus shouldered aside two of the wailing women and flipped the body over. It wasn't Caleb, but the man's dead face was still a shock.

"Who is this?" Nabonidus demanded.

One of the men stepped forward. "Alexander was just a fisherman trying to save the Jew who got thrown into the sea by that German giant. He didn't do anything wrong."

Nabonidus glared at him. "And what happened to the Jew?"

The man pointed toward the imposing arena only a short distance away. "They put him into a cart and took him to the arena. They said they were going to crucify him."

Nabonidus was already on the run by the time John caught the gist of what had been said. The posse gathered a few more recruits and joined the chase toward the city's main center of entertainment.

The rough wood against Caleb's bare back stung like needles as he opened his eyes to comprehend what was happening to him. The raw rope around his wrists bit into his flesh and threatened to cut off his circulation.

He realized that his naked torso hung from a cross beam, his feet dangling, his lungs hungry for air. Hundreds of people crowded around and then backed off to take their place in the stands. The rumble of voices sounded like a river avalanching through a forest during flood season. The crowd's energy was palpable and it carried the chilly edge of evil.

For years, Caleb had built crosses for the Romans. His childhood friend Yeshua had even died on the special cross Caleb had built from an olive tree—the cross he'd built for Barabbas.

Only in his nightmares had he imagined himself facing death in this way.

As Caleb squinted, he noticed the leering grin of the bearded Selsus. The man wore the olive crown of victory and sported a form-fitting golden breastplate and wristband with eighteen leather strands marking his kills. A dozen other watchers stood around as strong hands bound Caleb tightly. Two men carried a container of black tar which they set down near Selsus.

Caleb shook his head, trying and failing to make sense of the instructions being given.

A boy with a broom arrived and handed his instrument to Selsus, who dipped it into the tar. Stroke by stroke, the hot gooey substance was smeared on

Caleb's stomach, arms, and chest. Burning pain consumed him, but there was no escape from it.

A hideous masked sorcerer arrived, chanting and dancing around the cross that had been erected in the middle of the arena. Priestesses followed in their most seductive attire, and Demetrius trailed behind them with a cartload of silver icons. The priestesses placed the icons in a circle around the cross.

At last, a priest approached, leading an ox and a wagon of hay. The priest supervised as the hay was piled up under the cross.

The priest then placed one hand on the head of the ox and slit its throat with the other. The beast moaned and collapsed while the priestesses used vases to catch the blood pouring out of the wound. One after the other, the women uttered their chants and poured the spilled blood onto Caleb's legs.

As his breathing grew raspy and his mind dizzy from the strong oily vapor, Caleb noticed a cart upon which stood a barrel holding a roaring flame. The priestesses and dozens of others danced around the cart as it drew closer.

Deep regret filled Caleb's soul. Regret at his fight with Suzanna, regret that he would never know the joy of being a father, regret that the mission work they'd planned to undertake would never come to be.

Selsus raised a large wooden torch and joined the raucous parade. He was about to light the flame when Demetrius yelled out, "Wait!"

Everything froze in place. Caleb heard a woman screaming and glanced up toward the arena entrance. A woman, naked and tarred, was being dragged by two priests toward the group. Demetrius grabbed her by the hair and pulled her to stand before the cross.

He realized that it was none other than Asturex. She wept hysterically, pleading for her life.

"Look upon this wretched beast, you follower of Yeshua," Demetrius screamed. "This is the slave you purchased out of compassion. This is the one who betrayed you." He threw Asturex on the ground. "What shall I do with her? Shall I kill her quickly or slowly? By the knife or by the flame?"

Caleb shut his eyes and hung his head.

"Very well," Demetrius said. "You shall die hearing the screams of the one you tried to save."

Caleb opened his eyes at the moment Demetrius took the lighted torch and extended it to the screeching girl who was scrambling in the sand to escape. A wall of humanity blocked her every attempt to get away.

Demetrius raised the torch high and bellowed, "For the glory of Artemis and all the Ephesians!"

The flames leapt with demonic force onto Asturex and consumed her as she curled up, defeated and destroyed. Selsus ended her misery with a spear thrust. The roar from the crowd rumbled in the distance.

Every prayer Caleb could conceive of filled his mind, but no words slipped from his parched tongue save one. "Yeshua… Yeshua… Yeshua…"

Demetrius stood before him and shook his fist. "Stop it! Stop saying that name." He turned toward Selsus. "Bring the fire! The sacrifice must be given. There will be no mercy for this one."

Nabonidus burst into the arena just as Selsus delivered the spear thrust through Asturex's heart. The Persian man tore off his robe and sprinted at top speed while the German was thrusting his torch into the barrel and setting it aflame. He was within a spear's throw when Selsus passed the flame to Demetrius; he was a stride away when the flame was extended.

With his shoulder lowered, Nabonidus drove into the cross and knocked it over, rolling Caleb facedown in the sand. In the blink of an eye, he kicked the flaming torch out of the silversmith's hand. With his forearm, he clubbed Demetrius to the back of his head and left him unconscious next to the charred remains of the former slave girl.

When he regained his balance, he turned to stare into Selsus's fiery eyes. The German man's jaw and fists were clenched, his neck and shoulder muscles taut. He was a killing machine on home turf.

The priestesses scattered and kept their distance as the two men of war sized each other up. Caleb groaned, lying awkwardly under the fallen cross. He struggled to ease his nose out of the sand to catch his breath.

Selsus stripped off his golden breastplate. "So, we finally meet again, and this time without the nobility to cheer the true champion of the Ephesians." He held up his armband with the eighteen leather strands. "If only we had faced each other before you had become fat and lazy, living the good life of the rich and spoiled. If only the emperor himself were here to see what a wretch passed himself off as the champion of the Empire. This champion of Artemis is nothing but a weak betrayer who has chosen to worship a dead man rather than a living goddess."

Nabonidus hardly moved as Selsus circled. "I have only now realized the complete emptiness of Artemis, the foolishness of those who prostrate themselves in her temple, who lust after the flesh of helpless captives who have no choice but to fan your every foolish desire."

Selsus angled his way toward Caleb and Nabonidus knew he meant to kill if he got the chance. Using the momentary distraction to his advantage, and at great risk to himself, Nabonidus threw himself at the feet of Selsus and drove a kick to the side of the man's knee. The giant grunted and partially buckled as he twisted to avoid the follow-up kick.

His attention was now fully on Nabonidus. "So, you haven't forgotten everything I taught you," he said, grinning devilishly. "You won't get a second chance to try that. Before this day is through, I'll have you on a cross next to the one you came to save. How stupid you are to give your life for one who once enslaved you."

The German reached the wooden club that had been used to light Asturex on fire and flipped it up out of the sand with his foot. He caught it without taking his eye off Nabonidus.

"You probably know I gave you nothing more than children to fight and earn your glory," Selsus taunted. "I saved the real men for myself to destroy. All of Ephesus knows their true champion now. I shall claim your home, your girl, and your slaves for myself before this day is over."

Nabonidus watched the club swinging hypnotically in the hand of Selsus. The giant was using it as a distraction to set up his attack.

"You come as the champion of Artemis and I come as the slave of Yeshua," Nabonidus said. "I am nobody in myself. One day every man will stand and give account of himself before the throne of the Almighty. If my day is today, I'm ready."

Selsus stopped in his tracks and straightened up. "Let's consider something a little weightier for our final time in the arena. If I kill you, know before this week is over all those in that little church of yours will be rounded up and crucified in this very place. If you kill me, you can do what you will with Demetrius and all these priestesses."

He gestured toward the devotees of Artemis standing around the arena, watching the confrontation.

"I stand here only to protect those who are without a champion," Nabonidus said.

"You, the supposed Persian prince? You would die for a fool?"

Nabonidus saw Selsus burrow his foot into the sand and knew what was coming. When the sand flew toward Nabonidus's face, he was already sidestepping the death swing of the club aimed for his head. Selsus adjusted the arc of the club, though, and slammed it into Nabonidus's thigh. The pain burned like fire.

At that moment, John and the others ran into the arena and stopped in their tracks.

"Nabonidus!" the apostle called. "What is happening?"

Selsus smirked. "I see your followers want to make this easy for me. I won't even have to chase them down. Maybe they'll crawl up on their own crosses and take away your reason to fight. What a pitiful champion they have chosen."

The group of Christians moved forward and knelt over Caleb.

"What is happening here?" the apostle demanded again.

Selsus spat in John's direction. "Your champion has chosen to wager your lives in a death match against the champion of Artemis. When he dies, you too will join him before all of Ephesus. You will be a sacrifice to the goddess of the Ephesians."

Chapter Twenty-Four

Dark storm clouds gathered in a tumble of chaotic energy above the Ephesian arena as the two adversaries faced off to the death. Nabonidus ignored the chatter and flurry of those trying to revive and clean Caleb. The eyes of Selsus stared him down, waiting for the slightest distraction to open a point of attack. The pain in Nabonidus's leg throbbed, but it served to keep him alert. On his toes. Balanced.

Demetrius stirred, groaning as he rubbed the back of his head. He rolled onto his back and took in the fluctuating scene unfolding before him. As Nabonidus dodged Selsus's club swing, Demetrius pulled a dagger from under his cloak and tossed it to the German giant.

One of the priests behind Nabonidus scooped up a flagon of oily tar and tossed it at his back. Another priest approached with a torch. At the same moment, the priestesses rushed toward John, disrobing and screeching like demons. The chaos was paralyzing.

Selsus snatched the dagger up and charged at Nabonidus, who dodged behind the cart holding the pot of oil and overturned it on its side to form a barrier between them. Selsus darted out and grabbed the lit torch from the priest, then tossed it into the black tar. A bonfire leapt up.

Thunderclaps pounded across the hills, threatening to shake the city to its foundations. The ground shook as lightning bolts lit up the darkened sky. Wind swirled and spun the smoke into a twirling tower of cinder. The acrid smoke made everyone choke, and the combatants stumbled in opposite directions, fighting for breath. Selsus buried his nose into his forearm and wiped the stinging smoke from his eyes. Demetrius hunched over, retching. The priestesses raced away and the priests backed off, burying their faces in their robes.

John, Urbanus, and the others dragged Caleb away from the flames. Nabonidus hesitated to put them at further risk, so he moved away, circling toward the far side of the arena.

The growing crowd stomped their feet and chanted: "Death, death, death!"

Selsus glanced at the ragtag group dragging their friend away but addressed Nabonidus. "You're only delaying the inevitable. When you die, they will have no champion left. You should have run and come back to fight another day."

Nabonidus dropped to one knee and lifted his arms to the heavens. "Into your hands I commit my life, Yeshua, my God and Savior."

The German charged and plunged his dagger toward the throat of the kneeling Persian.

"For Artemis and the Ephesians," Selsus yelled.

Just then, a lightning bolt seared the air and hit the German man's raised blade. He bounced back as if hitting a stone wall and released the dagger, which suddenly felt as hot as burning coals. The icons of Artemis surrounding the cross melted into blots of silver.

Demetrius reached for the heavens. "Kill him, you fool! By the power of Artemis, strike the blasphemers who dare to curse your name!"

The silversmith reached for the Persian, but Nabonidus stood and wiped him away as if he were nothing worse than a fly. Demetrius lay writhing in the sand.

"Death, death, death!" chanted the crowd, on its feet now.

Nabonidus moved toward Selsus, a giant who appeared no more fierce than a pouting child.

"I give you Demetrius," Selsus offered Nabonidus. "You may reap your vengeance on him first."

"He is nothing but a pawn of forces he doesn't even understand," Nabonidus declared. "The crowd chants for death, but there will be no death where the Lord of life has shown his power. What hope is there now for the champion of the Ephesians when he cannot defeat an unarmed citizen? What hope is there now for a silversmith whose goddess has proven unable to protect and defend him?"

As the heavens rumbled and the crowd chanted, the distinct staccato of hundreds of legionnaires in synchronized march broke through. Nabonidus backed away from the smoldering cart, the charred Asturex, the writhing Demetrius, and the paralyzed Selsus.

Titius, dressed as the general again, arrived at the head of a full legion of Roman soldiers restless for action. Sensing that the show was over, the crowd scattered toward the exits.

A military physician rushed toward Caleb and worked with the apostle and Urbanus to clean him up. It would take a good amount of soap, olive oil, pumice stone, and lubricants to cleanse the affected areas—but Caleb had a chance now.

Nabonidus stood next to Titius and watched as Selsus disappeared into the tunnel that led to the gladiator's cells. The German would live to fight another day, but the Ephesian church had made a deadly enemy.

Ruth applied her healing knowledge to provide soothing creams and gauzes for the significant burns on Caleb's body. Suzanna hovered over her groaning husband as he fought for life and hope in the midst of pain. John, Urbanus, and the other members of the church took shifts praying and chanting psalms over the bedridden former cross maker.

On the third day, Caleb released an agonizing wail of agony. "Yeshua, take me home! Take me home…"

Suzanna lifted a cup of water to his lips. "No, my love. Your child must have his father. Do not quit this battle."

Caleb hung his head. "I wish I had died on that cross," he moaned. "How can I be a father when I cannot even manage this pain? This is a living death."

The servant girls had been picking up local gossip while they visited the market, and they shared news that talk against Christians was growing stronger. Demetrius and Selsus were accomplishing with their tongues what they hadn't been able to do with their weapons.

The light had hardly trickled down the hills of Ephesus when Ruth, Seti, Tryphena, and Tryphosa stepped off the donkey carts they had recruited for their mission. Ruth had done her best to dress in her priestess outfit, although she no longer felt confident and powerful displaying her body. An outward wrap helped ward off the chill of day and add some modesty.

The farm, as others called it, was a fenced-off section of land where ten domed buildings huddled in the center of a field. On the outskirts, running along the fence line, they encountered other structures, but nothing about the exteriors betrayed what went on behind the closed doors, although of course Ruth knew of the horrors inflicted here.

She had to stop it, once and for all.

Ruth led the small band of rescuers to the farm's front gate where two sentries lounged, barely awake.

"Awake, men, and greet your priestess," she said.

The sentries, both young men, bounced to their feet and bowed low, chanting their greeting. One of them, clearly the leader, straightened. "What brings the priestess to this sacred sanctuary of Artemis?"

Ruth drew herself to her full height and glared at the man. "Are you telling me the head priest hasn't told you of our need for more young girls at the temple?"

Both the sentries glanced at each other.

"No message has come while we've been on duty," the leader replied, shaking his head.

"You mean the girls haven't been roused and made ready? Do I have to do everything myself?"

By then, four other young men, sentries from other locations on the compound, arrived.

"Is this for the emperor's festival?" one of the newcomers asked after being informed of Ruth's need for the girls.

Ruth nodded. "We need all the girls—right now."

The newcomer shook his head. "All but five of the girls are locked in the purification chambers until next week. The priest knows this. Why hasn't he come himself to claim them?"

"Perhaps the old man is becoming forgetful." Ruth took a step forward. "I've just been reassigned to serve as matron of this farm. At least give me the five to bring to the temple. I'll explain the situation to the priest when I return."

"Perhaps, in exchange, you can leave your companions here," the leader of the sentries suggested, eyeing Seti, Tryphena, and Tryphosa. "They look experienced enough."

The three women stepped back, but Ruth held her ground. Her mind raced. This mission was becoming more dangerous by the moment.

"These women are needed to prepare the girls," Ruth said in her most commanding tone. "Now, bring the little ones out so we can carry out the priest's orders."

Two of the sentries peeled off and entered one of the nearby domed buildings. Within minutes, they came back outside leading five young girls no more than ten years of age.

The leader stood before the five girls, still glaring at Ruth.

"I'm not sure about this. Perhaps we should send someone to inquire of the priest about this odd request." The leader rested his hand firmly on the shoulder of one of the girls. "I still think we should keep one of your women as a surety until we know the priest's true purpose."

Ruth turned her back and started to walk away.

"Come," she said to Tryphosa, Tryphena and Seti. "It's clear that Selsus will have to come and deal with these upstarts himself. When even the word of a priestess cannot be trusted, only force will be understood."

The other sentries looked toward their leader.

"What are these five girls compared to the trouble we could gain for ourselves?" one of them asked.

Finally, the leader nodded, lowering his hand. "Go with the priestess, girls, and learn your craft well."

Ruth's heart leapt with joy and she could hardly contain herself. Although she hadn't been able to rescue all the girls, these five girls were better than nothing.

Within hours, she instructed the young girls on the importance of staying quiet. She then assigned Tryphena and Tryphosa to take the girls to stay with the believers in Sardis. The rest of the church would go on as though this rescue had never happened; they didn't need any further attention.

———————

On the Lord's Day, three weeks after the arena attack, John called the group together.

"It appears it may be time for some of us to move on," John said. "I will go with Mary, the Lord's mother, to revisit the Galilee until it's wise to return. Nabonidus and Daphne will marry soon and visit his homeland in Persia. Titius and Abigail are being called to Rome for duty. Urbanus has been compelled to team up with Apollos to reach the Greeks. Caleb and Suzanna need to find a safer place to heal."

"Where will we go?" Seti asked. "You have bought us and convinced us Yeshua deserves our lives, but now you leave us when things get hard."

The apostle bowed his head. "You ask good questions. There's a growing gathering of believers in Antioch. They're learning more about the teachings of Yeshua, and I would encourage you to go there until you're ready to return to Ephesus. The enemy here is real and he must be defeated by those who are strong in their prayer and sacrifice."

Daphne stepped forward. "But for now, we have a wedding to plan. Nabonidus and I have waited long enough."

Titius and Nabonidus sat under a tree on the crest of Mount Koressus overlooking Ephesus. A storm had dissipated, creating generous puddles around the city but leaving the mountaintop dry.

The Artemission, one of the seven wonders of the world, showed no evidence that one of its priestesses had abandoned her role and that a temple silversmith had lost his encounter with the forces of Yeshua. Instead the arena was setting up for a show featuring wild animals.

"Sometimes you need the big picture to escape being caught up in the little dramas," Titius said. "It makes you wonder what the big picture looks like to the Almighty from where he sits."

Nabonidus tossed a stone toward a tree trunk and watched it ricochet off its target. "Not even the little picture makes sense to me," he said. "Ruth converts to follow Yeshua just when the Almighty shows his power. Asturex gives in to her desire for a statue of Artemis, betrays us, and pays for it all with her life." He threw another stone off the tree trunk. "An innocent fisherman dies trying to save Caleb only to have Caleb almost killed anyway. Sometimes, none of it makes sense."

"Do you know the history of the city you've been fighting in?" Titius asked.

"I've heard stories but I never had any formal schooling."

Titius pointed toward a monument at the outskirts of the city. "Did you know you weren't the first Persian to be a champion here? Persia took over this whole area six hundred years ago." He pointed at another arch. "Alexander the Great beat off the Persians from this space until his general, Lysimachus, took it over." He pointed at a pile of ruins lying on the hill below. "The Egyptians conquered this land three hundred years ago, until Antiochus III gained it back for the Seleucids. That only lasted six years, though, until the area came under the rule of the Pergamons. Their king bequeathed the city to us Romans, and we've made it into the prosperous trading center you see today."

Nabonidus stood up and stretched. "If you Romans are all so civilized, why are there so many gods and goddesses fighting each other? Why do you confuse pleasure and beauty? Why does the god of fortune demand such a high price for your loyalty?"

Titius pointed to the caravan trains pouring in and out of the city. The endless line snaked into the hills and valleys. "North or south, east or west, we keep the roads safe so the world can meet here. Our peace has brought prosperity to the world."

"Your peace has brought slavery, death, oppression, and distrust," Nabonidus said. "Only the good news of Yeshua can bring the peace you imagine. Once I'm married, I will travel these roads to share it."

"It is good you will leave this place," Titius agreed. "The emperor has recalled me to Rome with the next galley and I cannot protect you here. Take the others and go."

"We will leave before this week is done," Nabonidus promised. "What kind of emperor do you obey?"

Titius shrugged and smiled. "No one expected Claudius to gain the throne. He's afflicted with a limp and is partially deaf." He glanced over his shoulder as if checking for a spy who might overhear him. "Claudius is the only Roman emperor born outside Italy. His deformities left him ostracized from public office, and when others were being assassinated he was overlooked."

"How in the world did he rise to the top?"

"The Praetorian Guard declared him after Caligula's assassination because he was the last man in the family still alive," said Titius. "He's been an efficient administrator and ambitious builder. He himself judges the significant court cases in Rome and many admire him."

"It's probably only a matter of time before someone takes his life," Nabonidus mused.

"That's the fear of senators everywhere. And he kills anyone who he thinks undermines him." Titius ran his fingers through his hair and stared into the distance toward Rome. "As long as I'm seen as a loyal general, I'll live. But if I were to somehow get promoted to senator, my life would be at risk."

"Perhaps his nephew Nero will provide more hope for the people."

Titius rose to join Nabonidus. "John knows that one day this city may be as great as Rome. He says that to reach the world, we must first reach Ephesus and Rome." He began walking again down the mountain trail. "No matter who is emperor, one day we must return. For now, my ship awaits."

"Let's go," Nabonidus urged. "I have a woman waiting for me and you only have two hours to tell me everything I need to know about marriage."

When they descended to the front door of the mansion, though, a messenger was waiting for them. The man approached with a sealed scroll.

"From Persia," the messenger said.

Nabonidus gave him a coin and then, once the man had gone, broke the seal. Titius stood waiting as he unrolled it and read.

"It's from Anoshiruvan's brother," Nabonidus said. "It seems his research confirms that there's a good chance I'm a prince of something. He wants me to confirm that I'm willing to claim my role as a prince, if it comes to that."

Titius gave him a man swat on the back. "A prince! It's a good thing you're free from the arena and ready to marry your princess. You better guard your life. After all, you might have a kingdom somewhere to rule!"

The apostle John broke the bread and distributed it around the crowded cellar. It had been months since any of the believers had needed to make use of the hiding place accessible through Daphne's inn, but now they all huddled inside.

There was a knock at the door—the coded knock—and everyone froze in place. As John set the communion tray down and moved to the door, a tsunami of silence fell over the group.

"Who is calling on the name of the Lord?" the apostle asked.

"All who believe," a voice responded. "The heart of Seti seeks entrance."

A collective sigh filled the cellar and John turned to the group with a smile. "It's been many years since I've played this game of hiding and finding. While I'm no longer a child, it's good to feel young again. If only the consequences of being found weren't so serious…"

Seti was welcomed with a sense of joy until the look on her face stilled the room again.

"They came at night," she said. "The home of Nabonidus was burned. All the fountains and pillars are smashed. The gardens have been overturned and covered with stones."

John held his hands in the air to regain silence. "It is as we feared. The enemy's forces are determined to drive us out." He paced back and forth and paused as if listening to an unheard voice. "We will go for now, as we planned."

"What about the wedding?" Seti asked.

The apostle turned and extended his hands toward Nabonidus and Daphne. "We'll have it now. It won't be as we dreamed, and the feast will consist of simple bread and wine, but the celebration of this union will ring through the halls of heaven."

Nabonidus and Daphne stepped forward into the small space created for them among the seated worshippers. Caleb hobbled forward with support from Suzanna and stood next to them.

John raised his hands toward the couple. "Who knows what ceremonies should accompany a Persian prince and a Greek innkeeper who have become Christians? Perhaps only God knows, and he has chosen not to show me. So we'll celebrate the way we know, with the joy of Yeshua binding us all together."

"I only wish Titius and Abigail could have been here," Suzanna said.

Nabonidus closed his eyes, tilted his head back, and waited to receive the blessings he hoped for. Daphne adjusted her shawl forward and glanced shyly toward her husband-to-be. She would be a wife more than a month earlier than expected, and she still had a lot of questions about what this ceremony would mean for her as a woman and a wife.

The apostle began to speak. "At Sinai, God himself performed his own ceremony in his marriage to the children of Jacob. For the followers of Yeshua, we see this as the marriage between Christ and his church. This is the holiest of days for Nabonidus and for Daphne. Today they will enter into a mutually binding covenant which will bring their bodies and souls together as one." John looked around. "We usually have a reception before this moment, to honor the bride and the groom. Their future will be fresh, because the Messiah has made it fresh. There has been no time of separation, but God understands their purity. The engagement contract and marriage contract will have to be signed in our hearts."

Nabonidus chuckled. "Does this mean I have no obligations toward Daphne? That she is victim to my whim?"

Daphne elbowed him lightly but kept her eyes focused on the apostle. "I'm not sure this wedding can be legitimate if we aren't dressed right."

John hushed the chatter with a wave of his hand. "In proper Jewish weddings, we usually veil the bride in harmony with Leah before she met Jacob. This shows that we cherish our bride not for her outer beauty alone but for her inner beauty. We need a marriage canopy, my friends."

Two of the young men beckoned to young women and the four of them took hold of a blanket at each corner and stretched it out over the couple. Nabonidus was so tall that his head rose up into the middle of the impromptu canopy. This generated another chuckle from the group.

John regained their attention. "The Lord Almighty promised our Father Abraham that his descendants would be as numerous as the stars. This canopy reminds us that our homes will always be open in hospitality to everyone."

"We need candles," Suzanna said, beckoning to the group behind her. Two young girls brought forward lit candles to the couple.

"Daphne, you need to walk around Nabonidus seven times," John instructed. "Like Joshua, you will bring the walls of his heart down and claim him exclusively as your own." He watched as she slowly danced around her man. "Now we must sing."

Half a dozen of the attendees joined in the chanting of Hebrews psalms while the others waited patiently for the traditional pieces to be done.

"Now we have to finish the betrothal and finalize the nuptials," John said. "Who has a ring we can exchange?"

Suzanna looked at Caleb and then held out her hand. He lowered his head and then nodded. She took off her own wedding band and handed it over.

"She can use this for now," said Suzanna.

John pointed at the jug of wine and motioned that a cup be poured. "This wine represents the joy marriage ensures. As I pour it, Nabonidus, put the ring on Daphne's finger. Repeat after me—'With this ring, you are consecrated to me according to the grace and love of Yeshua.'"

Nabonidus took the ring from Suzanna. With a smile, he took Daphne's hand. "With this ring, you are consecrated to me according to the grace and love of Yeshua."

John put his hand on Nabonidus and Daphne's. "This covenant is a legal and moral commitment that you are going to provide her with food, clothing, and affection. This is like the covenant God made with his people. Drink of this wine."

Nabonidus and Daphne took turns sipping the cup the apostle offered them.

"Now," John continued, "stomp on the glass to finalize your covenant."

Nabonidus crushed the cup under his heal.

"Mazol tov!" the Jewish believers yelled.

John shushed them, indicating the ceiling as a reminder that the world outside might hear. "Now, we will share the Lord's table as our reception."

Only a few moments later, a thunderous pounding sounded on the door above them and everyone hurried to escape into the safety of the tunnels.

In the residence above the Christians' hiding place, the elderly woman who owned the house shut the swing door that led to the cellar. Once closed, she placed a bench and flowers against it so that it looked no different than any other wall.

She paused, composing herself, and then went to answer the door. Before she had a chance to open it, the door burst inward.

The man she recognized as Selsus, the German giant, swatted her aside like a fly. She let out a cry of alarm as she bounced off a wall and fell into a heap on the floor. The shattering of glass and pottery testified to the rampage that followed as a half-dozen soldiers invaded the home, opening doors and tossing everything they could find.

The woman pulled herself to her feet with the help of a broom that had been lying next to her.

"Perhaps I can help you find what you're searching for," she said in a weak voice.

Selsus kicked over a bench. "I know they're here," he snarled. "There have been too many reports of singing and chanting from this building. If you show us where the apostates are hiding, perhaps you can avoid being the dinner for our lions!"

The old woman set the broom aside and turned the bench back right-side up. She set it against the false wall and sat down. "As you can see, I'm the only one here. If I sing too loudly, for that I am sorry."

Selsus grabbed the old woman by the shoulders and shook her. "The Persian! Tell me where I can find the Persian." When the woman fell, crying out, Selsus turned to the soldiers. "Bring her with us. We'll get her talking. One way or another, we're going to keep the crowds happy for the emperor's new festival."

Chapter Twenty-Five

Caleb and Suzanna sheltered in the tunnel, holding their breath with the rest of the group, while Selsus and his henchmen trashed the house where the church had celebrated its last communion. Despite his injuries, Caleb almost pulled open the door to defend the old woman screaming as she was hit and pushed around.

Suzanna squeezed his arm tightly.

"No, stay," she whispered. "We agreed to this plan. The church needs to survive."

Six hours after all was quiet, the group continued to huddle. Daphne and Nabonidus had taken the chance to sneak up into Daphne's inn, to make sure it was safe. When the coast was clear, the group breached the wall on the other side of the tunnel and crawled up the stairs into the inn. As they climbed, they were wary of any squeak on the wooden boards, any sound of movement which might betray them.

When they were certain that the Romans had gone, the Christians began to disperse in small groups out the inn's back door. They exited through the alley and walked into the darkness, the moonlight filtering through the cloudy skies. They skittered along in the shadows until they reached their homes in safety.

With dawn less than an hour away, Caleb and Suzanna were the last to leave. Caleb stumbled with the assistance of his cane as quietly as he could. The next refuge was two blocks away.

Nabonidus peeked out from under the tarp covering the cart in which he and Daphne had taken refuge as its driver rode through the countryside east of Ephesus. For two days, they had nestled together amidst the household goods they had managed to gather from friends. With their home destroyed, and with Selsus and Demetrius leading an all-out war to track down and eliminate the followers of Yeshua, there were few places to hide.

"Stop and let us out here," Nabonidus instructed the old man at the reins of the donkeys. "We can walk from here."

"It isn't safe to travel without a caravan," the old man warned.

"We'll walk beside you for a while," Nabonidus assured him. "I've travelled this road recently and can offer you protection."

"But what about those who seek your life?"

"They mostly want to claim Ephesus for Artemis. As long as I'm away from the city, they may not care to spend their energy chasing me."

The donkeys halted and Nabonidus assisted Daphne out from under the tarp. Soon they were stretching and basking in the sunshine.

"It was hot under there," Daphne said.

"Not much of a honeymoon suite, I'm afraid," Nabonidus muttered. "I never knew how hard it would be to practice self-control with you so close."

"Perhaps we can find our own space in a caravansary tonight."

"By the time we get to Tarsus, we should feel well married. By the time we get to Persia, we'll be ready for our mission to share the good news of Yeshua and what he has done for all mankind."

Daphne nodded. "Do you think this Saul of Tarsus you met would be willing to teach us?"

"If anyone knows how to take the good news across cultures, it's him."

Titius stood along the railing on the deck of the Roman galley and pointed Abigail toward the North African coast.

"Over there is Carthage, where Rome won the battle which made us the power of the seas," he explained. "Two hundred years ago, Hannibal took his elephants across to Gaul and attacked Italy from the north. He managed to destroy much of the Roman army, but we rebuilt and eventually won the Punic Wars."

Abigail soaked in the sun and watched a school of dolphins skipping through the whitecaps. "But wouldn't they rebuild, too, and try again?"

Titius smiled. "We dismantled their navy. We didn't want them to have any ships large enough to carry an elephant. If they can't get the elephants across the water, we don't have to fight them."

Abigail examined the massive sails billowing in the breeze above the deck. "How big is this thing?"

Titius pointed down the side of the ship. "It's a trireme, with three banks of oars. But we usually use four and five banks of rowers in battle. We have one hundred eighty men rowing when we need them. I marvel at how the carpenters use the oak, cedar, pine, and fir to knit the ship together."

"How do you figure out how to sail such a big thing?"

Titius leaned against the railing. "The craftsmen have to consider many things, including how to accommodate all our legions, rowers, and sailors. They must also think about how fast the ship needs to travel, how heavy it will be and where the waterline will be compared to where the openings are for oars. They have to make sure the ship is stable and strong."

The ship swung portside and headed for the island harbor where it would spend the night.

"I assume this is Syracuse," Abigail said.

Titius examined the roiling black clouds forming above the horizon. "Yes. Two nights until we get to Rome. Pray the emperor spares me and the Almighty gives me wisdom about how to respond."

The next hours involved a lot of activity as the oarsmen guided the ship into port. The first drops of rain fell as Titius and Abigail stepped onto the dock.

A nobleman, dressed in a toga edged with a purple stripe, approached Titius with a scroll in hand.

"I am Porpheus, my lord," the nobleman said. "The emperor wishes to invite you to join a special meeting of senators when you arrive in Rome. I'm here to assist with any of your needs."

The shiver running up Titius's spine caused him to freeze as he reached for the scroll.

"When am I expected at this meeting?" Titius asked.

"You have ten days," Porpheus replied. "The new general will take over your legion as soon as you arrive in Rome."

———————————

Ruth stood overlooking the Artemission from the rooftop of the home where she'd sought refuge after Selsus's raid. Merchants were setting up their booths in the temple courtyard; even Demetrius was busy unloading an oxcart of his precious silver icons.

She watched as the first of the priestesses emerged from the temple to troll for eager worshippers. Ruth shuddered as she remembered what it had been like to play that role in her own years as priestess of Artemis.

Dressed in a plain brown tunic and shawl, Ruth crept down the stairs of the building. No one gave her a second glance as she walked through the alley.

Before she got too far, however, two young girls leading a goat stopped her.

"We haven't seen you here before," the older girl said. "What is your name and where do you come from?"

Ruth crouched down against the retaining wall of a garden. "My name is Ruth, and I haven't been in this part of the city before. What are your names?"

The older girl pulled the rope on the goat a little closer and pushed the animal's nose toward Ruth. "If you offer her something to eat, she'll be happy."

Ruth fished into the pocket of her robe and pulled out a small apple. "All I have is this fruit." She extended her hand and let the goat chomp it down.

"My name is Aite," said the girl. "My name means 'good.' One day I'll be the most beautiful priestess in the Artemission."

The younger girl then stepped forward, with her hand on the back of the goat. "My name is Alexine. It means 'protector.' One day I will be a guardian of the temple."

Ruth continued to pet the goat as it nuzzled her robe for more food, but Aite pulled the goat away.

"This one is always hungry," Aite said. "She'll eat your robe if you're not careful."

Ruth stood and brushed away the goat's nose from her pocket. "Why do you want to become a priestess?"

Aite stood tall and faced the Artemission. "Every day I see the most beautiful women walking around the temple. They make the men so happy. My father says it is the greatest honor for a girl to become a priestess."

The girl spun in place with her hands raised over her head.

Ruth backed away from the girls. "I have been a priestess," she said. "Artemis demands much sacrifice. If I'd been able to choose, it would have been better to find a nobleman and marry. You would do well to find a kinder god."

Alexine rose on her tiptoes in defiance. "Artemis is great in Ephesus. There is no god or goddess greater. If anyone says she isn't great, they'll be fed to the lions."

Ruth smiled. "Dear, Alexine, you are indeed a protector. Do you think it's better to fear a god or love a god?"

"Which god have you ever loved?" Aite asked. "Gods and goddesses are to be honored and obeyed. They don't come near enough for us to love them. We love each other instead to show our worship."

"What if I told you I knew one god who did come close enough for us to love him?"

Alexine raised her fist toward Ruth. "If there was such a god, my father would have told us. Your lies will make you food for the lions. Leave us alone before we report you to the temple guards."

Ruth raised her hands and backed away. "The temple guards have been my friends since I was your age. There's no need for you to bother them when they're busy. Why don't you take your goat where she needs to go and I'll go where I need to go?"

Aite rested her hand on the goat's back and cocked her head inquisitively. "What is the name of this god who loves? How do you know him?"

"His name is Yeshua," Ruth said as she continued to back away. "If you pray to him, he will teach you about a love you can never find in the Artemission."

As Ruth turned to go, she could hear the girls arguing behind her.

Urbanus crouched in his hiding place behind a false-paneled cupboard as he heard pottery smashed in the main living room just outside. He was a fugitive hiding in his own residence, where Selsus was taking his fury out on the fountains and décor. Urbanus even thought he smelled smoke drifting through the cracks in the door. The terrified screams of his servants haunted his spirit, but he had promised to stay in place—and he would.

He had learned much from the apostle John in the years since his initial tutoring by Aquila and Priscilla in Rome. He had survived a theological bootcamp with Apollos and felt a calling toward Britannia and the cultish druids who kept the population there bound in dark fear. Much of the people of that land were terrorized by fear of gods and goddesses who enslaved them in superstition and sorcery.

Urbanus's knees burned in their cramped position and he attempted to divert his thinking by praying for each of the Christians who were even now attempting to escape the disaster which had befallen them. Nabonidus and Daphne, on their way to Tarsus, newly married, taking the good news of Yeshua to Persia... Caleb and Suzanna, still in hiding, hoping to take the message to Germania soon... Titius and Abigail, on their way to Rome, unsure as to what the emperor's bidding might mean for them... and Ruth, timid, daring, curious, eager, a woman in need of someone to guide and guard her...

The predetermined signal knock was so faint that Urbanus almost missed it. Still, he waited the required time, his knees and calves burning even worse than before. When he heard the second knock, as arranged, he released the catch and eased himself out of his hiding place.

As he cautiously poked his head out the door, a rough hand grabbed his hair and threw him across the room. Before he could move, vicious fists pulverized him into unconsciousness.

———————————

Ruth slipped in through the back door of the crude shack where she'd arranged to meet Seti. Just inside, she found the girl sobbing.

"What is it?" Ruth asked. "Why are you crying?"

Seti buried her head between her knees. Ruth hurried to her, dropped down, and tilted up the girl's face, which was bruised and bleeding. Her lip was swollen. Her eyes were swelling shut.

"This is a trap," Seti said. "They've beaten the others and found out where we all live. You shouldn't have come."

"What do you mean?" Ruth asked, thinking fast. She had to go. But where could she go? Was it safe to head to Daphne's inn?

The sound of footsteps behind her froze her in place.

"Too late, priestess," said a familiar voice. "We've already rounded up most of the apostates in this city."

"Demetrius," Ruth said. "Leave this one. Take me instead. I'm the one you want."

Demetrius dug his fingers into her shoulder and pulled her backwards. Before she could guard herself, he punched her in the face. She flung her arms up in vain and her nose snapped from the blow as blood gushed down.

The silversmith grabbed her by the hair and dragged her across the floor as she vainly tried to find her footing.

"Please, I'll go with you," Ruth blurted as he pulled her toward a fountain. "You don't need to do this."

"I'll do this and more. You were the best, the most beautiful. How could you dare betray Artemis?" Demetrius grabbed the back of her head and shoved it into the fountain water. She kicked and attempted to push herself out of the pool, but he was too strong.

When she went limp, he pulled her up and threw her on the ground.

"May the crows pick your bones clean," he roared. He then kicked her in the side and stomped out.

Seti crawled to her side, wailing. "Ruth, oh Ruth, what have we done to you?"

She wiped the steady gush of blood coming from Ruth's nose and tried to feel for breath. There was nothing… no rise and fall of the former priestess's chest. Seti pushed and pushed on Ruth's chest in a way she had once seen another slave help a person who had drowned.

When she could do no more, Seti laid her head on Ruth's chest and cried out in anguish to Yeshua.

Caleb and Suzanna had been on the way to the shack where Seti had told them to meet her when two of Selsus's henchmen stepped out from behind a hedge and clubbed them. Caleb threw himself between Suzanna and her attacker, but he only succeeded in drawing the ferocious anger of both of the ambushers. As he fell under their blows, he watched Suzanna scratch and scream.

He was still semi-conscious when his arms were yanked behind his back and secured with twine. His ribs screamed in pain as he was tossed like a sack of olives onto a wooden cart. He caught a glimpse of Suzanna being tied to the back.

"Walk, you wench," a voice mocked her. "You'll be a special treat for the wild dogs in the arena. We'll finish your husband's crucifixion and then he can watch the dogs enjoy themselves in front of all of Ephesus."

"We live for Yeshua and we will die for Yeshua," Suzanna declared defiantly.

Titius put a finger across his lips, a signal for Abigail to keep quiet. The two had acquired the garb of nobility as they slipped slowly down the alley away from the governor's mansion. His dress as a general would only draw unwanted attention at this point. Finding a ship leaving Syracuse without being seen was a near impossibility.

Porpheus's warning that the emperor was working to confirm Titius as a senator was a clear signal that the end was near. The years Titius had spent setting up a network of informants was paying off. It seemed that his stop in Syracuse was a trap, that in Rome he would be exposed and forced to commit suicide.

"Two more streets and then we'll enter the stables," Titius directed his wife. "The head groom knows our family and we can change our disguise there. In the meantime, walk like a noblewoman. Slow and dignified."

They adjusted their gait to flow with the pedestrians and stepped out of the way of an oxcart as they neared the stables. As they neared their destination, Titius noticed the flash of a legionnaire's uniform across the entrance to the stables, and he halted in his tracks, gently pulling Abigail by the elbow to press up against the bakery they were passing.

Titius and Abigail stepped into the shop and examined the fresh bread and delicacies. They purchased several buns and tried a piece of a fruit bread the baker offered as an enticement. They agreed to buy the loaf.

"Do you have any deliveries being made this morning?" Titius asked the man.

The baker glanced outside the shop and nodded. "Actually, my son is just about to arrive by cart. He'll be taking some fresh loaves to the temple priests. Why is that important to you?"

Titius smiled and looked at Abigail. "My wife is heavy with child and shouldn't walk far. We'd appreciate it if you could let us travel in the back of your wagon. We'll pay you well and not cause any inconvenience."

Arrangements were made and soon Titius and Abigail had slipped onto the back of the wagon amidst the most heavenly of aromas they could imagine.

"You better eat something to stave off your temptations," the baker suggested.

Titius handed over an extra silver coin. "There are others who may ask about us," he said. "This should help your memory think of other places we may have gone."

The baker frowned. "What about my son?"

"Your son will be safe," Titius assured him.

Chapter Twenty-Six

On their way to Tarsus, the rains poured down and hampered travel, so Nabonidus and Daphne chose to huddle down in the city of Magnesia. Nabonidus's nerves were on edge each time the sound of galloping hooves betrayed the approach of a significant group of newcomers.

Daphne busied herself with locating food and doing the best she could to settle the mind of her new husband.

"Nabonidus, rest, my love," she said. "You said yourself that Selsus was more interested in making sure Ephesus was being guarded for Artemis. We're out of his way now."

The big Persian man paced back and forth in their small room, glancing out the window each time he passed. The club he held in a death grip was grimy with sweat as he twisted it around and around. He'd had flashbacks throughout the night, ruining yet another chance for alone time with his new bride. The thought of what could be happening to the believers in Ephesus, who had been part of the church in his home, strangled any thoughts of love.

"If you're going to worry so much, we might as well be back there with them," Daphne said.

Nabonidus slumped down into a chair. "They're okay, right? They had a plan. If I went back now, it would probably make things worse."

Daphne stepped behind him and rubbed his shoulders gently. "Easy, my love. You've fought your fight. You've earned the chance to see your homeland again."

The former gladiator hunched and rotated his shoulders until he sighed and pushed back against Daphne. "I'm sorry you have to deal with all this. I should have finished things off in the arena with Selsus and Demetrius. How am I ever going to tell anyone about Yeshua when I can't even enjoy one night with my wife?"

Daphne soothed him with a warm cup of tea and a hearty meal of lamb stew and flatbread. She had run her hands through his hair, singing softly as he ate, and he got the message. He took her hand, kissed it gently, and rose to embrace her.

As he did, an urgent knocking sounded at the door.

Nabonidus pulled Daphne behind him and walked cautiously to the door. He opened it slowly and observed the young man standing there. To his surprise, it was one of the new believers who had been attending the church in his old home.

"Pelonius," he said. "What are you doing here? How are the others?"

The young man barged into the room and closed the door behind them. "Everyone has been captured," he said. "They've been beaten and taken to the arena. I saw Caleb in a cart, not moving, covered in blood. Suzanna was tied behind the cart being whipped by some of Selsus's men."

Daphne went to her husband immediately. "Nabonidus, hear me. I know you. You've already proven yourself as the Champion of Ephesus. And you might even be a prince somewhere in Persia."

He pushed her hands away and moved to the front of the room, looking out the window. "They're out there. They need me now more than ever."

Daphne moved to block his exit. "You've already proved that you think of others first. Now is the time to think of you. Of what Yeshua has for you in the future."

"Exactly. I always think of others first. If Yeshua wants me to become a prince in Persia, a prince who shares his good news, then he can take me through the fire ahead."

"Please… we've only just begun our lives together."

Nabonidus swung the club down hard on the windowsill, breaking it. The top half flew up and bounced off the ceiling, only to fall at Daphne's feet. She winced at the rage enveloping her husband. He was out the door and running before she could say a word.

Daphne went outside in the rain and watched her husband disappear down the street.

Pelonius came up alongside her. "What are you going to do? I think he's headed back to Ephesus."

Daphne turned and walked back into the building. She immediately started packing up her things. She was a married woman now, even if it didn't feel like it. Her place was with her husband.

"Find me a cart driver who can take me to Ephesus," she called over her shoulder to Pelonius.

Caleb regained consciousness but saw nothing through his swollen eyes. His jaw pulsed and his head throbbed like a drum beating over and over. His ribs burned like fire. The guttural laughter of Selsus in the distance was unmistakable.

Where is Suzanna? he wondered.

A twisting vice grip on his ankles released from him an involuntary scream. A pair of men dragged him out of the cart and dropped him on the paving stones below. One of them kicked him in the kidney, eliciting another scream as he attempted to curl into a fetal position.

Yeshua, help me.

The men picked him up by the hands and feet and half-dragged him across the rough ground to a place just off the road where they dumped him. The place stunk of urine and feces. Was he back in the arena?

A chorus of groans joined his own and he fought past his own pain to listen. If he concentrated, he thought he made out the voices of the other Christians.

Titius hung onto the railing as a storm raged against the small ship. Why hadn't he chosen a larger vessel, one capable of riding out a storm? The ship rose up one trough and dropped like a boulder into the next. Before long he was soaked to the skin and his grip was slipping along the slimy rail.

The captain of the junker was fighting a losing battle against the wind and waves. The vessel's single sail had been ripped to shreds.

Instead of crossing to Alexandria, as had been the plan, they were being driven back east...

He groaned. Right back toward Ephesus.

Titius pondered the dark night and yelled, "Yeshua, what are you doing?"

Suzanna stood chained to the bars of a cell. The darkness was thick with evil and shivers ran down her spine as she strained to decipher the faint sounds coming from elsewhere in the cavernous building. She had lost control of her bladder hours earlier and the discomfort and stench of the place, combined with her pregnancy, left her retching. The vomit splashed onto her bare feet.

A cool breeze from the storm outside found its way through the maze of underground passageways and touched the rips in the robe, put there by the whip of a depraved tyrant. As she stroked her lacerated back, she heard a deep whisper and lifted her head to listen.

Be strong and courageous, my daughter, the voice said to her. *I am with you. Your witness for me will be known and not forgotten.*

She bowed her head and let tears course down her cheeks and off her chin.

"Yeshua, I so wanted to be a mother," she said. "To hold this little one and tell him all I know about who you are… I wanted him to meet his father."

A hand touched her arm and she jumped.

"Don't be afraid," a girl's voice whispered. "Ruth sent me."

"Ruth?" Suzanna tried hard to peer through the inky blackness. She couldn't see the girl speaking to her, but she could feel the small hand holding her by the elbow. "Is she here?"

"She's in a place where there's no more pain. A place she has hardly dared to dream about. A place of peace and light."

"Who are you?" Suzanna whispered. "How did you find me?"

"I am a servant of Yeshua. I've come to take you with me."

The chains fell off of Suzanna's wrists and her arms dropped like lead weights to her side.

"Come!" the girl whispered. "Seti is waiting to shelter you."

"My husband, Caleb… I need to take him with me." But the girl kept tugging at her. "I need him."

"He has a different path to walk tonight. Follow me. Yeshua is alive in this place."

As they left the cell, every step was a lesson in enduring pain. The jagged rips in her skin split open and the blood flowed freely again. Her blistered feet screamed for her to stop walking. Even the child within kicked hard to draw attention to the chaos which had fallen on their world.

"Come!" the girl called.

The windswept vessel struck an outcropping of rocks within sight of the barren shoreline. The splintering of wood was like a thunderclap.

"Jump!" the captain yelled.

Titius stumbled toward the cabin and wrenched open the door where Abigail was curled up on the floor, covering her head. He grabbed hold of her and dragged her onto the deck the moment the ship lurched sideways under the power of the storm surge. Wave after wave washed over them as the boat disintegrated underfoot. Finally, there was no place to stand and Titius held Abigail tight as they were swept into the raging sea.

Twice the power of the sea almost wrestled Abigail from his arms, but Titius fought like the trained warrior he was, bobbing up from every dunking, sputtering and gasping but refusing to quit. On the surface, pieces of the wreck threatened to knock him senseless but he finally wrapped an arm around a section of rail and held on as the piece was driven toward the rocks.

His shoulder crashed into a boulder, forcing him to release his hold on Abigail. Her scream was choked off as she was swept back into the tumbling tower of water. Disoriented, Titius fought to surface and got his feet under him. He tumbled like a bundle of kelp until he washed up on the rocky beach.

He rolled away from the grasping reach of the sea and pushed himself to his knees. The pain in his shoulder was dizzying, but Abigail was somewhere out there. He half-expected a throng of spectators to appear, their thumbs down to see him executed.

But he wasn't done with this battle.

He waded into the water, searching in the dark for anything to help him find his beloved.

"Yeshua!" he screamed. "Yeshua!"

The cold, still body of a young girl lay next to Urbanus, unresponsive as the first tentative fingers of dawn light moved aside the cover of darkness in the gladiators' cells under the arena. The body's chilled flesh felt as lifeless as a fish. The girl's face had been mangled beyond recognition. It looked to Urbanus as though she'd been ripped apart by the jaws of a wild beast.

From the far side of the cell, he heard a woman's groan.

"Hello," he called softly.

"Urbanus?" the woman replied. "Is that you?"

"Yes. Who are you?"

"I'm Tryphena… Tryphosa is in hiding. The soldiers also brought Caleb and Suzanna…" She attempted to stand but didn't have the strength. "I heard Demetrius tell that German gladiator that Ruth is dead and that Seti's going to be lashed to death in the arena. How are you doing?"

Urbanus gently reached his free hand up to rub his temple. His scalp was caked in blood and dirt. Brilliant starlight kaleidoscoped through his vision despite the dimness of this stone prison. As he attempted to sit up, the drum beat reverberated through his skull, increasing in volume.

"Urbanus! I asked, how are you?"

"I've never been beaten this badly in my life," he admitted. "The apostle warned us we would have to pay the price for choosing Yeshua, but I never stopped to imagine how much it would hurt. Did they hurt you?"

Tryphena was quiet for a moment. "They hurt me like men hurt women. Over and over. I hoped I would die and wake up in heaven, but instead here I am. We had just come back from delivering the children from the farm to the believers in Sardis. We arrived at the house at the wrong time."

"I'm sorry. I'd always hoped Yeshua would prove his power by protecting us, but I guess if he didn't protect himself from the cross we cannot expect more. Can you remember a song to calm our spirits?"

As Tryphena hummed her psalms of lament, Urbanus mumbled the words designed for centuries to bring light into the deepest chambers of the darkness of an abandoned soul.

They were still sounding their prayers of hope when the first snarls of wild beasts sounded outside their cells.

———

Titius's heart skipped a beat when he saw a man's body twisted up with the wreckage and seaweed. He pushed his weary legs to stumble and fall, pulling at the body. It was the captain, breathless and lifeless.

On his feet again, he scanned the waves, still mocking him.

"Abigail," he called, then bent over in a fit of lung-searing coughing. The drying salt and sand in his wounds burned like fire. "Abigail!"

His sense of urgency pulled him away from the direction where he'd wandered. He pivoted and pushed himself in the opposite direction, scanning the sea as he went.

He almost ignored the boy standing at the water's edge sorting through the debris. Those planks, netting, half-basket, and stray bits of sail meant nothing to him.

"Abigail…"

The boy turned and faced him. As he prepared to pass by, the boy spoke up in Aramaic. "Do you seek a woman?"

Titius fell to his knees and took the boy by the shoulders. "Yes. Did you see her?"

"My father found her this morning. She wasn't moving." The boy pointed down the beach. "They carried her home."

Titius sprang to his feet. "Show me where. Take me to her."

Nabonidus used his rage as fuel to power his way through the last twenty miles toward the city. Traffic had been light when he started, but now the heavy procession of oxcarts, loaded donkeys, camels, and small, hand-drawn pullcarts filled every bit of the road.

He attempted to run along the side of the road, weaving between horses, dogs, and people using the shoulder to pass others. Twice, he twisted his ankle badly enough that he knew he should stop and give attention to the injury. Still he pressed on, ignoring the angry shouts of others who didn't appreciate being bumped or pushed out of the way.

He didn't even think of his new bride he'd left behind. He just pushed himself up hills and down slopes, eager to get his first glimpse of the Artemission. If all these people were going to the emperor's new festival, he was determined his friends weren't going to be the main attraction.

Several times he considered the possibility this was all a trap to get him to come back for a fight with Selsus. Each time, he convinced himself that if that were the case, he was ready to prove he was the true champion of Ephesus.

The argument in his head distracted him from noticing the dog darting away from the stick of a camel herder. The dog skidded under the front edge of a cart and darted right into Nabonidus's path. In moments, he was tumbling down an embankment while the dog yelped and barked above.

Daphne joined the long line of merchants, pilgrims, and curiosity-seekers on their way into Ephesus for the emperor's festival. Pelonius sat beside her at the back of the cart, legs dangling over the edge. The cart driver and his wife chattered among themselves and largely ignored their passengers.

The rains let up after noon, but they were already drenched. Smoke drifted in from a nearby field where a farmer was burning off the dregs of his crop; the shifting winds brought acrid plumes into the eyes, throats, and lungs of the travelers so they were soon choking and gagging.

"What will your husband do when he reaches the city?" Pelonius asked.

Daphne held a head scarf over her nose and mouth. "He'll probably try to rescue everyone. Yeshua has made him strong, like the old story of Samson, but he doesn't have the fear that might give him wisdom in dealing with our enemies."

"Will he go into the arena again?"

"Oh, I'm sure Selsus and Demetrius will try to provoke him into a public fight."

"Why does he put himself into so much danger?"

Daphne shifted for a moment before replying. "I think he doesn't yet fully understand there is only one Savior—and it isn't him."

"I need to stretch my legs." Pelonius hopped off the cart and walked along behind it for the next stretch of road. "Do you think he can win? Will you go to watch him fight?"

Daphne also stepped off the cart and started to walk. "Now that you ask, I'm not sure why I'm even going back. If Selsus is trying to destroy everyone in the church, he'll probably have people out looking for us. We're making it too easy for him to feed the lions today."

A commotion up ahead caught their attention, and Daphne sent Pelonius jogging ahead to find out what was going on.

Within a few minutes, he had returned.

"It's your husband," Pelonius reported. "He's been injured and is refusing help. I think his foot is broken."

Daphne jogged with Pelonius until she arrived at the spot alongside the road where Nabonidus still sat. He had a blood-stained rag wrapped around his head and a thick winding of other rags around his foot.

"It was a God-forsaken dog," Nabonidus said to them in greeting. "Why did you come? There will only be trouble ahead."

"Yes," Daphne agreed. "And you're determined to walk right into it. Perhaps Yeshua is giving you the chance to avoid another fight."

Nabonidus waggled his head back and forth. "They have no one. This was the church at my house. I believe Yeshua prepared me for this moment to stand up for him—"

"What about our mission to Persia?"

"It will have to wait. Today we have a mission with the people of Ephesus. They need to know there's a living God who's greater than Artemis."

Daphne motioned to the oxcart driver who was passing by. The cart halted long enough to allow Nabonidus to hop over and sit back on the cart. Daphne and Pelonius walked behind the cart, watching for the animal droppings scattered liberally on the roadway.

Daphne raised her head, saw Mount Koressus in the distance, and shivered. "Yeshua, be with us all."

Chapter Twenty-Seven

When Titius entered the darkened room where the boy led him, he immediately saw Abigail lying on a bed. The trained assassin, so familiar with death, threw himself on her and listened for signs of breath.

"She's alive," a man's voice behind him said. "I pumped the seawater from her lungs. My wife has changed her and warmed her. You're fortunate we found her."

Titius rose to his knees and turned toward the man. The recognition was instantaneous. "Julian!"

"Hello, General." The broad-chested soldier leaned calmly against a wall with his arms crossed. His thick flaxen hair was shoulder-length and wavy. He wore a loose brown robe to midcalf. His feet were bare.

Titius rose to his feet and faced his wife's rescuer. "The last time I saw you, you were giving me your sword in the governor's garden in Damascus. I'd assumed you had died."

"It appears to be a good thing I didn't. But as you know, all thespian assassins die to their past in order to better embrace their future."

"Are you still a thespian assassin?"

The military man uncrossed his arms and moved to the door. "I finished my last assignment. This new emperor is out to purge anyone who opposes him. Your name is on the list."

"Have you been tasked with ending my life?"

Julian motioned for Titius to join him. "Come, walk with me. My wife will watch her."

Titius followed Julian out the door and watched the storm clouds dissipating overhead. The first rays of sun broke through and touched his damp attire. The surface of the sea rolled gently. Gulls overhead glided on the breeze, and Julian's son had gone back to beachcombing.

"It's ironic, isn't it?" Julian asked, chuckling. "I came to hide here so I wouldn't have to find you, and yet here you are. We Romans believe in the fates, so it seems I'm meant to finish the task I was given."

Titius noted that Julian had a sheathed dagger. "How did you imagine you would take my life?"

Julian paused, his hand resting on the dagger hilt. "That's the funny part. I've imagined using poison, a dagger, drowning, even beheading… but in every case, I imagine you escape. I've known you too long to think you would fall prey to something unimaginative. What would you suggest?"

The two men stood side by side watching the waves roll in to the shore.

"There's a dead sea captain up the beach," Titius said. "Perhaps he could fit in with your plans for me."

"You're suggesting I could make it seem like that sea captain is actually you… make it seem like you died at sea." Julian paused, thinking about it. "Perhaps. What mark of identity might work to make them think this otherwise unidentifiable body might be you?"

"I have a family ring. If you put it on the decomposed body, the crest will convince anyone who sees it that the body is mine."

"You'll have to give up everything and never return," Julian warned.

"When my wife revives, we will leave immediately," Titius agreed. "I just have one quick task to complete in Ephesus. After that, I think Britannia is calling my name."

Tryphena stopped humming as she heard the slither of sandals on stone echoing through the cells. Someone was coming. Warmth and light penetrated the cold darkness in which Urbanus and she had suffered in anticipation of their end. The snarls of the beasts had quieted for a short time, but suddenly they increased again as the newcomer's presence grew more obvious.

Seti appeared, carrying a handful of barley loaves and a flagon of cheap wine.

"I bring gifts," she said. Her eyes went to the body of the dead girl lying next to where Urbanus was shackled. She bent over and examined the girl's swollen face. "Who's this? It's hard to tell. After those beasts attack, they don't leave much behind…"

"You look terrible, Seti," Tryphena observed. "May the Almighty strike back on those who did this to you."

Seti rose and stepped closer to her. "Bless you for your prayers. I've been given only a short time to bring you this food. I don't know yet whether they'll end my life with a whip in the arena or with the soldiers in their quarters." She handed a bun to Urbanus. "I feel nothing. This isn't how I imagined it would be to follow Yeshua."

"What will they do with us?" Tryphena asked.

"We've been scheduled as the finale for the current games," Seti said. "Our tormentors wish us to be gorged enough to give the snarly beasts something worth eating."

"I heard they were lions," Tryphena said. "Or are they wild dogs?"

Seti handed another bun to Tryphena, then glanced toward Urbanus. "You both look terrible, but not as bad as poor Ruth. Demetrius had no mercy on her."

"Are we to be eaten or crucified?" Tryphena persisted. "How did you get in here with all of this food?"

Urbanus broke off a small piece of the dry bread and stuffed it into his cheek to savor. "What's happened to the others?" he mumbled.

Seti slumped beside him and wept. "Ruth is gone. I saw four other bodies in the hall. But do you know who this girl is?"

Tryphena spoke up. "I heard Demetrius call her Aite. Her own father turned her in. Demetrius said that Ruth had polluted her mind with thoughts of a god who loves. He wouldn't allow a girl to have such thoughts, especially not one who wanted to be a priestess of Artemis. He beat her until she didn't move again."

The three sentenced to die mourned the one in their midst who had already fulfilled that sentence.

Nabonidus eased himself off the oxcart and thanked the couple who had facilitated his ride into Ephesus. They'd carried him right up to the agora.

"May the Almighty bless your business, your family, and your journey," Daphne said, adding her own words of appreciation.

Pelonius surveyed the crowded market. "I'll find a cane or a crutch of some form," he said as he went off toward a row of booths.

Nabonidus's first thought was to find a place to hide, but before he knew what was happening a group of four thugs, each man equal in size to him, stepped out of the agora and approached.

The leader bumped up against Nabonidus so they stood chest to chest. "Selsus says you have some unfinished business to complete in the arena this week. We're here to take you to your quarters. I'm sure you're familiar with them."

Daphne stepped up to her husband's side. "This man is married, and we stand as one. Whatever happens to him, happens to me."

Nabonidus put out his arm and pushed her back protectively. "No, I stand on my own. Leave her out of this."

One of the henchmen reached over and attempted to grab Daphne, but Nabonidus chopped at his wrist and brought back his elbow under the man's chin. One minute the man was standing and the next he was out cold on the ground.

Two other men charged Nabonidus, one low and one high. He kicked the lower one across the jaw but was leveled by the other. The leader of the group then brought his knee into the Persian's kidneys.

Before Nabonidus could catch his breath, he found himself lying facedown with his arms wrenched hard behind his back. The men tied his wrists together.

"Leave him alone," Daphne yelled, striking out at the men who knelt across her husband's neck and lower back. One of them knocked her off her feet, leaving her breathless.

A group of sailors suddenly jumped into the fray, punching and kicking the men who held Nabonidus. Men and women on the fringe cheered and jeered their encouragement as chaos reigned in the marketplace.

At that moment, Selsus stepped into the commotion and single-handedly threw off the fishermen.

"So, our little ploy worked," Selsus said. "The Persian couldn't resist coming back to play the role of savior. Ephesus and Artemis are finally going to crown their real champion."

Nabonidus arched his neck to look up at his nemesis. "I've already been freed. You'll have to find another to challenge for your title."

Selsus grasped the back of Nabonidus's neck. "A freed man, he says. Does anyone see the ivory pendant declaring this man to be free? I for one do not see any evidence of it."

Nabonidus was jerked to his feet, only to spot Pelonius standing right behind Selsus, smiling. "Welcome back, champion of Yeshua."

———————

The arena loomed large as Titius, dressed as a beggar, tapped his way through the crowd streaming into the cavernous space. A nobleman cursed the vagrant and lashed out with his own cane, catching Titius across his back. Apart from a slight stumble, Titius hardly reacted.

As he neared the entrance gates, he veered off and tapped his way alongside the wall toward the gladiators' entrance. No one paid him any heed as he slipped out of sight. In the dimness of the dingy passageways, he was almost invisible.

In the minutes that followed, a gladiator assigned to guard duty disappeared, a legionnaire strutting through the cells failed to show up at the exit where he was expected, a guardian checking in on the lions didn't return to confirm with his assistant that all was well, and the physician hurrying to alert someone that things weren't right didn't arrive at his destination.

Titius continued on until he reached the cells where Urbanus, Seti, and Tryphena knelt in prayer.

Seti rose to meet him. "We are ready to meet our maker. We have the peace of Yeshua to guard us."

Titius pulled back the hood hiding his face. "Good, because I'm here to get you out. Where are the others?"

Seti stood, her mouth open in surprise. Tryphena hugged Titius. Urbanus remained sitting, not comprehending what was happening.

"How did you get here?" he asked.

"I'll tell you later," Titius assured him. "I've brought you some clothes to change into. Put them overtop and keep your heads low as you follow me. Quick, before anyone notices you're gone."

The four—a limping gladiator, an armed legionnaire, a slight-framed physician, and a timid messenger—walked quickly into the sunshine and blended with the crowd until they veered off and away from the arena.

As the group slipped into an alley, however, Titius—now dressed as the armed legionnaire—turned and walked brazenly back into the gladiator cells. As he did, he was confronted by Selsus.

"There you are," Selsus bellowed. "The guardian for the lions is missing! Check and see that the beasts haven't already been fed. We have a feast for them."

Titius put his fist over his breastplate, nodded, and turned toward the caged lions without a word.

Selsus called after him. "When you're done, bring the prisoners to the cage so we can display them for the crowd."

The noise of the crowd grew as entertainers prompted responses with their lude displays of revelry. Titius walked quickly by the lions and confirmed the stain of blood left by the animals who sat comfortably in preparation for their post-meal naps. They had already eaten their fill.

On the other side of the arena, he saw a group of Selsus's henchmen. Nearby, Daphne and Suzanna had been tied securely to whipping posts. The men were making suggestive comments and taking bets on how long the women would last under the lashes.

Titius walked into the middle of the group without hesitation and untied the women. Daphne's mouth fell open in recognition and Suzanna was about to ask what he was doing there; he simply glared at her and put a finger to his lips.

One of the henchmen intervened. "What do you think you're doing?"

Titius looked him in the eye. "Are these the women Selsus wants whipped in front of the crowd?"

"Isn't that obvious?"

"Selsus ordered me to bring them to the cages up front where the crowd can see them. If you're the ones doing the whipping, you better get yourselves ready."

The henchman stepped closer. "We were about to have a little fun with them before their public appearance. We can bring them to the cages when we're done."

Titius drew himself up to his full height, staring. "If you want to face Selsus, and perhaps spend some time in the arena with the beasts for disobeying his orders, feel free. I would rather live another day."

The man backed off, but only after adding a few more crude comments to the women about his ambitions for what was about to happen.

Titius detoured the women into a small room below the arena where he tossed them a pair of beggars' rags. "Put these on. When we go, I'm going to chase you ahead of me out of this place. Just keep your heads low and act afraid."

"Where will we go?" Daphne said. "Nabonidus and Caleb are still in here somewhere."

"They may have to look after themselves once Selsus finds out we're all gone," Titius said. "Trust me and move where I tell you to move. Quickly."

Within minutes, the trio had escaped out into the sunshine. All the way, Titius chased after them, shaking his sword and screaming judgment on the beggar women who scurried in front of him. The crowd parted to make way as the chase continued into an alley.

When that legionnaire failed to return with the prisoners, Selsus raced through the cells looking for the group. Aite's dead body still lay where her father had dumped it.

"Save that one for the lions if we need it," he ordered one of his henchmen. "If we can't find the others, though, you and everyone else may be fighting those lions to make up for it."

When the German found himself standing before the cell where Nabonidus and Caleb were imprisoned, he calmed himself.

"At least the main attraction is still here," Selsus said.

Nabonidus stood up and grasped the bars. "Only a coward would harm women and children who only want peace."

Selsus smashed his club against the bars, making Nabonidus jump back to save his fingers.

"Today may be your lucky day, gladiator. Your women have somehow disappeared." Selsus pressed his face to the bars and whispered in a rage. "The child you claimed for Yeshua is already dead. We'll find them all, and any others you're still hiding in this city. Great is Artemis, goddess of the Ephesians."

Selsus turned on the guards standing nearby.

"Your life for theirs," he bellowed, pointing at the prisoners. "I want them in the front cages where everyone can see them. And I want the lions right next to them. If anything goes wrong, you'll all be the main attraction."

Titius followed Daphne and Suzanna through a half-opened door off the alley where he had previously taken the others he'd freed. Once inside, he quickly shed his Roman breastplate and leggings.

"Quickly," he urged. "Around the corner, you'll find steps leading down to a cellar. Abigail will show you what to do. Go and change into the clothes Abigail has for you there. Urbanus will take you to safety."

He could see that Daphne and Suzanna looked very worried as they peered back in the direction they'd come.

"You will have to trust your men to Yeshua," he said to the women. He then turned specifically to Daphne. "If you get a chance to speak with Nabonidus, tell him I'm going to the children's farm."

Selsus was in a rage by the time the opening acts of the games were completed. He sent his men to the governor's dungeon with large bribes so that the jailers would release a dozen prisoners.

He then hurtled to the arena's entrance, where a group of four physicians had gathered. They were ready to claim the injured bodies of the fallen combatants.

"Remember the law," Selsus reminded them. "The victims must be alive still if you're to dissect them. You may each select one man. The rest will receive the hammer of Thor to their skulls and be carried to the realm of the dead. Choose wisely, when you can, and don't get caught in the action."

In the distance, Selsus heard the announcer whip the crowd into frenzied chants: "Artemis of the Ephesians! Artemis is great! Artemis of the Ephesians! Artemis is great!"

He stepped forward to get a better view of the acts, each of them framed as a contest between the goddess of the Ephesians and the god of the Jews. The name of Yeshua was being blasphemed and cursed over and over.

The final acts, Selsus reflected, would be billed as a showdown between those loyal to Artemis and those loyal to Yeshua.

Selsus could hardly wait to see it.

As Nabonidus and Caleb entered the arena, they saw that all the prisoners were being labeled as the traitorous followers of Yeshua, even though most of them weren't. The two of them were shoved into a cage first, then the others were marched around the arena for a while before joining them.

Three of the prisoners were chosen to go first and subjected to the whips, with the crowd betting on how many lashes it would take before they were declared dead. The chanting and counting with each stroke nauseated Caleb, so he turned away.

Nabonidus had a different strategy. He tried to convert the other prisoners in the cage with them.

"You're being labeled followers of Yeshua," Nabonidus said. "You're going to die for him soon. Let me tell you about him so you have a chance to live even if you die."

The Persian continued to preach at the remnant even as another four were chosen to run from a pack of wild dogs. They didn't last long and the crowd jeered.

Next, the lions were released into the arena. It took some time for the lions to dispatch the wild dogs, who had no intention of fighting the larger beasts. The crowd jeered some more.

The remainder of the prisoners were released at last, and each given two sharp sticks with which to defend themselves. These men formed a defensive circle as the lions paced around them.

"Great is Yeshua!" one of the men shouted. "Great is Yeshua!"

The lions responded in an unexpected way, and one by one they lay down. The beasts appeared suddenly fat and satisfied, uninterested in chasing anything that didn't show fear or try to run away.

"Kill them, you lazy beasts!" they heard Selsus raging from the entrance of the gladiator cells. Nabonidus eyed the German as he turned to the jesters with their long lances. "Go out there and force those beasts to get those men!"

The jesters danced and prodded the beasts, but the lions did little more than snarl. When one jester got too close to one lion, and turned his back on another, the latter beast rose up and swatted him into the sand. In a moment, the jester was finished.

The other jesters backed off as the lions chose to face them instead of the prisoners. In the melee which followed, two lions and four jesters met their end. One jester escaped into the stands, despite the jeering of the crowd.

It seemed Selsus had finally had enough, because he sent a dozen men with lances out to chase the remaining lions back into their cages. Soon two dozen gladiators stepped into the arena and the crowd burst into ecstatic roars again.

"We who are about to die salute you," said the gladiators as they faced the sponsors of the games. "For the honor of the emperor and Artemis, we give our lives today."

The announcer then declared that the so-called followers of Yeshua, with their sharp sticks, would fight with the gladiators for the right to face the champion of Ephesus. Six other prisoners were added to the five who still lived, but only one survivor would be crowned before the final event. The crowd responded with enthusiasm for this promise of blood.

Nabonidus and Caleb bowed their heads and ignored the chaos. All around, bets were cast as people chanted for their favorite fights.

As one warrior after another fell in battle, Caleb turned to Nabonidus, noticing how swollen his foot had become.

"That foot is so swollen, you can't even walk on it, never mind fight," Caleb said. "I'll fight for you."

Nabonidus gripped the cage bars as he focused on the action in the arena. "Yeshua has brought me this far. He'll have to heal me or help me. This is my fight, not yours."

As they prayed to Yeshua for strength and courage, Selsus stopped outside their cage.

"Cowards," Selsus snarled. "Watch and see how real men die fighting for their honor. You will be the last to die. Watch and learn how to die well."

The German grabbed a lance and poked it through the lion's cage to torment the beasts. He kept jabbing at them until all four were snarling and batting at his weapon.

"Now you're ready for the arena," Selsus shouted. "Lazy beasts."

The mix of fighters, both those who were unwilling to die and those who had been trained to kill, kept the crowd entertained for almost an hour. The prisoners attempted to form the same tight protective circle as they had with the lions, but the gladiators, armed with spears, easily got past them and wounded those in the middle. The rest of them were attacked with tridents, nets, and swords.

After a couple of the prisoners had died, and even a couple of the gladiators, the prisoners were motivated to run as a pack. Despite the crowd's mocking, they chose to strike and flee in guerrilla-style combat.

The sun grew hot overhead and the malnourished prisoners eventually lost their energy. One after another fell. When the prisoners had all died, the gladiators settled on facing each other. There was no mercy given to those who bared their neck.

The physicians scurried like ants at a picnic, looking for the best candidates for dissection. There was one whose heart still beat despite having largely bled out.

Finally, only a pair of gladiators remained—an Ethiopian and an Egyptian. The Ethiopian carried a net and trident while the Egyptian carried a large shield, spear, and dagger. For ten minutes, they fought to avoid being trapped. The crowd jeered again.

When it seemed as though the bout had reached a stalemate, Selsus stepped into the arena in full combat gear. His golden breastplate shone brightly, marking him as the emperor's champion. The twenty-one leather strands on his right wrist marked his kills. His golden helmet captured the sun's rays and drew everyone's attention. A ripple of excitement rushed through the crowd as they noticed this new dynamic.

Selsus led a pair of glistening black Arabian stallions harnessed to a chariot. His aide held up a long spear and a bow with arrows for him. Without hesitation, Selsus climbed into the chariot and acknowledged the roar of the crowd. While the two remaining gladiators paused their combat to figure out what was happening, Selsus rode around the perimeter of the arena.

At last, four gladiators-in-training opened the cage holding Nabonidus and Caleb.

Caleb turned to his former slave. "You are now my champion, and the champion of Yeshua."

The gladiators-in-training tossed combat gear into the cage and Nabonidus slowly put it on. As he did so, the anticipation spread like wildfire through the hundreds of thousands who had been waiting for Selsus to prove himself against the former champion.

The announcer took his place and waited for the crowd to quiet. "Sons and daughters of Artemis, there will be a slight change to the program. The surviving gladiators from our last match will both be offered their freedom should they survive a match against the current champion of Artemis." He paused to await the ripple of reaction. Immediately the people began placing wagers. "We also have the battle of the ages, between the former champion, representing the forces of Yeshua, and our current champion, representing the true sovereign, Artemis of the Ephesians."

The crowd's roar of approval thundered across the city.

Nabonidus ducked out of the cage and entered the battleground with a trident, net, and dagger tucked into his belt. He and the Ethiopian were identically equipped.

Caleb hardly resisted as he was tied to the cross and turned to face the crowd. This time, there was no hay to light on fire. He would die another way.

The announcer motioned for the people to quiet. "The vows have been made. The battle is ready. Now, who is your champion?"

The crowd erupted in volcanic fury. "Artemis! Artemis! Artemis!"

Selsus whipped his horses into a furious pace around the perimeter. As he crossed in front of Caleb, he drew his bow and sent an arrow straight into the center of the former cross maker's open right hand. Caleb screamed in pain, but Selsus just whipped the stallions and raced around the arena for another pass.

Nabonidus quickstepped, as best his hobbled foot would allow, to place himself directly in the path of Selsus's next attempt. The two other gladiators stood by, uncertain as to their role in this contest.

Meanwhile, a jester stepped over to the lions' cage, released the catch, and swung the door open.

Selsus didn't appear to notice the lions, but reacted quickly to seeing Nabonidus blocking his way. He drew his bow and attempted to shoot a bit earlier than anticipated, but the arrow hit the crossbeam less than a finger's width from Caleb's left hand. Selsus swerved away from Nabonidus and urged his mounts to go around the arena for another pass.

The third pass resulted in a third arrow, this one landing even farther away; it thudded into the base of the cross a full hand's width under Caleb's dangling feet.

One of the surviving gladiators, the Ethiopian, attempted to throw his net into the wheels of Selsus's chariot, but instead the net tangled in the axle and pulled the gladiator off his feet. His trident flew in an arc and embedded itself in the sand, wobbling for a moment as if unsure whether to remain in place.

Selsus aimed his bow and sent an arrow into the Ethiopian's unprotected neck. The man's body dragged along behind the chariot as the horses responded to the sting of the whip by picking up their pace. The crowd roared at the heroic son of Artemis in action.

When Selsus was well away from the others, he halted the chariot and got down to cut away the net and the dead gladiator. The final gladiator, the Egyptian, anticipated the move and ran quickly toward Selsus, his spear extended. His shield easily blocked the arrow Selsus shot his way and, with deadly force, the Egyptian smashed the bow with his spear.

Selsus shielded himself behind the chariot.

With those two engaged in combat, Nabonidus plucked the abandoned trident from the ground. Armed with two, he now backed toward Caleb and pulled the arrow out of the restrained man's hand.

As Nabonidus prepared to cut Caleb down with his dagger, though, he noticed the first lions emerging from the cage.

Selsus twisted the horses toward the gladiator attacking him, but the man was agile of foot and refused to be manipulated into a compromising position. When the horses reared up, the Egyptian gladiator plunged his spear into the haunches of the closest beast. The animal bellowed in pain and launched forward, and the chariot wheel caught the gladiator's shield. He fell hard on his knee. The impact spun him around, leaving him vulnerable to Sestus's spear. He twisted to get away, but he wasn't quick enough to avoid the German man's experienced arm. The throw was aimed at the Egyptian's midsection, and the spear struck him on the right side—a crippling blow.

Selsus stalked the last gladiator relentlessly, dodging the man's increasingly feeble spear thrusts, raining blow after blow on the shield. The gladiator knew he was in trouble and backed purposefully toward Nabonidus in the hope of finding an ally.

In the way of the lions, though, Nabonidus had to abandon his attempt to save Caleb. Taking a trident in each hand, he moved to put some distance between himself and the four lions who had now all exited the cage.

Selsus focused on Nabonidus and the failing Egyptian. He wielded his spear like a battering ram, driving the Egyptian gladiator back on his heels. The wounded gladiator, now desperate, pushed back one more time to unbalance Selsus, but the attempt failed and left him unprotected. At last he stepped backwards, tripped over the body of the fallen Ethiopian, and lost hold of his shield. Selsus thrust him through.

Nabonidus remained near Caleb, watching the lions cautiously out of the corner of his eye. However, Selsus still didn't seem to have noticed the lions. Oblivious to their approach, his chest heaved from the victory of his latest skirmish. He drank in the chants of the crowd: "Selsus! Selsus! Selsus!"

The German picked up the fallen Egyptian's spear and raised it toward the crowd. Behind him, Nabonidus raised both of his tridents.

The two men began to circle each other, twenty feet apart. Selsus dodged back and forth, threatening to throw his spear. Nabonidus, hobbled, just did all he could not to be caught off-balance.

When Selsus finally threw his first spear, it nicked Nabonidus's right shoulder. The Persian man ducked and rolled before the second spear could be launched. Meanwhile, the lions crept toward the cross where Caleb was fastened, calling out to Yeshua.

Selsus, growing agitated by the prayers, yelled for Caleb to shut up. Still Caleb cried out.

Selsus circled to get closer to the cross, but Nabonidus forced him to keep at a distance. Anxious, Selsus took hold of his dagger and tossed it at the crucified man. He missed his mark.

Finally, Nabonidus charged Selsus, brandishing his two tridents. Selsus ran in an attempt to outflank Nabonidus's position in front of the cross, and the movement caught the lions' attention. One of the lions took off in a streak of tawny terror, and within ten powerful leaps he had catapulted onto Selsus's back. Having noticed the attacker at the last second, Selsus rolled and avoided the full weight of the beast.

The cat spun on its haunches, clawing at air, but Selsus rolled again and sprang to his feet. By then, though, another of the lions had entered the fray and sprang for his throat. He ducked but didn't escape the beast's raking claws across his back and shoulders. The attack knocked him off-balance.

Selsus spent his spear fending off the attack of the third lion, but that left him with nothing to defend himself. The pride sprang on him in unison.

In moments, the battle was over. The crowd grew silent.

Nabonidus hobbled toward the cross, cut Caleb down, threw him over his shoulder, and walked calmly out of the arena. No one followed as they crossed the street and stepped into a stable, where they met Titius, dressed as an old bearded shepherd.

The streets were soon filling again with disillusioned spectators who had watched the champion of Artemis get consumed by lions. Those who had bet much had lost much. Mobs of ruffians and disillusioned citizens went on the rampage, rioting, looting, and destroying anything rumored to be connected with Yeshua. The city authorities stood guard over the Artemission and shrines set aside to honor Artemis. Her reputation had suffered enough for one day.

Within minutes, Titius was urging a horse-drawn carriage, carrying his friends to safety.

Chapter Twenty-Eight

Once Titius had ensured the safety of his friends, he secured a horse and galloped toward the location of the children's farm. He couldn't leave Ephesus without completing this one last task. After all, Nabonidus had rescued those who were special to him; now he would rescue those who were special to Nabonidus.

His disguise as a shepherd was designed to get him close enough to the farm without arousing suspicion. Whether he could breach the compound's defences and rescue the remaining children there was uncertain. He prayed for a miracle.

As Titius approached the front gates, he saw six sentries loading girls onto a pair of oxcarts. Six of the girls didn't fit, and it seemed they would be made to walk behind. He watched silently as those last six girls were tied together and fastened to the back of the cart. Where were they being taken?

Titius dismounted, tethered his mount, and slipped behind some bushes bordering the gate. He quickly spotted a pair of Persian girls, looking confused and angry, for they had been among the six who would have to walk. No doubt those were Anoshiruvan's daughters.

Rescuing them wouldn't be easy.

Two of the sentries stood nearby with bows, the arrows nocked. Another two wielded spears and short swords. The final two took their place on the carts, driving with one hand on the reins while holding daggers in the other.

Titius shook with frustration. What had he been thinking, coming out here alone?

The first cart started off with its load of girls, and four of the sentries went with it, two riding up front and two standing in the back with the girls. The driver of the second cart whipped his ox to get through the gate and then waited as the final sentry locked the gate behind them. The six girls on foot, including Adrina and Atossa, stumbled forward.

When the first sentry posted to the second cart looked away, and the other became preoccupied with fastening the gate, Titius stepped quickly out from the bushes and used his dagger to slash the throat on the man at the gate. He silently dragged the man into the bushes before anyone noticed.

But Adrina and Atossa saw. The girls stared at him, wide-eyed. He motioned them into silence, then once the dead sentry was hidden away he crept up behind the cart and cut them loose.

Suddenly, the driver of the second cart called back to his comrade—and obviously he received no response. The driver stopped the cart's slow forward movement, dismounted, and walked around the wagon to investigate.

Titius silenced him, too, with his dagger. He then carried the body into the bushes to join his comrade.

Moving as quickly as he could, Titius gathered the two Persian girls and led them through the bush toward his mount. Once they were safe, he then turned back to see if he could rescue the others, but by now the first cart had noticed the absence of movement in the second cart, whose load of girls had begun screaming. Three of the sentries were already running toward them.

Frustrated and disappointed that he couldn't do more, Titius set the girls on the horse and raced away. His friends were waiting.

Titius was half a day's journey from Ephesus before he removed the false beard and head covering. Nabonidus slipped out from under the tarp on the cart and joined him up front, his foot still throbbing despite the potion he'd been given. Caleb lay stretched out in the bed of the cart, nursing his wounded hand.

"Did you find the children's farm?" Nabonidus asked. "Did you find Adrina and Atossa?"

"The place was well guarded," Titius said. "I was only able to save the two. They will meet us up ahead."

"It is enough for now," Nabonidus affirmed. "My promise to their father is complete."

As nightfall shrouded the landscape, the trio pulled into a wayside inn where a jubilant Daphne burst out of a side door. She ran to envelope Nabonidus in a hug, and he swung her around as they chuckled in joy.

"Perhaps now we'll have our honeymoon," he said. "Persia awaits."

Suzanna hobbled tentatively a few steps outside their room and waited for Caleb to reach her. Five months of pregnancy had taken its toll, and their embrace was tentative. She reached for his hand, in its blood-soaked wrapping, and cradled it against her cheek.

"Are you sure you still want to spread the good news in Germania?" Suzanna asked. "There may not be anyone there to rescue you from a cross."

"There was no one to rescue Yeshua either," Caleb reminded her. "If there's one thing I've learned, it's that somehow we're immortal until God calls us home."

Titius released the horses and handed them off to a stable boy, then turned to see Abigail, also heavy with child, framed in the doorway. She was talking over her shoulder to others inside.

He picked up the pace as she stepped into her sandals and opened her arms in welcome. After a sustained kiss, he held both of her cheeks in his hands.

"My love, I don't think Rome is ready for us yet," Titius said. "Perhaps we will try Britannia to start our next church."

As they walked into the inn, they discovered Urbanus, Seti, Adrina, Atossa, and a dozen others huddled together on a blanket, sharing platters of food. Titius served up a flagon of cheap wine, pouring cups for everyone. As the last cup was filled, he raised his own and the room fell silent.

"Today we celebrate the greatness of Yeshua. He has declared his name before the throne of Artemis at great cost." Titius surveyed the battered group, desperate for hope. "Today we will remember the first martyrs of Ephesus—our sisters Ruth and Aite. Ruth was raised as a priestess of Artemis, and she knew Yeshua just long enough to share him with a young girl. Both honored their faith through death. They knew the truth and the truth set them free. Today we have given our blood and our tears together."

"Thank you, Titius," Urbanus said on behalf of all who listened.

Titius turned and gestured toward Nabonidus. "Thank Yeshua for his mercy. Thank Nabonidus, the Persian prince, the cross maker's champion. May Yeshua raise up his champions to bring freedom once again to this land."

Other Books In This Series

The Cross Maker
ISBN: 978-1-4866-1856-9

First-century Palestine is a hotbed of political, cultural, and religious intrigue. Caleb ben Samson, a carpenter from Nazareth, and Sestus Aurelius, a Roman centurion, both want peace. Can this unlikely partnership accomplish what nothing else has accomplished before? Can they bring about peace through the power of the cross? And what role will Caleb's childhood friend Yeshi play in a land that longs for hope?

In *The Cross Maker*, Jack Taylor weaves a tapestry of creative history, powerful characters, and dynamic dialogue to bring to life a shadowy world. In a land where tragedy is as common as dust, triumph is about to make itself known.

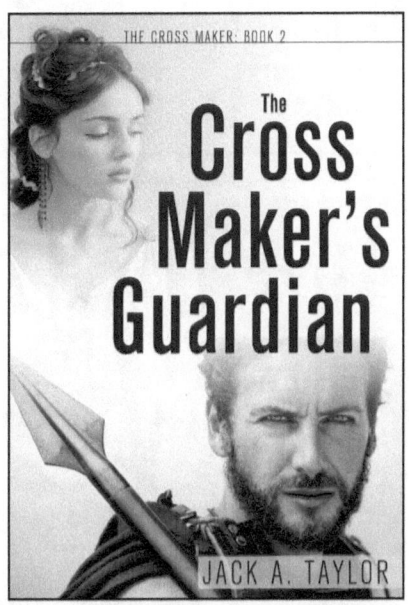

The Cross Maker's Guardian
ISBN: 978-1-4866-1858-3

Roman legions thunder across first-century Palestine, seeking to use the power of the cross to crush the lightning strikes of the zealots led by Barabbas. Behind the scenes, a secret squad of thespian assassins are being trained—and Titius Marcus Julianus is caught up in this silent whirlwind, conscripted to be the new guardian of the crossmaker, Caleb ben Samson.

Titius is fuelled by vengeance and love as he seeks to regain his stolen Roman estate and the young Jewish slave who once captured his heart. Meanwhile, voices from his past and present wrestle for control of his heart and mind.

In *The Crossmaker's Guardian*, Jack Taylor unveils the clash between the Roman and Jewish civilizations as they battle for life in a world suffused with international intrigue. Descriptive narrative, biblical history, and powerful characters all come alive in this thrilling read where death and love are only a blink away.

Other Books by Jack A. Taylor

One Last Wave
ISBN: 978-1-7706-9261-9

Katrina [Katie] Joy Delancey has staked her life on keeping the past and future away from her heart. But she is no master of fate or captain of her own journey. *One Last Wave* is a story about being discovered by faith and love no matter where you are, no matter where you've been, and no matter what you think may lie ahead.

No Place to Run
ISBN: 978-1-7706-9786-7

No *Place to Run* continues the adventures of Katie Delancey, begun in *One Last Wave*. It's a story of rediscovering faith, hope, and love when the maze of life seems to close in around you... about realizing that the whispers of the past can be keys to your future.

Stretching for Home

ISBN: 978-1-4866-0996-3

A blissful love nest amidst a brutal Minnesota winter turns into a fiery ordeal of grief and terror as Katie is caught up in the never-ending pursuit of human traffickers who want to eliminate her from their deadly game. *Stretching for Home* is an education into the heart of missionary kids searching for healing as life tumbles in around them. Their quest for home can be as elusive as a rainbow's pot of gold. Finding old roots and spreading new wings can be a challenge.

www.ingramcontent.com/pod-product-compliance
Lightning Source LLC
Chambersburg PA
CBHW030108260626
47156CB00008B/2577